Pandemics, Authoritarian Populism, and Science Fiction

With a focus on *I Am Legend* and *Day of the Dead*—two series of film remakes of popular science fiction stories—this book addresses the social origins of the recent surge in authoritarian and populist social movements. Exploring the ways in which the themes of tribalism, confidence in medical science, and confidence in military violence changed over the years in the process of re-telling these stories in popular culture, the author identifies the shift towards a narrowing of moral scope, an embrace of military violence and a distrust of medical science with three elements of authoritarian populism: tribalism, distrust of rational elites and their institutions, and willingness for violent coercion. An engaging study of popular culture that sheds light on contemporary political attitudes, *Pandemics, Authoritarian Populism, and Science Fiction* will appeal to scholars of sociology, social theory, and cultural studies with interests in critical theory, film studies, and science fiction.

Jeremiah Morelock is an instructor of sociology at Boston College, USA, and the Director of the Critical Theory Research Network. He is the editor of *Critical Theory and Authoritarian Populism* and *How to Critique Authoritarian Populism: Methodologies of the Frankfurt School*.

Visual Modernities

Series Editor:
Martyn Hudson, Northumbria University

The sociological imagination of modernity is entangled with our senses and, primarily, with vision, yet the process of being able to see something is often extraordinarily complex. Marx's attempt to visualise commodities, Durkheim on totems of religious life, Simmel on money and the metropolis, Elias on social taste, are all projects which attempt to see beyond the empirical and into levels of abstraction and immateriality that lie beyond the senses. Visualisation is part of the making of modernity and a response to it.

This series explores and elaborates upon our experiences of modernity. It offers ways of seeing from the margins of our world and from its exemplary sites of industry and urbanisation. Grand narratives of human history mix with micro-histories that are embedded across our globe. Using multi-disciplinary methods, it seeks to expand upon our knowledge of global and local visual cultures, whether in architecture, painting, photography, theatre, film and other cultural forms. Examining the material and the tangible as well as the immaterial and the imaginary it aims to offer the best of sociological thinking and thought: literally re-visioning our social world.

Visual Modernities welcomes new studies that have visualisation at their heart and embed new ways of perceiving our shared world and our multiple and complex experience of modernity. It seeks to publish works that are innovative, multi-disciplinary in scope and which challenge and rupture the classical social sciences with new ways of looking at method, theory and our social futures.

Pandemics, Authoritarian Populism, and Science Fiction

Medicine, Military, and Morality in American Film

Jeremiah Morelock

Routledge
Taylor & Francis Group

LONDON AND NEW YORK

First published 2021
by Routledge
2 Park Square, Milton Park, Abingdon, Oxon OX14 4RN

and by Routledge
605 Third Avenue, New York, NY 10158

Routledge is an imprint of the Taylor & Francis Group, an informa business

British Library Cataloguing-in-Publication Data
A catalogue record for this book is available from the British Library

Library of Congress Cataloging-in-Publication Data
Names: Morelock, Jeremiah, author.
Title: Pandemics, authoritarian populism, and science fiction : medicine, military, and morality in American film / Jeremiah Morelock.
Description: New York : Routledge, 2021. |
Series: Visual modernities | Includes bibliographical references and index.
Identifiers: LCCN 2020043278 (print) | LCCN 2020043279 (ebook) |
ISBN 9780367435103 (hardback) | ISBN 9781003003779 (ebook)
Subjects: LCSH: Science fiction films--United States--History and criticism. |
Epidemics in motion pictures. | Authoritarianism in motion pictures. |
Populism in motion pictures.
Classification: LCC PN1995.9.S26 M63 2021 (print) |
LCC PN1995.9.S26 (ebook) | DDC 791.43/750973--dc23
LC record available at https://lccn.loc.gov/2020043278
LC ebook record available at https://lccn.loc.gov/2020043279

ISBN: 978-0-367-43510-3 (hbk)
ISBN: 978-0-367-72057-5 (pbk)
ISBN: 978-1-003-00377-9 (ebk)

Typeset in Bembo
by Taylor & Francis Books

Contents

Introduction

Films are known for showing us to ourselves, sometimes couched in thick and spectacular metaphor, sometimes quite realistically. Through films, just as through our dreams, we play out our fears and fantasies without risking the repercussions that might occur in the real world. Indeed, the film is a pseudo-reality that we passively experience, riding the highs and lows much like a dream; and although we do not literally dream up the films we see, the emotional resonances of films speak to the same deep well of internal stirrings that the metaphors of dreams emanate from.

As the dreamer of a dream, I generate the imagery out of my own "dream-work"—through condensation and displacement I translate my latent thoughts into experienced dream content—and I experience the imagery according to the same lexicon of connotation that guides my dream-work into existence. The "dreamer" both creates and experiences the dream, and both acts (creation and experience) happen simultaneously, according to the same logics of association. As a viewer of a film, I am only individually on one side of the event. I do not create the film, but I experience it in a very similar way to how I experience a dream—it activates the same lexicon of connotation as the dream. I do not generate the film-as-dream. A collection of other people does that, largely guided by the aim of creating a film-as-dream experience that will resonate with the minds of as many people as possible. In this sense, writers, producers, actors, and other industry professionals generate it on behalf of "society" as a whole; or perhaps society generates the dream through writers, producers, actors, and other industry professionals. Yet I do experience the film-as-dream, in my own way, according to my own psychology, my own repertoire of fears, longings, experiences and associations, embedded as I am in my time, place, society, and social location.

In science fiction, we can indulge our imaginations in broad and dramatic representations of the limits of human existence. Here the longing for utopia and the fear of dystopia have fertile soil (Sontag 2001; Jameson 2005), and so we can venture further into them with science fiction than with more "down to earth" genres. Indeed, the extremes of science fiction lend it even more of an obvious dream-like quality in the sense that its anything-goes unrealism is part of its ostensible glamor.

The sci-fi genre is extremely wide, and yet all throughout its history, stories about threatening Others—often "humanoid," meaning human-like but biologically distinct from "us"—are invariably a central component. It happens in many guises, and the specifics of these Biological Others can vary considerably: A mad scientist creates a living monster out of the body parts of dead people. A mad scientist accidentally genetically combines himself with a housefly. Apes, gorillas, and orangutans develop the capacity for speech and abstract reasoning and overtake humanity. Machines or robots become sentient and strive to obliterate humanity. Extra-terrestrials invade and try to destroy us, or we encounter them as hostiles during our space travels. The list goes on. "Biological horror," or "bio-horror," greatly overlaps with the science fiction genre, the latter of course being much broader. In bio-horror, some sort of biological anomaly—whether brought on by nature, scientific experimentation, divine punishment, or the environmental impacts of war—threatens the safety of (normal) humanity.

The threat of Biological Others often takes the form of an invasion, colonization, or genocide. Simplified, the Other will control us, kill us, or both. There are many variations within this basic trope. Sometimes, as mentioned above, the Other is humanoid. In this case, the encounter between Us and the Others is likely to take the recognizable form of war, although mind control is also a possibility. Sometimes, the Other is a parasite. In this case, the threat has two levels: the parasite, and the inhabited human host. The parasite might simply kill the host, in which case the threat of the host to other people is simply the possibility of the parasite spreading. In other renditions, the parasite takes over the host's mind (and hence body). Then, both the invading parasite and the controlled human bodies might be actively hostile to "normal" people. This means two threats of Others—the parasite and the Inhabited Others. Sometimes the Other is an infectious disease. This version is much like the parasite stories, only now the original Other is invisible. The two threats are the disease, and the Diseased Others, the latter of which might spread the infection and might be actively hostile to normal people.[1] In the latter case, the modern zombie is the quintessential example.

What is it about these narratives that are so compelling to us, even perhaps timelessly relevant? One possible answer is that threats of hostile Others, of war, and of disease have been with humanity from before it was humanity, i.e., that they have been so ingrained through our evolutionary and social histories that they are part of our deep, phylogenetic inheritance, just like fear of the dark, of heights, of snakes, etc. In *Plagues and Peoples*, Historian William H. McNeill says:

> Skill and knowledge, though they have profoundly transformed ordinary encounters with disease for most of humankind, have not and in the nature of things never can extricate humanity from its age-old position, intermediate between microparasites attacking invisibly and the macroparasitism of some men upon their fellows.
>
> (McNeill 1998, 294)

At different points in history, however, good arguments could be made that various stories signify very specific social currents. Over the past few decades, authoritarian populism has become a major social and political force and the science fiction genre has risen in popularity to become overwhelmingly the most prolific genre in the United States. It is perhaps not coincidental that the zombie trope has risen in popularity over the same time as America has turned toward tribalism, becoming especially popular in the years leading up to the turbulent election of Donald Trump. Zombie sci-fi has risen in popularity to the point where *The Walking Dead* was the most popular television show in America from 2012 through 2016—four consecutive years (Katz 2016). Consider the main theme of almost any zombie story: a virus erupts which turns a segment of the population into abject, undead living dead in/humans. The remaining normal people must fight back the abnormal infected ones from continuing the spread of the virus and from killing and overtaking the entire normal population. Protagonists generally adopt the conviction that Foucault articulated as typical ideology behind modern state-sanctioned mass killing: "society must be defended" (Foucault 2003). The zombie apocalypse is a biopolitical tribalism nightmare.

To the extent then that the zombie story reflects popular tribal anxieties, the level of confidence in medical science and the military exhibited in these stories may also reveal something pressing about what institutions and methods people trust, feel protected or threatened by, and are given to turn to or blame in their nightmares of biopolitical urgency.[2] The modern zombie is afflicted by a virus and poses a violent threat to the human population. Thus, both medical and military responses may be warranted in combatting (or attempting to combat) the disease, and zombie stories tend to prominently involve some relative combination of these two arenas of response (Pokornowski 2013). Invariably, the methods by which "society is defended" in the zombie story are medical science and military violence. And it is not only the conclusion to the outbreak that concerns these two domains. Frequently, doctors, scientists, or military are culpable in the origin story of the pandemic as well.

What to expect

There are certainly numerous ways of sociologically studying authoritarianism and populism, numerous enough that they do not require full illumination here. I will just say that they run the gamut of qualitative and quantitative approaches to research and analysis in sociology generally. Although populism and authoritarianism are ostensibly political tendencies, I am especially interested in the beliefs and impulses circulating in the larger cultural mind that may feed into authoritarian populism in America. Here I use a psychoanalytic methodology to interpret popular film, in the tradition of the early Frankfurt School. The basic idea is that films can be analysed as having latent, covert meanings that reveal various fears, hopes, and preoccupations of the societies they were made in at the times they were made (see Morelock 2021; Kellner 2010; Wood 2018).

In Part I, I introduce a conceptual framework in layers. The framework is largely a multifaceted empirical and narrative history that brings together pandemics, authoritarian populism, and science fiction film, through a variety of pathways. I discuss a political shift where the right-wing became aligned against science and the left-wing has been consistently split or ambivalent towards it, although very recently becoming more aligned with it. At the same time, the right-wing became increasingly positive about the US military. Medicine went from its "golden age" when infectious diseases were apparently being overcome and doctors had virtually unchecked professional dominance, to the current period where medicine is steeped in much bureaucracy and regulation, consumers demand more say in their treatment, and infectious diseases have returned to become major medical threats. I also discuss changes in tribal splits in society, primarily concerning race and political values. I explore how aspects of these developments are reflected in American science fiction film defined broadly, with special focus on film series (e.g., *Planet of the Apes*, *X-Men*, etc.) to illustrate change over time. I argue that moving across the decades, the films represent a moral narrowing toward simple personal loyalty and risk assessment, with a consistent ambivalence about science and scientists. I then briefly outline what I call "Diseased Others films," which combine themes of pandemics and tribalism in a very direct way.

In Part II, I provide two detailed case studies, using Diseased Others films that were remade multiple times. The two "remake series" I use are *I Am Legend* and *Day of the Dead*. I explore each rendition of the stories regarding what moral attitudes are portrayed concerning confrontation between rival groups, whether and how medical science and the military respectively operate to the benefit or detriment of humanity, and how these representations change over time. I provide transcribed dialogue from the various film renditions, explaining the dialogue in terms of how they express moral attitudes toward intergroup relations (i.e. tribal moralities), as well as in terms of the relative helpfulness or harmfulness of medical science and the military in the story of the origins of the disease and in the attempts to quell the disease. I discuss these changes in light of the historical context of the films' release, as well as in light of comments about the films from the cast and crew.

In the conclusion to the book, I provide further theoretical reflection on pandemics, authoritarian populism, and science fiction—particularly the Diseased Others films from the two case studies. I suggest an overall chronological picture reflected in the films of increasingly volatile medical science, increasingly positive military violence, and narrowing moral horizons toward a focus on charged personal loyalties. Consulting ideas from Zygmunt Bauman and Anthony Giddens, and information about demographic changes in the United States since the 1970s, I outline a conjuncture of trends that together have influenced the rise of the far-Right.

Notes

1 In the case of parasites and diseases, note that there may also be a diabolical villain behind the outbreak, such as a terrorist or terrorist organization.
2 Studies of national survey data indicate that since the middle of the twentieth century self-reported confidence in science and medicine has continued to decline, yet self-reported confidence in the military has increased (Pescosolido, Tuch and Martin 2001; Gauchat 2012; Twenge, Campbell and Carter 2014; Montenaro 2018).

References

Foucault, M. (2003). *"Society Must Be Defended": Lectures at the Collège de France, 1974–1975*. New York: Picador.

Gauchat, G. (2012). Politicization of Science in the Public Sphere: A Study of Public Trust in the United States, 1974 to 2010. *American Sociological Review*, 77(2), 167–187. doi:10.1177/0003122412438225.

Jameson, F. (2005). *Archaeologies of the Future: The Desire Called Utopia and Other Science Fictions*. New York: Verso.

Katz, B. (2016). 'The Walking Dead' is TV's No. 1 Show for 4th Year in a Row. Retrieved from *HNGN*: http://www.hngn.com/articles/195957/20160409/the-walking-dead-tv-1-show-4th-year-row.htm.

Kellner, D. (2010). *Cinema Wars: Hollywood Film and Politics in the Bush-Cheney Era*. Malden, MA: Blackwell.

McNeill, W. H. (1998). *Plagues and Peoples*. New York: Anchor Books.

Morelock, J., ed. (2021). *How to Critique Authoritarian Populism: Methodologies of the Frankfurt School*. Leiden, The Netherlands: Brill.

Montenaro, D. (2018). Here's Just How Little Confidence Americans Have in Political Institutions. Retrieved from *National Public Radio, Inc.*: https://www.npr.org/2018/01/17/578422668/heres-just-how-little-confidence-americans-have-in-political-institutions.

Pescosolido, B. A., Tuch, S. A., & Martin, J. K. (2001). The Profession of Medicine and the Public: Examining Americans' Changing Confidence in Physician Authority from the Beginning of the 'Health Care Crisis' to the Era of Health Care Reform. *Journal of Health and Social Behavior*, 42, 1–16. doi:10.2307/3090224.

Pokornowski, S. (2013). Insecure Lives: Zombies, Global Health, and the Totalitarianism of Generalization. *Literature and Medicine*, 31(2), 216–234. doi:10.1353/lm.2013.0017.

Sontag, S. (2001). *Against Interpretation and Other Essays*. New York: Picador.

Twenge, J. M., Campbell, K. W., & Carter, N. T. (2014). Declines in Trust in Others and Confidence in Institutions among American Adults and Late Adolescents, 1972–2012. *Psychological Science*, 25(10), 1914–1923. doi:10.1177/0956797614545133.

Wood, R. (2018). *Robin Wood and the Horror Film: Collected Essays and Reviews*. Detroit, MI: Wayne State University Press.

Part I

Chapter 1

Politics and pandemics intertwined

What is authoritarian populism?

Stuart Hall birthed "authoritarian populism" as a specific term in his work of the late 1970s (Hall, et al. 2013). Hall's notion was rather situated in space and time, as a diagnosis of Britain's move toward Thatcherism. He characterized this sort of movement as a combination of fervent nationalism in rhetoric with neoliberalism in politics. Hall's concept is thus pretty broad, and the term "authoritarian populism" has endured into the present day, such as in recent analyses of Trumpism and other far-right phenomena in the United States (Norris and Inglehart 2019; Kellner 2016).

The definition I use here of "authoritarian populism" is arguably wider than Hall's original term, although Hall's notion is certainly consonant with it. When I speak of authoritarian populism in this book, I mean it in the more intuitive sense that a person unfamiliar with Hall's work is more likely to interpret the term. I simply refer to movements that are simultaneously authoritarian and populist. One might imagine a Venn diagram of authoritarianism, populism, and their intersection. Yet the terms "authoritarianism" and "populism" are still very slippery in their meanings. To be more explicit about the meaning I am using here, I offer the following brief working definition of authoritarian populism:

> In the pages that follow, to be "authoritarian" is to seek social homogeneity through coercion. "Populism" is defining a section of the population as truly and rightfully "the people" and aligning with this section against a different group identified as elites. Together, "authoritarian populism" refers to the pitting of "the people" against "elites" in order to have the power to drive out, wipe out, or otherwise dominate Others who are not "the people." Generally, this involves social movements fueled by prejudice and led by charismatic leaders that seek to increase governmental force to combat difference.
>
> (Morelock 2018, xiv)

While neither authoritarianism nor populism is specific to right vis-à-vis left politics, authoritarian populism is generally more explicit on the Right (Morelock and Narita 2018, 2019). Correspondingly, in this study I am interested first and foremost in American far-right authoritarian populism, which is generally associated with Trumpism, the Alt-Right and contemporary white nationalism. So, when I refer to "authoritarian populism" here, it is intended to broadly signify those movements.

Being a broad grouping of tendencies and phenomena, the term "authoritarian populism" needs to be broken down more in order to address it effectively—otherwise it stays on very general and vague terms. There are many ways to break up and analyse such an "object,"[1] and any one way of analysing it is probably incomplete. For purposes of some degree of analytic clarity, in this study I break up "authoritarian populism" according to three "elements." These are not the only ways to break it up and analyse it, but they do have background in the literature and they are the ones I chose to organize my study so as to be able to address—even if only partially—the broad phenomena of authoritarian populism. I introduce the elements below.

Three elements of authoritarian populism

Tribalism

There is in-group/out-group alignment and antagonism. In the terms of Nazi political theorist Carl Schmitt (2005), this is the "friend-enemy" distinction. This can occur on a variety of axes, including race/ethnicity, political belief, religion, class, gender, age, and so on. For purposes of parsimony, in this study I frame tribalism in terms of racial and political difference, and I am particularly interested in how these divisions can operate in tandem. Popular political alignments in the United States today tend to run along racial lines, with the Alt-Right touting white nationalism, and the Left touting #BlackLivesMatter. At least in this country, tribalism along racial and political lines frequently appears like one axis of division. This is not to say that the political Right are all white and the political Left are all people of colour. Rather, more of the non-white vote typically goes to the Democrats, and the majority of Republican voters are overwhelmingly white. This became especially marked in the 2016 election, when white racial anxieties contributed greatly to Trump's victory.

Distrust of rational elites and their institutions

This is the most complicated of the three elements I am outlining here. Those people who are identified as "elites" can in principle vary in a complex society. Populist political movements will predictably identify the political establishment, at minimum. But it tends to go far beyond just this. Authoritarian populist movements typically involve a claim to directness and authenticity that the entrenched establishment lacks. The rhetoric of the movement often speaks to casting off the shackles of modern rationality as it is deployed to manage the population ("regular people") by specialists and technocrats. "The people" seek to bring society back to earlier times, when their "way of life" was not under threat by the constant impingements of "experts" who use their stocks of knowledge as a claim to the right to overturn traditional culture in favour of the rule of them and their cadre. The authoritarian populist leader is typically a "great little man," exhibiting traits of a strong leader as well as a down-to-earth "regular person."

The far-Right (and others) often point to the University as a bastion of liberal elitism and political correctness (Harris 2010; Shapiro 2010; Kors and Silverglate 1999; Lukianoff 2014). College students, college professors, and college graduates are all by this reasoning part of the American educated elite, at least to some degree. The vitriol is especially directed toward the humanities, which—unable to boast of a non-academic job skill set or career track—are *only* used to further human understanding. Learning for learning's sake is pure intellectualism, and the language of the academy ("academese" or "jargon") is a mark of separation from the culture of "the people." Traces of this way of thinking extend beyond the far-Right. Consider the adage "those who can't do, teach," or the term "academic" when it is used to disparage a complex logical argument as removed from reality and hence discreditable.

While in the University the humanities are most decried in such terms, the "scientific community"—a circuit that intersects with the University but is not confined to it—is also often targeted. The grounds are typically religious or political, and again have to do with an alleged elite group of educated liberals pushing their own agendas and rendering conservatives oppressed. During the COVID-19 pandemic, Trump severed ties between the United States and the WHO, held political rallies with no social distancing measures enforced, and ignored the analyses and warnings of top scientists at every turn. Many of the Right rejected wearing masks in public, viewing the act as one of defiance against an oppressive medico-technocratic liberal elite. In connection with the intertwining of racial and political alignments mentioned above, note that the sickness and death of COVID-19 in the US fall disproportionately on communities of colour. One should be careful in deciding exactly what this means, but at the very least, the pattern persists—for the Left to wear masks and follow social distancing protocol simultaneously positions them as listening to scientific experts and caring about the well-being of racial minorities. The most consistent religious dividing line is the debate about teaching creation vs. evolution in schools. Here, science is on one side, and religion (Christianity) is on the other. The science behind evolution is not only discredited by the far-Right, it is also taken to be a threat to Christianity. Climate change is another area where science and scientists are decried outright as liberal elites who are pushing a liberal agenda (Otto 2016).

The rejection of the scientific community extends into a rejection of Western medicine, which of course is rooted in science. Christian Scientists, for instance, believe that illness is caused by unhealthy thinking, and that prayer and right thinking will cure illness instead of scientific medicine (Schoepflin 2003). Some evangelicals also advise against Western medical practices, and suggest turning to Jesus instead (LaMotte 2018). A more aggressive rejection comes in the form of religious objections to abortion and reproductive technologies such as IVF (Sallam and Sallam 2016). Religious objections also extend into stem cell research and the prospect of human cloning (Evans 2002). Sometimes backed with religious fervour, many people are avoiding and protesting vaccinations (Dubé, Vivion, and MacDonald 2015).

To authoritarian populists, science is not all bad. Again, it is not scientific knowledge per se that is the problem; it is elite scientists and scientific intellectuals who allegedly try to use their elite status and esoteric knowledge to control "the people" and destroy traditional ways of life. In this sense, scientific advances can be very useful if they do not make waves in the traditional culture, and are not promoted by "elites" as tools for steering society. In this way, technicians who use technologies for practical ends may be celebrated. For example, carpenters who uses power tools are not classified as scientific elites, nor are they shamed or shunned for using electrical equipment. To take another example—and this leads to the next "element"—advancements in military technology are not railed against, as they do not impinge on the rhythms, customs, and values of everyday life. They are simply more effective ways of killing, and most of their deployment happens toward Others. Military personnel who use the advanced equipment for killing, are not considered part of the controlling "elite," and the military is not decried as an elite institution.

Willingness for violent coercion

Finally, the acceptance or even romanticizing of coercion and violence as political tools is an important element. The Trump presidential campaign carried with it a couple of refrains that pointed in this direction, namely "lock her up" and "build that wall" (Kellner 2016). The shootings at abortion clinics point more violently in this direction (Franklin and Ginsburg 2019). Or consider the famous pick-up truck driver who intentionally ran into left-wing protestors at the 2017 Unite the Right rally, followed in 2020 with numerous instances of people running their cars into #BlackLivesMatter protestors. The acceptance (even if ostensibly in irony at times) of Nazi imagery is another case (Hartzell 2018). The right-wing general stance against gun control can also be considered a hint in this direction (Berlet 1995), while the public display of firearms by right-wing protestors during the COVID-19 pandemic is a clear sign. The fact that American popular culture is often so enamoured with guns is another indication, and the frequency with which shootings in schools and other public places have started to happen only further suggests this (Kellner 2015).

Metaphor

As cognitive linguist George Lakoff has shown, everyday language and cognition are infused with metaphor, whether we are consciously thinking metaphorically or not (Lakoff and Johnson 1980; Lakoff 2014). Even when we do not "mean" the connotations attached to our words, even if they remain invisible and unarticulated, even unconscious, they are still tapped. While the typical use of the term "metaphor" is to refer to one thing standing for another thing in a unidirectional relationship, scholars from a variety of disciplines are turning to the notion that "bidirectionality" is a staple of metaphorical cognition, rather than being exceptional (Goodblatt and Glocksohn 2017). When object A and object B are brought into metaphorical relation, they typically both become coloured with or framed by the other. And these metaphors can be powerful influences on our politics and other values. With this understanding, it is easy to see how disease narratives and Othering could be so entangled in one another, how Others could be described as "parasites" or "cancers" and how illnesses of public concern so often have "War" declared on them in popular and political parlance.

There are different types of metaphor. There is a more direct, denotative type, such as "A is like a B." Then there is the more metonymic type which can be more indirect and connotative. For instance, when somebody says, "give it a little elbow grease," this refers to muscular force, not literal "elbow grease" (whatever that would be). This type is more like association due to proximity or attribution, while metaphor taps more into direct comparison of shared traits. "Synecdoche" is like metonymy and has to do with associations of parts and wholes, in either direction. Basically, if A is often a part of B, then when A is encountered or mentioned, B is evoked. It can be the reciprocal direction as well, so that when B is encountered, A is evoked—and in the common case of bidirectionality, then both would certainly be the case simultaneously.[2] To note that on the one hand metaphor—including metonymy and synecdoche—is a deep aspect of everyday cognition, and on the other hand metaphorical cognition is bidirectional, is to note that everyday cognition is framed in and structured by complex chains of reciprocal connotation.

This is significant for the present discussion especially when it comes to different and even seemingly paradoxical meanings apparently signified in the same object. Wholes are invariably made up of multiple parts, which means that in bidirectional synecdoche, the significations of the various parts influence one another because each is influenced by the whole that they all feed into. Each part is mediated by the whole, and the whole is mediated by the entire collection of the parts. By extension, the parts bleed into one another.

There are deep connections between pandemics and authoritarian populism. This is true on the level of metaphor, and on the level of reality, of history. This is not to say that the one causes the other, or that they are inseparable. They are different animals entirely, yet both take place for us within the murky and malleable realm of human understanding, which is forever subject to the dominating shadows and directions of the unconscious. And in the unconscious, their logics are commensurate.

Historian William H. McNeill (1998) suggests that stretching back even into humanity's prehistory, our societies have been characterized by shifting dynamic interrelations among (a) deadly disease outbreaks, (b) intergroup conflict, and (c) technological change, or in other words, scientific progress. Regarding the last of these, techno-scientific advances in areas such as food production would often lead in two directions. First, population growth, which could inspire geographical movement and conflict with outside groups. Geographical movement, conflict with outside groups, and of course the combination of the two, could also expose people to new diseases their immune systems are unequipped to handle. Second, disruption of local ecosystems, which would also lead to disease outbreaks. From the start of humanity's story, the twin threats of plagues ("microparasites") and Other peoples ("macroparasites") have been central elements, deeply intertwined with scientific advancement. Jared Diamond (1999) makes a similar claim—geography has shaped the destiny of different societies and the interactions between them, via military violence, disease outbreaks, and urbanization/technology. If, as Marx once wrote, the "tradition of all past generations weighs like a nightmare on the brains of the living," this nightmare must be saturated with concerns about pandemics, Others, and the role of science in society.

In the last several years, "tribalism" and "polarization" have risen to become raging topics at the forefront of public discussion across the political spectrum. Around 2018, several political commentators and academics released books focusing on these notions, in application to American political and social life (Chua 2018; Abramowitz 2018; Mason 2018; Goldberg 2018). "Tribalism," when kept on the general level, is a neutral term—in the sense that there is no designated "good" or "evil" side, rather the affliction is the social antagonism, which cuts both ways. By contrast, many will point out that equating the two sides is grossly misleading. For instance, it is a false equivalency to group under one heading the contemporary sense among many white people of persecution and "extinction anxiety," perhaps the threat of affirmative action and like policies, with the black history of being on the victimized side of slavery, imprisonment, systemic underprivilege, and police brutality. The protest against "false equivalence" surely has axiological and ontological merit. And yet still, a more general form of *protecting one's own group against threatening Others* is applicable in either case. On this issue, as with so many others in American political discourse today, there seems to be a kind of splitting impasse. But there is a philosophical way out, although it provides no clear guide for action in itself. This way is Theodor Adorno's (1966) way—acknowledging and even embracing contradiction rather than trying to avoid it, seeing the general and the particular as mutually generative and dependent, and yet as irreducible to one another. To put this in a more direct way: tribalism is a very broad concern in the US these days, that is not limited by political alignment Left vs.

Right. Within this trans-partisan form, there are different experiences, perspectives, and dynamics that are more appropriately understood as on this or that side of the tribal divide, and in fact this "general" tribalism can only be understood as constituted by a combination of these particular, localized experiences and perspectives.

In the COVID-19 era, tribal alignments arose over the question of if, how, and when to lockdown, quarantine, and "open up" the economy again. In essence, the Left wanted caution and restraint, and the Right argued against it. The mask took on a special symbolic role in this rivalry, almost like a gang emblem. In most cases, differences of opinion over the wearing of masks did not escalate to violence, but there are a variety of documented cases where they did. Of course, part of the right-wing discourse, promulgated by Trump, was blaming the virus on the Chinese, as he adopted names for it such as the "China virus." And in turn, anti-Asian prejudice and violence rose considerably, specifically surrounding this issue of blame for the scourge. On more of the left-wing side, Social Darwinist metaphors abounded, about the inferiority of people who refuse to wear masks or social distance—nature will weed these "stupid" people out with the sickness, by killing more of them than those who take the recommended precautions.

Historically speaking, prejudice toward some population (racial or otherwise) in reaction to pandemic illness is very common. For instance, Jews were routinely driven out, killed, even burned at the stake, during the Black Death in Europe. In different locales and different times, cholera was blamed on different scapegoated groups. The nineteenth-century global cholera outbreak of 1826–1837 is often referred to as "Asiatic cholera." In England during the 1830s and 1840s, blame was placed on the poor, who were truly at much greater risk for contracting the disease because they were forced to live and work in horribly inhumane conditions (Alcabes 2010; Engels 1993). In several places, including New York, cholera was often blamed on the Irish (Shah 2016). Sontag (1989, 169) reports of "incarceration in detention camps surrounded by barbed wire during World War I of some thirty thousand American women, prostitutes and women suspected of being prostitutes, for the avowed purpose of controlling syphilis among army recruits." The global flu outbreak of 1918–19 is often referred to as the "Spanish flu," despite there being no evidence of it originating in Spain or disproportionately impacting people of Spanish descent (Rolfsen and Tworek 2020). In Los Angeles in the early twentieth century, Mexicans were repeatedly quarantined as a protective measure against multiple diseases, e.g., smallpox, typhus, and pneumonic plague (Honigsbaum 2019). During the late twentieth century, in the early decades of HIV and AIDS, the ailment was sometimes referred to as the "gay plague."

Susan Sontag (1989) explains that this notion of blaming a disease outbreak on a subpopulation, and at the same time associating that population with the disease and with having the disease, has a long history stretching back to ancient times. Diseases like HIV inherit the "plague metaphor," whereby they are viewed as divine punishment for the alleged moral transgressions of some subpopulation. Tendencies follow from this—the splitting of the population into healthy vs. sick, confounding this split with an associated demographic division (it could be ethnic and/or sexual, etc.) and moral judgment. Hence on one side we have a group associated with health and moral salience, and on the other side we have a group associated with sickness and moral depravity. And important to note—the former group are not immune to the pandemic; they are vulnerable. Maybe they suffer it less because it is really meant as a punishment for the latter group. In some sense though, the whole society is morally polluted because of the presence of the transgressing subpopulation.

This was the story during the Middle Ages, first with the exclusion of lepers and then with the treatment of Jews during the Black Death, as mentioned above. With the denotation of AIDS as the "gay plague," some of the same religious sentiment was involved. Yet the literal belief in "God" is not necessary for the basic nature of the plague metaphor to be active. For Sontag, the metaphor of plague can still involve a condemnation of the ill that has something of an unconscious religious flavour. Many in England during the time of cholera believed in the theory of "miasma" as the cause of disease. According to this theory, diseased air—probably with rancorous odour—was the cause of illnesses such as cholera. Despite the material explanation, the poor could still be held as to blame for the scourge. Only now, some combination of organic inferiority and unsavoury behaviour could be assumed. In essence, it is still the fault of the afflicted, but now without the intermediary of divine judgment. With the rise of Social Darwinism and the Germ Theory of illness, the characters changed but the story remained the same. To be ill signified some combination of being genetically more susceptible, thus of an inferior caste, and having brought the scourge upon oneself due to licentious behaviour, or being a drunk, etc.

Moving through the twentieth century, the trend toward focusing on the *individual's* (often sexual) "deviant" behaviour, as the alleged moral violation that almost "karmically" brings sickness upon oneself, rose (Alcabes 2010). The discourse moved toward a discussion of "risk factors" and "at-risk" groups. This new individualization of risk, focusing on personal behaviours rather than group characteristics, may have muddied the waters somewhat but the tendency to Other and to blame Others remained strong. Not only did those who engaged in (or who were assumed to engage in) "risky" behaviours thereby become members of an "at-risk" group, but also the same old racism could just be translated into this new language. For instance, during the AIDS crisis, African Americans were associated with a greater tendency to engage in risky behaviours—one could say that in this case the pairing of race with blame was only *mediated* by the *language* of risk.

Not only do blame and stereotype operate here, but the notion of moral failing is also still operant. In the case of AIDS, promiscuity, homosexuality, and intravenous drug use were all identified as primary ways to contract the disease. Sontag notes that all of this dovetails elegantly with conservative attitudes already present, about these activities being morally repugnant, and for religious conservatives, against the will of God. Thus, issues of moral "pollution" and divine punishment comingled with modern secular and medical notions of "risk" behaviours. And arguably, the discourse of "risk" shared with religious discourses a core thread of moralization, condemnation of transgression, social categorization, and exclusion. Anthropologist Mary Douglas suggests this to be the case—that today, when disease is associated with "risk" behaviours, the notion of "risk" functions akin to the notion of "sin" (Douglas and Wildavsky 1983; Douglas 2013; Washer 2010).

Foucault says some commensurate things. In *History of Madness* (Foucault 2009) he identifies ancient origins of psychiatry and psychiatric thinking today in the exclusion of lepers from society in Medieval Europe. Through ritualized procedures, people who suffered from the disease were morally segregated and physically expelled from "normal" society—a pure and stark form of Othering, specifically revolving around the contraction of illness. Although contents and styles have changed over time, the Othering of the diseased has been a constant. Foucault (1990; 2006) also discusses the transfer of authority and style of power from religion to medicine. For instance, he sees the function of the religious confession transferred to the medical or psychiatric assessment—the authority of the priest in the ways of God to the authority of the doctor in the ways of scientific medicine and the body. In both cases, we inhabit a safe space, in confidentiality, to fully divulge our transgressions and impurities, and to seek absolution or relief from suffering by the words and edicts we receive. Whether religious confession or doctor's appointment, divulgence of sexual "deviance" (e.g., promiscuity, homosexuality, etc.) may be part of either scenario.

Douglas also views responses to "risk" as falling within general patterns of social Othering. Hence the classification of "at-risk" groups, and the moral stigmatization attached to them via the condemnation of "risk" behaviour, is intimately connected with the sort of drawing of social boundaries that underlies racism and tribalism.

> [W]hen the new disease AIDS appeared, symbolic boundaries were constructed between healthy self and diseased *other* that functioned to apportion blame. The people in the category of *other* were then seen as responsible for the genesis of the disease; and/or for "bringing it on themselves"; and/or for "spreading" it.
>
> (Washer 2010, 176)

This is more or less the same conclusion as Sontag's identification of the "plague metaphor" in the AIDS-related homophobia of the 1980s (Sontag 1989). Douglas also notes that when outsiders (Others) are not blamed for disease, oftentimes *elites* are. Blame tends to flow in one or both of these directions, toward one or both of these targets (Douglas and Wildavsky 1983; Douglas 2013; Washer 2010). As discussed above, in the case of authoritarian populism the combination of these directions is the direction of the vitriol of "the people."

The kinship is very strong here between authoritarian populism and popular reactions to disease outbreaks. The connection between authoritarian populism and movements to protect the health of "the people" can be illuminated further using Foucault's ideas concerning the rise of Nazism in the twentieth century. Foucault (2003) stresses that two types of "racism" came together in an explosive way in the early twentieth century: (a) ethnocentric, and (b) biological or eugenic. The meeting of these two racisms facilitated the Nazi ideology which saw the Aryan people as superior to other races not just culturally but in a biomedical sense. And it is this more biological form of racism that, for Foucault, really provided the ideological justification for genocide. It is through the biological form of racism that medical rationality could fuse with military rationality, and the atrocities of Nazi Germany such as extermination of millions of people could be rationalized as in the interest of the health of the nation. The basic dichotomy between essentialized categories of normal people and abnormal people, and the institution of measures to protect the normal from the abnormal (the superior from the inferior, the healthy from the sick, the sane from the mad, the clean from the dirty, the law-abiding from the criminal, etc.), typifies the "biopolitical" logic of the Nazis, and persists in many guises today, all over the world, the United States included. It is alive and well in our institutions and popular narratives.

Sontag notes as well that popular discourse about disease often adopts militaristic language. Talk about a "fight" or "war" against disease is beyond the point of cliché—it is so familiar it almost feels literal. On September 16, 2014, President Obama revealed he would be sending US troops into West Africa to help combat Ebola, setting up a "military command center" in Liberia (Obama 2014). Hence, consonant with what the governments of Liberia, New Guinea, and Sierra Leone were already doing in the face of the outbreak, medical assistance was fused with military presence. A recent op-ed in the *New York Times* reads: "How Americans Lost the War on COVID-19" (Krugman 2020). Consonant with Foucault's diagnosis of Nazi biopolitical reasoning, Sontag warns of this tendency for military and medical metaphors to mix, as the conjunction is often used by demagogues—or "agitators," as Löwenthal and Guterman (1970) called them in their seminal work on authoritarian rhetoric *Prophets of Deceit* (Löwenthal 1987)—to identify a subpopulation as something society needs to be "cured" of, through force. In other words, when a group of people is viewed not just as suffering from disease but as *being* a disease, and logics of war are invoked, the door is opened to genocidal reasoning.

The status of medical rationality in authoritarian populist discourse, however, should not be understood in too rigid a way. In Nazi Germany, medical science was an integral part of the movement, and yet romantic irrationalism—anti-modern and anti-intellectual—was an overriding source of authority and inspiration. Hence the movement displayed plenty of distrust toward rational institutions, yet maintained a central place for scientific medical experimentation, as horrific as so many of the experiments of the

Nazi doctors were (Lifton 1986). In the United States today, the far-Right tend to lean more toward religion, tradition, and "common sense" as legitimate sources of knowledge and authority, while scientific reason is valuable insofar as it serves to further utilitarian ends or technological achievements with market value. These are not the only times that medical professionals attracted distrust and ire during a disease outbreak. Shah (2016, 125) reports that during the "Asiatic Cholera" pandemic:

> When cholera hit Europe in 1832, rumours that hospitals were in the business of killing patients to rid society of those deemed "surplus" made the rounds. People stoned and assaulted local physicians, accusing them of killing cholera victims for the express purpose of dissecting their bodies [...] During cholera outbreaks in New York, mobs attacked quarantine centers and cholera hospitals, and blocked health officials from removing cholera-struck corpses from their tenements.

During the Ebola outbreak of 2014, governments in West Africa responded with many coercive controls, including mandatory treatment facilities, outlawing traditional burial practices, and the dispersion of military personnel. There were a variety of conspiracy theories about healthcare workers, including that they were intentionally spreading Ebola, and even that they were "cannibals or harvesters of body parts for the black market in human organs" (Snowden 2020, 498). Conspiracy theories about COVID-19 are prevalent today: that the disease is a myth or at least is hyperinflated as a coordinated attack on Donald Trump by the Democrats (i.e., the elite political establishment), that part of this ruse is the gross distortion of death counts from COVID-19 to label many deaths actually from other causes, as due to the Coronavirus (i.e., "the doctors are in on it"), the idea that when a vaccine comes out it will contain a microchip for the government to track you. These are conspiracy theories that thrive on populist urges; still, recognizing this fact, the fear of medical science being part of a larger system of social (authoritarian) control has precedent.

In *Discipline and Punish*, Foucault identifies the medieval plague-stricken town as the origin and perhaps haunting archetype of modern methods of control and surveillance. The plague town is divided into parts, and each part is watched over by an intendent, each street watched over by a "syndic." Records are taken and kept on the people of the town. Individual movement is strictly controlled.

> If it is absolutely necessary to leave the house, it will be done in turn, avoiding any meeting. Only the intendents, syndics and guards will move about the streets [...] Each individual is fixed to his place. And, if he moves, he does so at the risk of his life, contagion or punishment.
>
> (Foucault 1995, 195)

Foucault explains that the medieval plague town is in a temporary situation—"normal" life is not supposed to be within this state of crisis, nor within the strictures undertaken to ward off the chaos of disease and death. In the modern period, however, surveillance, in the form of record keeping, assessing, partitioning space, and controlling movement, has seeped throughout society into so many spaces that it characterizes an ongoing situation, rather than an exceptional one. The severity of the control in the medieval plague town is greater than typical in modern life, but the methods of what Foucault calls "disciplinary power" are constant and far-reaching. If the plague town is something of an ancient microcosm of modern surveillance, it is not unreasonable to fear that if the exceptional situation were to return (e.g., a modern plague town), so might some of the severity of the exceptional situation.

Nazi political theorist Carl Schmitt (2005) believed that the sovereign—the central ruler—should be invested with the authority to declare circumstances abnormal and in need of emergency responses, and then to order those emergency responses without recourse to checks, balances, and democratic deliberations. Giorgio Agamben (2005) warns that the distinction between a "state of exception" and normal circumstances has largely eroded today. In the United States, the frequency of Donald Trump's executive orders (more the rule than the exception) attests to Agamben's point. The immigrant children held indefinitely in detention camps speak of this condition as well.

When COVID-19 was first becoming a concern in Italy, Agamben criticized the government's control measures on the grounds that this was exactly the sort of "state of exception" scenario he warned about. Part of his claim was that the state was dramatically over-reacting. At the very least, this latter assumption was an unfortunate misunderstanding on his part, and he has received quite a bit of criticism for his early statement. When faced with the question of control measures against COVID-19 in the United States, Trump and his cadre protest the protective measures promoted by the Democrats and the scientific community (e.g., the CDC, the WHO, Dr. Fauci, etc.), sometimes with the heated claims that these measures—no doubt suggested and implemented in the sense that we are in exceptional circumstances—are totalitarian inroads. Not wearing a mask is touted as an act of defiance against oppressive authority. This is the sense in which Trump's brand of neoliberal authoritarian populism is at least not now promoting the sort of total surveillance that the term "totalitarianism" implies. And yet in questions of the economy, "opening up" becomes no less coercive than "locking down," as the onus is on the individual whether and how to go back to work in many cases. The absence of state control in this case is also an absence of state support, and in the abdicating of responsibility to intervene on behalf of supporting the medical safety *and* economic security of workers, the state facilitates the situating of most of the country in a very constrained situation where the "choice" to go back to work is not much of a choice at all, it is a threat of unemployment and destitution if one does not adhere to the admonition to work no matter the health risk.

Clearly these issues are complex, and yet repeatedly, medical science and military violence occupy important positions in the debates that permeate and surround authoritarian populist movements. The question of the impacts and legitimate uses of medicine, science, and the military, as well as their relation to larger forces of authoritarian control, can come out with urgency in pandemic times. Compliance and resistance can be understood dialectically regarding this issue. Libertarian "resistance" to the advice of scientific experts and the left-wing voices who support compliance and government intervention, often supports Trump's tendency to ignore influence from qualified sources and exercise his own alleged "resistance" against control by Democrats and technocrats—and Trump's resistance to "elites" and "experts" manifests in exercising his own autocratic rule. To put it simply, in a two-party, roughly equally divided country, "resistance" of the Right to the Left, just as resistance of the Left to the Right, translates easily into authoritarianism when viewed from the other side. When science is allied with one side of this divide—as it is allied with the Left in the early twenty-first century—then it participates in this dialectical dance of liberty and oppression, of liberty of "us" from the oppressions of the Others. This is one of the pathways by which, at present, infectious disease is deeply intertwined with authoritarianism and populism. And as described above, relationships between pandemics and tribal/populist authoritarianism are many. Overall, the connections between the two are thick and well-worn over time.

Priscilla Wald (2008) seminally articulated the notion of the "outbreak narrative," which should be intuitively familiar to many people in the twenty-first century. Essentially, in this narrative, there is a large epidemic or pandemic, and society must mobilize in some form to counteract the threat by containing the spread and hopefully devising a cure or vaccination. Wald shows how this narrative embodies and is embodied by various social issues of the day. For instance, the Red Scare carried with it a fear of Communism as a social contagion, while *Invasion of the Body Snatchers* followed an outbreak narrative and carried with it Cold War metaphors of the threat of Communism. Much like Sontag's discussion of military metaphors in disease narratives and disease metaphors in military narratives, Wald's analysis of the relationship between sociopolitical and epidemiological understandings runs in both directions.

In this chapter, disease outbreaks and three elements of authoritarian populism were shown to be historically intertwined through a variety of pathways, some material, and some narrative. Next, twentieth-century history will be recounted from a different, but related angle, focusing on a few more layers: social histories of science and medicine in fact and in Hollywood fiction.

Notes

1 See Morelock and Narita (2018, 2019, 2021).

2 I would like to suggest that what is true historically might tend to become true culturally and thus true psychologically, for many people. History, culture, and psychology like to operate in tandem, and the tropes of history often become tropes of popular discourse and of the unconscious.

References

Abramowitz, A. (2018). *The Great Alignment: Race, Party Transformation, and the Rise of Donald Trump*. New Haven: Yale University Press.

Adorno, Theodor W. (1966). *Negative Dialektik*. Berlin: Suhrkämp.

Agamben, G. (2005). *State of Exception*. Translated by Kevin Attell. New York: Columbia University Press.

Alcabes, P. (2010). *Dread: How Fear and Fantasy Have Fueled Epidemics from the Black Death to Avian Flu*. New York: Public Affairs.

Berlet, C. (1995). The Violence of Right-Wing Populism. *Peace Review*, 7(3–4), 283–288.

Chua, A. (2018). *Political Tribes: Group Instinct and the Fate of Nations*. London: Penguin Press.

Diamond, J. (1999). *Guns, Germs, and Steel: The Fates of Human Societies*. New York: W. W. Norton & Co.

Douglas, M. (2013). *Risk and Blame*. New York: Routledge.

Douglas, M., & Wildavsky, A. (1983). *Risk and Culture: An Essay on The Selection of Technological and Environmental Dangers*. Berkeley, CA: University of California Press.

Dubé, E., Vivion, M., & MacDonald, N. E. (2015). Vaccine Hesitancy, Vaccine Refusal and the Anti-Vaccine Movement: Influence, Impact and Implications. *Expert Review of Vaccines*, 14(1), 99–117. doi:10.1586/14760584.2015.964212.

Engels, F. (1993). *The Condition of the Working Class in England*. Oxford: Oxford University Press.

Evans, J. H. (2002). Religion and Human Cloning: An Exploratory Analysis of the First Available Opinion Data. *Journal for the Scientific Study of Religion*, 41(4), 747–758. doi:10.1111/1468-5906.t01-1-00151.

Foucault, M. (1990). *The History of Sexuality. Vol. 1: An Introduction*. New York: Vintage.

Foucault, M. (1995). *Discipline and Punish: The Birth of the Prison*. New York: Vintage.

Foucault, M. (2003). *"Society Must Be Defended": Lectures at the Collège de France, 1974–1975*. New York: Picador.

Foucault, M. (2006). *Psychiatric Power: Lectures at the Collège de France, 1973–1974*. New York: Picador.

Foucault, M. (2009). *History of Madness*. New York: Routledge.

Franklin, S., & Ginsburg, F. (2019). Reproductive Politics in the Age of Trump and Brexit. *Cultural Anthropology*, 34(1), 3–9. doi:10.14506/ca34.1.02.

Goldberg, J. (2018). *Suicide of the West: How the Rebirth of Tribalism, Populism, Nationalism, and Identity Politics is Destroying American Democracy*. Danvers, MA: Crown Forum.

Goodblatt, C., & Glocksohn, J. (2017). Bidirectionality and Metaphor: An Introduction. *Poetics Today*, 38(1), 1–14.

Hall, S., Critcher, C., Jefferson, T., Clarke, J., & Roberts, B. (2013). *Policing the Crisis: Mugging, the State and Law and Order* (2nd ed.). Accessed July 18, 2020. http://oro.op en.ac.uk/37679.

Harris, L. (2010). *The Next American Civil War: The Populist Revolt against the Liberal Elite.* New York: Palgrave Macmillan.

Hartzell, S. L. (2018). Alt-White: Conceptualizing the "Alt-Right" as a Rhetorical Bridge between White Nationalism and Mainstream Public Discourse. *Journal of Contemporary Rhetoric,* 8(1/2), 6–25.

Honigsbaum, M. (2019). *The Pandemic Century: One Hundred Years of Panic, Hysteria, and Hubris.* New York: W.W. Norton.

Kellner, D. (2015). *Guys and Guns Amok: Domestic Terrorism and School Shootings from the Oklahoma City Bombing to the Virginia Tech Massacre.* New York: Routledge.

Kellner, D. (2016). *Donald Trump as Authoritarian Populist.* Accessed July 18, 2020. http s://link.springer.com/chapter/10.1007/978-94-6300-788-7_6.

Kors, A. C., & Silverglate, H. (1999). *The Shadow University: The Betrayal of Liberty on America's Campuses.* New York: Simon & Schuster.

Krugman, P. (2020, July 6). How Americans Lost the War on COVID-19. *The New York Times.* At https://www.nytimes.com/2020/07/06/opinion/covid-19-trump.html.

Lakoff, G. (2014). Mapping the Brain's Metaphor Circuitry: Metaphorical Thought in Everyday Reason. *Frontiers in Human Neuroscience,* 8, 958.

Lakoff, G., & Johnson, M. H. (1980). *Metaphors we Live By.* Chicago: University of Chicago Press.

LaMotte, S. (2018, February 7). "Inoculate Yourself with the Word of God": How Religion Can Limit Medical Treatment. *CNN.* https://www.cnn.com/2018/02/07/ health/religion-medical-treatment/index.html.

Lifton, Robert Jay. (1986). *The Nazi Doctors: Medical Killing and The Psychology of Geno- cide.* New York: Basic Books.

Löwenthal, L. (1987). *False Prophets: Studies in Authoritarianism.* New York: Routledge.

Löwenthal, L., & Guterman, L. (1970). *Prophets of Deceit: A Study of the Techniques of the American Agitator.* 2nd ed. Palo Alto, CA: Pacific Books Publishers.

Lukianoff, G. (2014). *Unlearning Liberty: Campus Censorship and the End of American Debate.* New York: Encounter Books.

Mason, L. (2018). *Uncivil Agreement: How Politics Became Our Identity.* Chicago, IL: University of Chicago.

McNeill, W. H. (1998). *Plagues and Peoples.* New York: Anchor Books.

Morelock, J., ed. (2018). *Critical Theory and Authoritarian Populism.* London: University of Westminster Press.

Morelock, J., & Narita, F. Z. (2018). Public Sphere and World System: Theorizing Populism at the Margins. In J. Morelock (ed.), *Critical Theory and Authoritarian Popu- lism.* London: University of Westminster Press.

Morelock, J., & Narita, F. Z. (2019). *O Problema do Populismo: Teoria, Política e Mobili- zação.* Anhangabaú: Paco Editorial.

Morelock, J., & Narita, F. Z. (2021). A Dialectical Constellation of Authoritarian Populism in the United States and Brazil. In J. Morelock (ed.), *How to Critique Authoritarian Popu- lism: Methodologies of the Frankfurt School.* Leiden, The Netherlands: Brill.

Norris, P., & Inglehart, R. (2019). *Cultural Backlash: Trump, Brexit, and Authoritarian Populism.* New York: Cambridge University Press.

Obama, B. (2014, September 16). Remarks by the President on the Ebola Outbreak. *Centers for Disease Control and Prevention.* At https://obamawhitehouse.archives.gov/ the-press-office/2014/09/16/remarks-president-ebola-outbreak.

Otto, S. L. (2016). *The War on Science: Who's Waging it, Why it Matters, What we Can Do about it.* Minneapolis, MN: Milkweed Editions.

Rolfsen, E. & Tworek, H. (2020, February 5). When a Virus is the Cause, Racism is often the Symptom. *UBC News.* At https://news.ubc.ca/2020/02/25/when-a-virus-is-the-cause-racism-is-often-the-symptom/.

Sallam, H. N., & Sallam, N. H. (2016). Religious Aspects of Assisted Reproduction. *Facts, Views & Vision in ObGyn,* 8(1), 33.

Schmitt, C. (2005). *Political Theology: Four Chapters on the Concept of Sovereignty.* Chicago, IL: University of Chicago Press.

Schoepflin, R. B. (2003). *Christian Science on Trial: Religious Healing in America.* Baltimore, MD: Johns Hopkins University Press.

Shah, S. (2016). *Pandemic: Tracking Contagions, from Cholera to Ebola and Beyond.* New York: Sarah Crichton Books.

Shapiro, B. (2010). *Brainwashed: How Universities Indoctrinate America's Youth.* Nashville, TN: WND Books.

Snowden, F. M. (2020). *Epidemics and Society: From the Black Death to the Present.* New Haven, CT: Yale University Press.

Sontag, S. (1989). *Illness as Metaphor and AIDS and Its Metaphors.* New York: Picador.

Wald, P. (2008). *Contagious: Cultures, Carriers, and the Outbreak Narrative.* Durham, NC: Duke University Press.

Washer, P. (2010). *Emerging Infectious Diseases and Society.* New York: Palgrave Macmillan.

Chapter 2

Science, medicine, and society from the "Golden Ages" to 2020

1950s–1970s

Several retrospectively titled "Golden Ages" coincided in the middle decades of the twentieth century. Generated in the post-World War II economic boom, we had the "Golden Age of Capitalism" from 1945 to 1975. In this same time frame, and no doubt related to the economic trends of the time, the white middle-class "American Dream" was forged, which included the "nuclear family." Hence, some people on the political Right have referred to this as the "Golden Age of Family." This economic boom and fetishizing of suburban patriarchal life also overlapped with what has been called the "Golden Age of Medicine" (Light 2004) or "Golden Age of Doctoring" (McKinlay and Marceau 2002) the "Golden Age of Hollywood," the "Golden Age of Television," and the "Golden Age of Science Fiction."

The reasons for all these alleged "Golden Ages," and their flavours of Goldenness, are different in each case. As mentioned, the rise of the American Dream that included the nuclear family had much to do with the economic boom following World War II, but also with the "baby boom" that followed the war, and the optimism and patriotism that flourished in the wake of the defeat of German fascism. In the case of science fiction, the "Golden Age" was part of an era where short sci-fi stories were published in popular magazines. Many authors who are still very well renowned got their start publishing in such magazines. *Astounding Science-Fiction*, under the editorship of John W. Campbell, Jr., was especially significant. Campbell himself wrote the novella *Who Goes There?* (Campbell 1938/2009), which is the story that inspired the various films on *The Thing*. Campbell basically took what was, before him, a very pulpy genre of magazine fiction and breathed new life (i.e., quality) into it.

No doubt some of the impetus behind the boom in sci-fi was the wealth of scientific and technological advances that happened in the industrial revolution and continued over the first half of the twentieth century. Some of these involved improvements in transportation, like the locomotive, the automobile, and the aeroplane. Some involved communication technologies such as the telephone and the radio. All these rapidly changed the contours of everyday life. The photograph, the motion picture, the television, satellite technology, and early forms of the computer, all made their debut over this period. There were also major innovations in weapons technology, notably in radar technology and the atomic bomb. Science was unequivocally celebrated in mainstream America prior to World War II, but when the United States dropped atom bombs on Hiroshima and Nagasaki, considerable guilt and forebodings were evoked. Apocalyptic visions came to the front of popular consciousness, and general concern about the negative consequences of humanity's technological advances. And yet it was also clear in a non-partisan mainstream consciousness as well as federal fiscal priorities, that science was a tremendous asset in the war, and would continue to be so after the war. Science became something immensely important and dangerous. It goes without mentioning that this new charged vision of science could only add fuel to the imaginations of science fiction writers and fans.

In the time of economic prosperity following World War II, there was considerable investment of public money into science, including medicine. The country's medical infrastructure boomed, as did the public's faith in science and medicine (Starr 1982). There were major innovations in medicine during the early and middle decades of the twentieth century, especially in the treatment and prevention of various infectious diseases, through antibiotics and vaccines. These advances were so profound, in fact, that by the middle of the twentieth century the leading causes of death moved from infectious to chronic illnesses, such as cancer, heart disease, and so on. Especially in the post-war period, these major victories fed into much optimism about professional medicine and medical science. This is where the "Golden Age" of medicine/doctoring coincided with the "epidemiological transition" from an "infectious disease era" to a "chronic disease era."

While medical science was devising cures for a variety of infectious diseases, the medical professions were on an upward trajectory for some different reasons as well. In 1910, the "Flexner report" assessed every medical school in the United States. Its results being negative for all but three schools (Stevens 1971), the report was very influential in getting medical schools to uphold higher standards for training doctors. If the schools wanted funding, they had to comply with consistent standards set by the Council on Medical Education for their teachers, their graduates, and their facilities (Light 2004). As the training for the profession solidified, the American Medical Association (AMA) became active in promoting doctoring as an autonomous practice which should be sovereign from outside interference or regulation. Several different trends coincided: the sense of professional authority, the aura of esoteric knowledge and training, and so on, rose to prominence in the same decades as the solidification of medical training, the apparent victory over infectious disease, and massive federal spending on medicine. By the middle of the century, the physician was accountable almost solely to professional peers. In Eliot Freidson's (1970) terms, it was an era of physicians' "professional dominance."[1]

According to Thomas Szasz and Marc Hollender (1956), doctors and their patients at the time generally interacted in a hierarchical manner when the presenting issue was infectious disease, but in a more collaborative fashion when chronic illness was the focus. Since with the conquering of infectious diseases, chronic diseases became more common and of greater concern, the medical advances of the early twentieth century naturally led to an increasing prevalence of collaborative interaction between doctor and patient. Still, the more common assumption in the 1950s about the physician-patient relationship was that it was properly hierarchical, that patients should be compliant and respect physicians' professional knowledge and authority.[2]

With public investments in science and medicine, there rose an increasing number of scientists and medical professionals. But more than this, the booming economy meant a blooming and growing middle class. The general rise of the American middle class during this period was not just about family structure—it was also about a new era of occupational prestige for a growing portion of the population. While the development meant greater opportunities for work that was simultaneously intellectually engaging and financially lucrative, it also meant a greater amount of control invested in positions of professional power and influence. The open frontier of possibilities for technological progress and its marvels was marked, as also was the fear of society becoming administered by elite technocrats, as well as the fear of total annihilation. Jacques Ellul famously lamented the dawn of "technological society," where efficiency becomes the prime virtue (Ellul 1954/1964). The Nazis may have been defeated, but the Cold War with the Soviet Union remained. Now there was one clear evil geopolitical menace—Communism. A major element of this was an ongoing competition in science and technology to establish dominance, especially through weapons technology, but also through capabilities for space travel (Agar 2012). The role of science here, in relation to the threat of authoritarianism, is charged and ambivalent. The threat of being ruled by technocratic "experts" was a rising concern while the development of science and technology for military purposes was necessary in order to rival and hopefully outpace the Communists.

The competition for military, scientific, and technological prowess was coupled with the competition to ally with as many countries as possible, the allied countries being thus ostensibly invested in either Communism or capitalism as a global order. The Soviets were a formidable rival in this race, and with Mao's rise to power in 1949 and the Korean War's start in 1950, the fear that Communism could engulf the world gained in intensity. This was the era of the "domino theory"—that a country "falling" to Communism would result in surrounding countries doing the same—and the second Red Scare, where government surveillance and blacklisting ran rampant domestically, in an attempt to weed out suspected Communists and Communist sympathizers. Along with the international domino theory, there was a fear that domestically people could be manipulated or seduced into supporting Communism. For all the surveillance and blacklisting, the anti-Communist McCarthyites saw themselves as defenders of freedom and democracy. Both the domino theory and the fear of local indoctrination and recruitment have a structure similar to concern with infectious disease. Proximity could lead to infection, and you cannot always tell who is sick. At any moment, the virus could enter your home and infect your life, take your children away from you, and so on. In science fiction, anti-Communist metaphors abounded, mixed into narratives that also included fears about annihilation and technocratic authoritarianism. The tribal sentiments of capitalism vs. Communism were buttressed by the fact the Communist threat was consolidated in non-European countries across the Atlantic Ocean, and so the West/East binary was easily fused with the capitalism/Communism binary. In this matrix, anti-Communism inherited Orientalism. In the cinema, the rampant Communist metaphors were frequently associated with the exoticized East, further underscoring the Communist as foreign, backward, mysterious, non-rational, and Other (Hendershot 2001; Said 1979). And reciprocally, the stereotype of the non-rational, exoticized, non-Western Other was laced with anti-Communist paranoia.

Of course, the tragic irony (to put it lightly) of the Red Scare is that the anti-Communist measures were themselves founded in paranoid group-think, glaringly authoritarian, irrational, and thus a very real, immediate threat to many people in the United States. The threat of the authoritarian Communists had its counterpart in the threat of the authoritarian anti-Communists. Each side feared the authoritarianism of the other. What Hendershot identifies as rampant anti-Communism in 1950s sci-fi, could also be read as rampant anti-McCarthyism. This is not to say that Hendershot is wrong. Rather, the point is that different positions, experiences, perspectives, etc., even radically diverging along the political spectrum, had a similar enough broad form that these films could speak in metaphor to both sides of the divide using just one set of omni-resonant imagery and thematic. The metaphors were socio-politically *overdetermined*.

For mainstream white America a primary *intranational* Other besides the Communist was the person of colour, who may have inherited some of the friend-enemy dynamics from Orientalism and anti-Communism. As the Civil Rights movement gained momentum into the 1960s, with protests, riots, and so on, a common fear for white America may have been the notion of a mob of black revolutionaries, of a black uprising to overturn white privilege and extract violent retribution, possibly to the extent of white genocide reminiscent of the Haitian revolution. Partly out of this nexus of fearful Othering on the part of the conservative white population, black America was victimized by considerable violence during the 1950s and into the 1960s, perpetrated by the Ku Klux Klan and other white supremacists, often acting in mob formation.

In her essay "The Imagination of Disaster," Sontag wrote "The typical science fiction film has a form as predictable as a Western" (Sontag 2001, 209). She then identifies three different scenarios in sci-fi films, which contain considerable overlap. In each of them, a struggle against threatening Others takes a central role. Whether battling a race of extra-terrestrials or the catastrophic results of scientific experimentation gone wrong, in these films the normal must defend society against the abnormal. Us (the friends) must defend society against Them (the enemies). She sees considerable sadistic gratification in these films, claiming they are not so much about science as they are about disaster, being "concerned with the aesthetics of destruction, with the peculiar beauties to be found in wreaking havoc, making a mess" (213). There is a sense of freedom in the sci-fi disaster scenario because it "releases one from normal obligations" (215). The moment of disaster creates a kind of anarchic space which is cognitively freeing, and in addition we get to indulge in:

> extreme moral simplification—that is to say, a morally acceptable fantasy where one can give outlet to cruel or at least amoral feelings. In this respect, science fiction films partly overlap with horror films. This is the undeniable pleasure we derive from looking at freaks, beings excluded from the category of the human. The sense of superiority over the freak conjoined in varying proportions with the titillation of fear and aversion makes it possible for moral scruples to be lifted, for cruelty to be enjoyed. The same thing happens in science fiction films. In the figure of the monster from outer space, the freakish, the ugly, and the predatory all converge— and provide a fantasy target for righteous bellicosity to discharge itself, and for the aesthetic enjoyment of suffering and disaster.
>
> (215)

The dramatization of "freaks" or "Others" allows us to satiate our "hunger for a 'good war,' which poses no moral problems, and admits of no moral qualifications" (219). Hence military violence can be fully honoured, in an all-out war between friends and enemies, with no reservations, because on screen the Others are not really people. And yet the fact that this is an attractive experience for viewers indicates a desire to be free of moral scruples and wage all-out war in general, against some group that can be deemed outside of moral consideration due to sufficient difference. We watch it happen to aliens or zombies because on some level we want to do it to people. In the "good war" of the sci-fi film, we can fully indulge this desire through metaphor, without having to acknowledge the desire in any direct way.

Sontag also notes the ambivalent role of science and scientists in the typical sci-fi films of the era. She says that these cinematic scientists are almost never purely revered. There is a strong moral thread in such films about "the proper, or humane use of science, versus the bad, obsessional use of science" (216). Note the common trope of the "mad scientist," the deranged genius drunk on their own ingenuity, messing with things they should not be messing with, ultimately unleashing something horrific upon humanity. Sontag notes that this instability and potential depravity relates to their status as intellectuals, hence the sci-fi films reveal a species of anti-intellectualism that includes the educated ("elite") scientific community. The problem, hence, has less to do with science per se, and more to do with the "scientist-as-intellectual" (217), being overall "both satanist and saviour" (218).

The suspicion of the scientist-intellectual is central in *The Thing from Another World*, which came out in 1951. The film includes scientists and military characters, as well as a dangerous humanoid Other—"the thing." The scientists consist of a genius with a visage reminiscent of V. I. Lenin, and his underlings. Although not visibly a "mad scientist" per se, he is dangerously fixated on an alien life-form that the group uncovered from underneath the ice, and its plant-like offspring. He breeds the offspring, keeping it a secret from the military. The fact that the thing is extremely hostile to humans and powerful, does not deter him because he is so curious and fascinated by the life-form. He is so enraptured by his intellectual pursuits that he lacks common sense and concern for human safety. When the military set out to kill the humanoid, the scientist is willing to kill people to protect it.

Sontag's essay came out in the 1960s, and this was a time when popular estimation of physicians—and doctors' cinematic representation—was also just starting what would become a long decline, for a variety of reasons (Dans 2000). First, as the chronic disease era set in, so too did patients' general expectation of a collaborative relationship with doctors, rather than the hierarchical model that was more common over issues of contagion. According to Leo G. Reeder (1972), the shift in treatment from acute diseases to chronic diseases was also a shift from curative to preventive medicine, and hence also from a "seller's market" to a "buyer's market"—patients had to be persuaded to come in. Some of the physician's "dominance" was lost to the patient. This was the dawn of the "consumers movement" in health care; the hierarchical doctor-patient relationship evolved into the more equal relationship between "provider" and "consumer."[3]

The epidemiological transition from the "infectious disease era" to the "chronic disease era" coincides with what, from a Foucauldian perspective, might be understood as a change in the power relations that the doctor embodies. In Jewson's (1976) terms, it was a transition between "medical cosmologies," from "Hospital Medicine" to "Laboratory Medicine." In the former case, doctors have considerable power, and patients are dependent upon them. In the latter case, the doctor is under the direction of scientific tests (the patient is still dependent). The doctor no longer has autonomous "professional discretion" under the dominion of laboratory science. Another status-subverting aspect of the switch from infectious to chronic diseases is that doctors had built up an aura of effectivity that they could not sustain. Having risen to high esteem on the heels of medical advances in curing infectious disease, doctors began failing to live up to their reputations, since they could not so readily "cure" chronic conditions such as heart disease, diabetes, and cancer.

The counterculture of the 1960s was a complex of elements—besides the Civil Rights movement there were also significant feminist and anti-capitalist, back-to-the-land sentiments, a movement toward intentional communities and alternative lifestyles, a movement for peace, against the Vietnam War, a movement for "free love," the embrace of psychedelic drugs. A wide rebellion against the stifling conformity of the 1950s white middle class life extended through all of this. And relatedly, many young people advocated dropping out of society, seceding from the institutions and mores of contemporary society. Herbert Marcuse (1964), who rose to a well-loved position among the counterculture, warned of the creeping "one-dimensionality" of "advanced industrial society" during this time. At this point the New Left often took a stance against science and technology. Yet the relationship to science of the 1960s counterculture tended to be ambivalent overall, some protests being directed against scientific advances such as nuclear technology, other protests—such as against rampant pesticide use—being facilitated by scientific research (Agar 2012).

This ambivalence toward science can be seen in the original *Planet of the Apes*, which hit the theatres in 1968. The friend-enemy scheme is a central problematic here, within a framing that is both progressive and pessimistic. It is progressive because an anti-Othering message is glaring at the centre of the narrative. It is pessimistic because hardly any of the characters can overcome their tendency to Other, to be anything but callous or cruel. The non-human primates harbour a belief that humanity was immoral, dangerous, and hubristic with its science, and that the civilization run by apes is a much better one. We are forced to conclude that the apes are largely correct about what was wrong with human civilization, but also that they are wrong about being superior—their civilization is much the same. The ambivalence toward science and scientists is also clear. In the first part of the film, our human protagonist, Taylor, and his crewmates suffer inadvertent time travel during an adventure in outer-space (in this sense it is their own fault: if they had never ventured into space, they never would have gotten stuck in the future). Taylor—the only one of the astronauts whose character is developed, is a cynic and a nihilist. And yet the apes who are able and willing to accept him—Cornelius and Zira—communicate with him, and ultimately save him, are scientists.

In *Beneath the Planet of the Apes*, released in 1970, even more emphasis is put on the bleak message that human "progress" is destructive and amoral if not immoral. We encounter the last surviving humans, who have evolved to be super-intelligent and communicate psychically. They are also stubborn, emotionless, and cruel. The film ends when the planet is destroyed with a nuclear weapon. Then in *Escape from the Planet of the Apes*, Zira and Cornelius avoid the apocalypse by going back in time, where they are placed in a zoo. Throughout the film, Zira and Cornelius are assisted by two human scientists who watched them at the zoo. They are also fatally manipulated by the President's Science Advisor. In the course of the film, they become degraded celebrities, go on the run to avoid forced abortion and sterilization, and finally are shot and killed by government agents, but not before Zira gives birth to a baby who is hidden from the government by a circus keeper. The story revolves around Othering and tribalism, with two scientists positioned as the best friends to the apes, and another scientist—this one occupying an especially influential and elite position in society—as a villainous liar.

In the second half of the twentieth century, as doctors became increasingly beholden to scientists, so scientists became increasingly oriented to the body. For practising physicians, power was slowly delivered from the autonomous professional physician to science and scientists. For scientists, the bulk of research and development began a long swing from the physical sciences to the life sciences (Agar 2012). And alongside this sweeping change, the political Right would become increasingly hostile to science, the political Left increasingly embracing of it. No doubt this has much to do with the evolution away from spending primarily on bombs, radars, and rockets, and toward increasing reproductive choice and studying climate change. Birth control pills were approved for contraceptive use in 1960, abortion was legalized (through *Roe vs. Wade*) in 1973, and in 1978 the first baby was born from in vitro fertilization (IVF). Rachel Carson's landmark book *Silent Spring* came out in 1962, bringing to public awareness the damaging effects on health and the environment of industrial pesticide use, and setting a precedent for future environmental scientific research. Otto describes:

> On one side of the political schism over the biological and environmental sciences, we see the elements that became the modern US Republican Party, and that influence conservative parties in many Western countries: an anti-regulation, anti-reproductive-control, and pro-corporate marriage of old industry and old religion. On the other side we see the elements that became the modern US Democratic Party, and that influence the attitudes of progressives across the Western world: a pro-environment, prochoice, and anticorporate marriage of government scientists, environmentalists, and activists.
>
> (Otto 2016, 267)

Heading into the 1970s, sociologists announced the beginning of "post-industrial society," where service occupations eclipse manual work in the scope of the economy, and experts become more numerous and more powerful, playing an increasingly central role in decision-making in many spheres, medicine included, but also in politics in general (Touraine 1969/1971; Bell 1974). Yet as Bell suggested, there would also be social tensions specifically against this knowledge/ expertise stratification. Starting in the 1970s, as the consumers movement in health care grew, so also grew a movement to involve lay constituencies' perspectives and concerns in the negotiation of science policy (Agar 2012). The sense of individualism implicit in 1960s nonconformism and rebellion against institutions remained a central cultural trope, but it became consolidated increasingly with rugged individualism and self-gratification. The 1960s hippies became the 1970s "me generation" (Otto 2016). This type of anti-establishment culture is reflected in the portrayal of medicine in films from the 1970s such as *The Hospital* (1971) and *One Flew Over the Cuckoo's Nest* (1975). Frequently the hero of such a story is one who rebels against the inhuman bureaucratic control of the medical establishment (Dans 2000). When doctors turn out to be heroes, it is the ones who go rogue and disobey their regulations.

During the 1970s the health care industry bulked up considerably on government regulation through professional standards review organizations (PSROs) to oversee Medicaid and Medicare, and health maintenance organizations (HMOs). Large, for-profit health care organizations grew in prevalence during the 1970s and the 1980s (Starr 1982), which entailed more bureaucratization. This has been referred to as the "proletarianization" of physicians and the "corporatization" of health care (McKinlay and Arches 1985; McKinlay and Stoeckle 1988). In the scientific community, significant advances and newfound interests in the management of biology were taking place. The genetic code was completed for the first time in 1967, and early in the 1970s, further progress was made in manipulating DNA, facilitating rudimentary genetic engineering. Multinational corporations (including large pharmaceutical companies) invested heavily in biotechnology, and before long it was booming. Just after World War II, government funding poured into scientific research, primarily—but not exclusively—to enhance military capabilities. Now, public funding for science was on the decline, and private funding for research and development was on the rise, for biotech (Agar 2012).

The fear of domination by a technocratic elite is expressed in *Conquest of the Planet of the Apes* (1972). The story is set in a technocratic, dystopian slave society—the apes are slaves to the humans, who have them under surveillance. The apes are treated inhumanely, and apparently only two humans see the problem with this: a former circus keeper and an aide to the Governor. Caesar—the talking ape who is close with the circus keeper—leads the apes in an armed revolt, and ultimately to victory. And when Caesar is finally victorious, he reveals a deep bloodlust for revenge against humanity. Caesar has the potential to be a terrible tyrant, but when Caesar's girlfriend yells "no" as he is about to execute a human, he stops himself and proceeds to proclaim loftily that the new ape civilization will not display the barbarism of human civilization. Like the other films in the series, concern over tribalism and authoritarianism is central. Friend-enemy binaries are subverted yet pessimistically maintained. The old order deserves to be destroyed, but the new order will probably be just as bad. And the destruction of human civilization was brought on by humanity's moral failings.

Again, in Ridley Scott's *Alien* (1979), rebellion against the technocrats plays a central function in the story. The crew, aboard a commercial spaceship carting tons of ore, are woken up from their hibernation pods earlier than anticipated, due to a distress call from a nearby planet. Regulations—presumably from their employing company—require them to investigate any distress call. Once on the planet, some of the crew investigate an abandoned alien spacecraft. A face-hugger latches onto one of them, and those with the unconscious, latched-onto man bring him back to the ship. Ripley, played by Sigourney Weaver, argues that according to quarantine regulations from the science division at their company, they are not allowed to bring the facehugger onto the ship. She warns about the potentially life-threatening danger to the entire crew. Ripley refuses to let them back on the ship with the facehugger, but Ash (who we later discover is an android) lets them in anyway, going against Ripley's authority. Ripley condemns Ash for disobeying orders and being risky and unorthodox. The facehugger dies of its own accord, but a new alien pops out of the man's chest, and this new alien grows to be very large and kills almost everyone aboard the ship. Eventually, Ripley and the rest of the surviving crew discover that Ash is an android who was conspiring to bring back the alien, at the secret request of their employing company. Ash was directed to make sure the alien makes it back, all other considerations secondary, including the lives of the crew. During their final moments with Ash, between fighting with him, knocking his head off, and disconnecting his wires, Ripley speculates that the company wants the alien "for the weapons division," and Parker hears Ash calling the alien a "perfect organism" and expressing admiration for its lack of morality. Now, Ripley calls for the crew to abandon the ship and to blow it up with the alien inside it. Ripley shifts her position from sticking to the quarantining guidelines of the company to protect everyone, to turning against the company and ordering a massive explosion to protect everyone. It is a transition from compliance with medical scientists and bureaucrats, to going rogue against them and initiating massive destruction. Before, she was acting reasonably, except that she was being duped by the technocrats, whose safety guidelines were a ruse when compared with their hidden dark agenda.

1980s–1990s

The anti-establishment attitudes of the 1960s and "me generation" individualism of the 1970s transitioned into the neoliberalism of the Reagan and Thatcher era in the 1980s.[4] At the same time neoliberalism was beginning its triumph, the autonomy and "dominance" of physicians were in a process of deepening curtailment, often referred to as physician "deprofessionalization" (Ritzer and Walczak 1988). This trend was the product of trends that had grown in health care since the 1960s—commodification, corporate bureaucracy, government regulation, consumer advocacy, changing norms of doctor-patient (provider-consumer) interaction, etc. While the AMA was the guiding voice of the profession in the middle of the century, the trend over the latter half was for a multiplicity of "countervailing powers"—groups with different interests (e.g., consumers' groups, the state, insurance companies, etc.) having influence over health care (Light and Hafferty 1993; Light 2000).

The HIV/AIDS crisis showed doctors in the United States to be relatively powerless in the face of infectious disease for the first time in decades. The United States began to recognize AIDS in 1981. The following year, John

Carpenter's *The Thing* came out. The set-up of the film was very roughly akin to a sequel of the 1951 film *The Thing from Another World*, although the alien was very different, and in 1981 the original group who discovered "the thing" did not survive. This time, the alien works very similarly to the aliens in *Invasion of the Body Snatchers*—it duplicates itself and after killing other living things, it replicates them and uses their form as disguise. The doctor who first figures out the gravity of the situation, is also quick to have a mental breakdown. A combination of scientific knowledge and military violence are taken up to combat the thing, and clearly both are necessary; however the thing is ultimately too powerful and, in the end, the whole operation has to be burned down in order to have a hope of saving humanity, which constitutes suicide for the dwindling number of humans still alive at the outpost.

The ambivalence toward the scientist as both "satanist and savior," or in "risk society" terms as a source of catastrophe as well as necessary aid and expertise, is echoed in the *Back to the Future* trilogy, from 1985, 1989, and 1990. The first film of the trilogy opens with shots of a complex series of interlocking machines designed to take human labour out of someone's morning breakfast routine. The machines are very inventive, but also fail to work in a helpful way, at least now, with nobody home. Toast is burnt, a disgusting heap of dog food falls onto a dog bowl, etc. Soon after, Marty McFly, played by Michael J. Fox, is turning up all kinds of dials on a guitar amplifier, which contains one excessively humungous speaker. Upon playing his first note, Marty is sent flying across the room into a bookcase, and the speaker cracks apart. These inventions were all presumably made by Dr. Emmett Brown, played by Christopher Lloyd, who has the wild hair and eyes of a 1930s "mad scientist" (Frayling 2005). Dr. Brown's central creation of the film is a time machine, which runs on plutonium that he stole from Libyan terrorists. Dr. Brown is clearly erratic and messy. His haste in stealing plutonium leads to his getting shot down by the terrorists he stole from, as well as Marty's accidental time travel to 1955 as he desperately flees from them.

Marty enlists the Dr. Brown in 1955 to help him get back home to 1985. Dr. Brown in 1955 gives Marty a warning about the dangers of time travel, that anything he does could disrupt the space-time continuum. Much of the drama from there to the end of the film revolves around Marty's need to—before he (hopefully) goes back to 1985—undo the damage he has inadvertently done by traveling back in time and intervening in his parents' lives—damage which, if left unfixed, would mean he and his siblings would never be born. Eventually Dr. Brown and Marty fix everything, and their interventions even make Marty's family more functional and happier. In the remainder of the series, Dr. Brown and Marty skip around in time to fix Marty's family's problems in the future and Dr. Brown's murder in the past once he accidentally goes back in time to 1885. Their primary opposition in the future as well as the past, is a bully named Biff Tannen and his family—Biff's son Griff in 2015, and Biff's grandfather Buford in 1885. In the second film of the series, Marty gets a sports almanac from 2015 and plans on going back to 1985, placing winning bets, and striking it rich. Biff from

2015, however, discovers the almanac and the time machine, steals them, and travels back in time to give the almanac to his younger self from 1955. This results in the Biff of 1985 being Marty's ruthless, conniving, and authoritarian stepfather who murdered Marty's biological father George.[5]

By the end of the third film in the series, Dr. Brown is convinced that once they resolve their current set of self-inflicted problems, the time machine should be destroyed. It is destroyed accidentally, but Dr. Brown converts a locomotive from 1885 into a new time machine anyway. Evidently, for all the disruptions Dr. Brown and Marty caused with their time travel, they were able to solve all their problems, and improve their lives. Marty's family is better off than before, and Dr. Brown has fallen in love. Science and technology have clearly been "both satanist and savior" in this saga, with the power to be both very harmful and very helpful.

In the 1990s, there were several Ebola outbreaks in Africa, and although there was no such outbreak in the United States, the lethality of the illness and the lack of a cure earned it media attention and the status of a terrifying, if still distant, threat. Evidently, the AIDS crisis would most likely not be the last time the United States would be powerless in the face of infectious disease. In the middle of the decade two very popular books were published that may have added to popular concern over contemporary pandemics. These were Richard Preston's (1994) *The Hot Zone*, and Laurie Garrett's (1995) *The Coming Plague*. In 1999, the West Nile Virus made its United States debut (Preston 1999). George Armelagos and Kristen Harper (2016) believe that the "epidemiological transition" away from infectious disease and toward chronic disease has ended, and that instead we have entered another epidemiological transition where the problem of infectious disease returns. In similar terms, others have referred to the present as the "eco-epidemiology" era, in contrast to the preceding infectious disease and chronic disease eras (Susser and Susser 1996a; 1996b).

Regulation of medical practice evolved into "managed care" in the 1990s. The core of managed care is "utilization management," where "third party payers"—e.g., insurance providers, HMOs, PPOs, and managed care organizations (MCOs)—exercise oversight of medical practice through reviewing medical records, requiring prior authorization before services rendered or hospitalization, etc. Treatment provided should be "evidence-based" and "medically necessary" to be reimbursed by insurance. Managed care has persisted to the present time. While mainstream medical practice has become more standardized and accountable to laboratory science in the form of evidence-based practice protocols (Timmermans and Berg 2003), so Complementary and Alternative Medicine (CAM)—chiropractors, naturopaths, acupuncture, yoga, reiki, massage, over-the-counter supplements, etc.—has also risen in popularity (Goldstein 2000). In other words, while doctors are under increased scrutiny and control from outside sources and "countervailing powers," more and more consumers are losing faith in them and turning away from mainstream medicine.

In the 1980s and 1990s, as scientific medical practice became increasingly bureaucratized and people became increasingly disenchanted with it, an anti-science movement developed in the universities: postmodernism. In postmodern thought, the hegemony of science was contested on several grounds, e.g., the pretention to objective truth claims, its place in Euro-centric narratives and cultural colonization of non-Western cultures, its fixation on empiricism and formal logic, and so on. Starting in the late 1950s, a long-lasting rivalry developed in the university between science and the humanities, between positivism and interpretivism, etc., which reached an apex in the 1980s (Otto 2016). Postmodernism took up the torch vehemently in these "paradigm wars," launching a powerful attack on positivism (Guba and Lincoln 1982; 1994). The rejection of scientific rationality, objective truth, and the Western canon became staples of the postmodern Left. All the while, scientific research was making great strides in environmental and life sciences, which increasingly aligned science with the political Left, against the political Right (Agar 2012; Otto 2016). With both the sciences and the humanities on the Left, conservatism in the academy dwindled. And with the sciences on one side and postmodernism on the other, the academic Left was split.

The Right, on the other hand, suffered no such epistemological schism. Alienated from the university, the rejection of scientists and humanities scholars could coalesce into a wholesale rejection of the "academic elite." As far as the Right was concerned, the technocrats and the postmodernists were both part of the problem. Instead, the Right held onto religion, tra-dition, and "common sense," and touted these as moral goods against the degradation and hubris of the liberal academy. Although in different ways, positivism and postmodernism both spurned an engagement with "grand theory" and with the Western philosophical and literary canon. For positi-vists, grand theory could not be scientifically tested, and always took spec-ulative leaps that could not be empirically substantiated. Classical philosophy and literature both failed to provide any practical guidance for modern sci-entific inquiry. For postmodernists, grand theory was a totalitarian imposi-tion derived from Western minds who sought to project their agendas and their experiences onto the rest of humanity, silencing cultural differences and local knowledges. The ambition to objective truth, to somehow "accurately" enclosing the world within a clean, systematic philosophy, was also rejected as impossible and hubristic. Classical philosophy and literature were all taken from the dominant Western culture constructed by "dead white men," in other words not just outdated, but also dominated by white, male, Western, heterosexual and gender-normative voices. Sur-rounding the university there developed a political tribalism: The Right was aligned against both science and the humanities, while science and the humanities were pitted against one another.

2000s–2020

September 11, 2001 was a turning point in the history of American tribalism. The Cold War, the primary friend-enemy frame from the end of World War II until the Soviet Union fell in 1991, had not been replaced with any coherent threatening group of Others. Anti-immigration picked up considerable pace in the 1980s. Suddenly, when terrorists hijacked two commercial planes and flew them into the twin towers of the World Trade Center, destroying the buildings and killing thousands of people, that situation changed. The bombings were tied back to Al Qaeda and their leader Osama bin Laden, and suddenly people from countries in the middle east such as Iran, Iraq, and Afghanistan were suspected as possible terrorists. George W. Bush declared a "War on Terror," and identified Iran, Iraq, and North Korea as the "axis of evil." The response of the Bush administration was to consider the terrorist threat a state of emergency, and colour-coded, state-designated levels of terrorist threat became common parlance. The violent excesses of the Bush administration ostensibly in the protection of freedom and democracy included bombing civilian areas, suspension of habeas corpus for suspected terrorists, indefinite detention, torturing, and generally inhumane treatment of political prisoners.

The *X-Men* film series, spanning the early twenty-first century, revolves around issues of normalcy and abnormality, tribalism, and the moral rivalry between the pacifist, peace-loving Charles Xavier, and the militant, revolutionary, mutant supremacist Magneto. At times, Charles Xavier's X-Men and Magneto's Brotherhood square off over differences concerning whether, in the face of humanity's persistent discrimination against mutants, to try to make peace with humanity or to wage war. At other times, the two sides cooperate to defeat a major joint threat. In the first three films, *X-Men* (2000), *X2* (2003), and *X-Men: The Last Stand* (2006), Magneto is hardly a sympathetic character. The protagonist group is Charles Xavier's moderates, Magneto's extremists periodically fighting on the side of "good" (defending mutants when mutants are attacked, including Dr. X and his group) but placing the human Others beyond the boundaries of moral consideration. Despite these periodic transgressions into "good" territory, Magneto is always untrustworthy and ruthless, and all the films end with Magneto's and Charles' group butting heads, and Dr. X's group winning. The two are often compared respectively to Martin Luther King Jr. and Malcolm X. The comparison is not perfect, but it is consistent as a metaphor that fits with the late twentieth-century and early twenty-first-century mainstream American narrative that Martin Luther King Jr. was a true American hero and a peacemaker, and Malcolm X was a little too militant and confrontational.

Regardless, in some sense Dr. X promotes working for change within the system, which is often the American national narrative. And Magneto promotes war and victory over the Other, which—although also thick in American history—is typically cast as what authoritarian governments in Other nations do, quintessentially Germany under Hitler. As a revolutionary who is sympathetic and looks to empower his group who have been subjugated by "normals," Magneto is like Malcolm X, but in his touting of biological supremacy and his support for the domination or obliteration of humans by mutants, he is like Hitler. Magneto is something of a condensation of both figures, capable of simultaneously signifying black power and white power movements. Considering these films came out surrounding Bush's "War on Terror," one could also reasonably read into them a story that reflects some Leftist criticisms of American hegemony, yet emphasizes it is important not to become "radicalized" by terrorist groups, such as Al Qaeda. Magneto's revolutionary agenda is always too far, and so the lesson is always to stick with the moderate Dr. X, who stands for working within the system and making peace rather than making waves.

In 2011, Magneto has become more sympathetic. Marvel introduce a younger version of the characters in X-Men: First Class, and in this film, we get an origin story about the X-Men, the Brotherhood, and the friendship of Dr. X and Magneto. It is moreover an origin story about Magneto himself. The Nazi connection is stronger now, as the film opens with child Magneto in a concentration camp, getting separated from his family. A high-powered Nazi played by Kevin Bacon has Magneto's mother executed in front of him, as part of a training experiment, because he likes Magneto's powers and wants him to gain mastery over them. Once an adult, he meets Charles Xavier by having his life saved by him. The two become close friends, and Magneto's support of mutants becomes very clear, as he argues that they should not be ashamed of nor hide their differences; in sociologist Erving Goffman's (1963) terms, they should not feel the need to "pass" as normal by hiding their "stigmas." In giving great sympathy to Magneto throughout the film, we know from early on that he will kill without any moral scruples, but he also consistently does so after being wronged by humanity. His actions may be extreme, but time and again his position appears warranted. Dr. X, on the other hand, appears both idealistic and unrealistic, his pacifism functioning like a dogma that clouds his judgment and risks sabotaging himself and his cause of protecting mutants.

When the Nazi from Magneto's youth returns, recruiting mutants to join him and become empowered by waging war on humanity, Magneto fights back against him with the X-Men. But while Dr. X wants to spare the Nazi's life, Magneto goes rogue and murders the Nazi, after confessing to him that he agrees with everything he said, but since he killed Magneto's mother, revenge must be taken. Several elements are significant here—Magneto takes over the Nazi's place, organizing his own brotherhood, with much the same mentality. He is positioned as a victim of the Nazis, as fighting against the Nazi, and yet also as taking up the Nazi's mantle. He is both fascist and anti-fascist. In all, loyalty moves Magneto, and may be his only ethic. The loss of family is the trauma that truly motivates him, and now he is very loyal to mutant-kind, including his old friend Dr. X who is often fighting in opposition. He does not appear to condemn humanity on any moral grounds. He simply detests them and does not trust them, due to his history of trauma—the loss of family—at their hands. Magneto's framework is a strong friend-enemy binary, and loyalty to those closest to him, fighting for his own kind, is his sole mobilizing principle.

Not long after the 9/11 bombings, letters containing anthrax showed up at the White House, which immediately raised the threat of bioterrorism in minds throughout the country. And in 2002, a lethal epidemic dubbed Severe Acute Respiratory Syndrome (SARS), caused by a novel coronavirus, hit the world and caused a great deal of fear. It was by far most destructive in East Asia in general and China in particular, but by the time the epidemic was over, Canada had over 200 cases and the United States had 27 (WHO 2004). In the twenty-first century the list of new or newly recognized infectious diseases has already included avian flu, swine flu, Middle East Respiratory Syndrome (MERS), Methicillin-Resistant Staphylococcus Aureus (MRSA), Zika, and COVID-19.

Overall, the ambivalence toward science that was released with the dropping of the atom bomb has continued to the present time. Sociologists Anthony Giddens (1991a; 1991b) and Ulrich Beck (1992) have identified this anxious duality as a central feature of our "risk society," which is marked by the dependence on massive, "abstract systems" that seem out of our control and generally beyond our comprehension, where global disaster is a perpetual possibility waiting around every corner. Whether nuclear annihilation, cataclysmic climate change, emerging infectious diseases, terrorism, or some other apocalyptic scourge, we are dependent upon science, technology and globalization, which simultaneously threatens to end the world as we know it, if not our species.

The same year as *X-Men: First Class* came out, a revisioning of *Conquest of the Planet of the Apes* also came out, under the title *Rise of the Planet of the Apes* (2011). While *Conquest* was overtly political and concerned the systematic barbarism perpetrated against the apes under technocratic human rule, *Rise* is more focused on personality and loyalty. The issue of technocracy is gone, but the space of science is very ambivalent. Human experimentation on animals is very cruel in the wrong hands, but in the right hands, while still volatile, it can make amazing things happen. The story begins with a biotech company testing potential pharmaceutical cures for Alzheimer's disease on primates. On a trial subject, the drug is effective, but the chimpanzee becomes violent and out of control after giving birth, being protective of her new son. She is shot and killed, but one of the scientists, named Will, takes the baby chimpanzee home, and the baby turns out to have inherited the intelligence-boosting effects of the drug his mother was given. The highly intelligent ape Caesar and Will are intensely loyal to one another, and this loyalty punctuates the arc of the story. Caesar proves to be a danger to humans after he assaults a neighbour, biting off two of his fingers. His reason for assaulting the neighbour was based on loyalty, as the neighbour had been speaking and gesturing in a hostile, threatening way to Will's father Charles. Caesar is then locked up with other apes, where he and they might even be okay, were they not sorely mistreated by a young, sadistic employee of the facility. Will administers the Alzheimer's cure to his father, and it works, temporarily. Will's supervisor develops a more powerful, aerosolized version of the cure. Caesar gets his hands on the aerosolized cure, and while freeing the other primates he unleashes it on them, raising all their intelligences. The new cure acts as a pandemic virus to humanity, and so the escape of the apes from captivity (which turns violent) coincides with the beginning of a pandemic that extends all over the world through air travel, and that wipes out most of the human population.

"Risk society" themes are also very prominent here. Humanity's downfall is caused by scientists messing around with biotech. Globalization anxieties are brought in at the end of the film, when the spread of the pandemic is represented using a digital map, including dotted lines showing its dispersion between distant countries, presumably through air travel and aided by a globalized society. Humanity played God with medical science and caused its own global downfall.

Beginning in *Rise*, and a major theme in *Dawn of the Planet of the Apes* (2014), Caesar develops a rivalry for control with a militant, innately aggressive bonobo named Koba. The rivalry is very similar to that between Dr. X and Magneto, with Caesar seeking peaceful coexistence between apes and humans, and Koba seeking war between apes and humans. Once again, the divide is akin to the popular narrative of the divide between Martin Luther King Jr. and Malcolm X. At times Koba's perspective appears warranted, considering the consistent maltreatment of apes by humans. One of Koba's rhetorical tactics is to decry Caesar's loyalty to apes. Yet Koba is also manipulative, out of control, and in the last instance, only values the lives of apes who comply with his leadership. Koba's role is partly inherited from the Planet of the Apes films of the 1970s. In that earlier series, gorillas were innately predisposed to conflict, as a species. Now in the 2010s, it is only Koba who bears this problem. In the conclusion to the newer series, *War for the Planet of the Apes* (2017), Koba is gone, and with him the rivalry of attitudes toward humans. Caesar has come closer to Koba's original position, and peaceful coexistence between humans and apes is no longer considered. A young human girl displays some bridging behaviour when she brings food and gives her doll to Caesar during a time when he is tortured and caged by humans. Her compassion and the bridging surrounding it is not politically framed or backed with an explicit moral discourse. The girl's bridging behaviour is compassionate, but also personal and idiosyncratic. Later, Caesar's highlighted moment of compassion is to let a man commit suicide instead of killing him.

In *X-Men: Apocalypse* (2016), Magneto tries to maintain a normal life and keep his condition a secret, but when it is revealed, government agents come to his home and kill his family, and Magneto responds by killing the agents. Apocalypse, a recently awakened ancient mutant who used to be worshipped as a god, brings Magneto to Auschwitz, and convinces Magneto to join him in his quest to destroy civilization and begin anew, to "build a better one." He convinces Magneto by having him fully realize the extent of his powers, a process which involves flashbacks to his traumatic moments of losing his family. Magneto destroys Auschwitz, punctuating his alignment with Apocalypse. In one sense, this suggests that the holocaust was such an abomination that it proves human history has been horrific, humanity is guilty, inadequate, etc. Yet Magneto is not swayed by a moral or political argument. It is his personal sense of loss, the murder of those closest to him, that drives him. This is Magneto's general trend in the X-Men films of the 2010s: the trauma of personal loss moves him to militancy—not far from Hitlerism—to promote and defend mutant-kind, and the only thing that sways him from his dark tendencies is new personal loyalties. Ultimately, Apocalypse wants to become dictator of the world and enslave humanity. Magneto is finally convinced by Raven to fight alongside the X-Men against Apocalypse, but her convincing takes a very personal tone, rather than exhibiting any coherent moral principle or political value. It is Magneto's connection with the mutant Raven and his loyalty to mutants in general that inspires him to shift his position.

In 2017, the latest instalment of Ridley Scott's Alien films was released—*Alien: Covenant*. Along with the central friend-enemy binary of humans vs. aliens (and eventually androids), the "moral" deliberations of the film revolve around personal loyalties and risk assessment. The film is something of a hybrid between remake and prequel in relation to the first *Alien* film, from 1979. This time, instead of transporting raw materials for pay, the crew of the ship are trying to get to a new planet to colonize, since the Earth is no longer inhabitable (later on, the android David will indicate this is humanity's fault). As before, the crew wake from their pods before they were originally planned to, and land sooner than expected in order to respond to a distress call from a nearby planet. Before, regulations from the technocrats at "the company" required they stop and investigate. This time, it was a dangerous and unnecessary decision of the default captain, for reasons of personal insecurity. There are two androids, David and a doppelganger named Walter. Now, we are given an origin story for the central aliens of the film series. The aliens were created out of a bioweapon containing a virus/parasite that enters the body and aliens hatch from their human (or other animal) form like an egg, as in what happens after a human is conquered by a facehugger. David originally released the bioweapon, and from there, after doing some genetic engineering, he was able to create the aliens we have known in the series for the past four decades. Wariness of biotechnology and the life sciences is combined with the threat of pandemic viruses and bioterrorism, on top of the basic tribal rivalry for survival between the humans and the aliens. Like Magneto, David is militant about being free from human control—which tends to also mean genocide, i.e., killing every human and animal except for his genetically engineered aliens, which he considers to be a "perfect" species. He has some desire to unite with other androids in a friend-enemy pact, as evidenced by his attempts to bring Walter into his fold. If the Nazi insinuations were not blatant enough, David also has a love of Richard Wagner. In the closing scene we witness him, the lone awake member of the ship, listening to Wagner, and interacting with symmetrical forms and patterns—storing miniature alien eggs into a clean drawer of perfect, symmetrical circles, and strolling through a room filled with symmetrically arranged, hanging sleeping pods. The combination of Wagner's music and people arranged in replicated patterns harkens back to techniques Leni Riefenstahl used in the Nazi propaganda film *Triumph of the Will*.

The latest film in the X-Men series, *Dark Phoenix* (2019), is less moral and political than *X-Men: Apocalypse*, even more narrowly focused on personal and familial loyalties. Magneto has let go of his vendetta against humanity, but it is framed in terms of him having stopped killing because it did not ease the pain of his prior traumas—there is no political or even moral frame. His only real disagreement with Dr. X is over whether to kill Jean, one of the X-Men who is out of control and killed Raven. Jean's problematic condition started when Dr. X had some of the X-Men go up into outer space and rescue some humans from a shuttle that was being torn apart by a solar flare. Despite Raven's voiced misgivings about Dr. X putting mutants in danger to stay in humanity's good graces, Dr. X asks them to go, and in particular asks Jean to go out when time is running thin and one human is left aboard the shuttle. Jean physically internalizes the solar flare, and almost dies. Later, after Jean accidentally kills Raven, the mutant Beast yells at Dr. X that Raven's death is his fault, and that he should admit to being wrong. Beast turns to Magneto and the two partner up to seek revenge by killing Jean, out of loyalty to Raven. Jean proves much more powerful than Magneto, so his attempt to kill her fails. Dr. X is able to get through to her, and turn her against an alien who is trying to enlist her in a transcendence of her humanity through the force of the internalized solar flare; the transcendence seems like it will involve killing many people (and mutants) using unstoppable powers. Dr. X can convince her to resist the seductions of the alien and the destructive power by letting her see inside his mind, which reveals his memories about taking her in as a child. The sense of family loyalty brings Jean's full consciousness and conscience back into control. When she eventually faces off against the alien, she describes it as "protecting my family."

By the early twenty-first century, during the Bush administration and beyond, hostility of the political Right toward science became more palpable, and in 2005 Chris Mooney seminally articulated the situation in his book *The Republican War on Science* (Mooney 2007). Science was leading society toward reproductive technologies, environmental regulations, teaching evolution (not creation) in schools, and a generally atheist, materialist worldview. Although explicitly an "objective" and "disinterested" enterprise, it had become an implicitly Leftist purview. By the mid-2010s, postmodernism had fallen from grace. Its remaining residue was primarily in movements to diversify beyond the Western canon: intersectionality, feminism, critical race theory, queer theory, postcolonialism, decoloniality, etc. The American legacy of anti-Communism was mobilized to combat this in right-wing conspiracy theories about "Cultural Marxism," which boils down to a claim that Left-wing identity politics are totalitarian in the academy—especially in the humanities—and derive from postmodernism, which is in many ways a closeted form of Communist Marxism. It is allegedly a conspiracy to institute global Communism (no doubt in the image of the Soviet Union under Stalin) by undermining Western civilization and was set into motion by the Frankfurt School (Jamin 2014; Mirrlees 2018). Not just the anti-science and anti-intellectual far-Right tout this idea, but also some political moderates who leverage the conspiracy theory to defend the place of free thinking and scientific reason in the academy and society (Pluckrose and Lindsay 2020). Somewhere between the two camps is the public intellectual Jordan Peterson, who has probably done more to popularize the theory of "Cultural Marxism" than anyone else (Burston 2020).

In theory, the conspiracy narrative about "Cultural Marxism" would have the potential to swing the scientific community toward the Right; but this is not what is happening. Instead, the Left of the humanities no longer rails against science. The legacy of postmodern scepticism and anti-science has evidently passed to the far-Right, where a combination of religious faith and anti-intellectualism can thrive on the destruction of the legitimation of scientific objectivity that postmodernism wrought. Donald Trump thrives upon this, since without the need to appeal to evidence, he can make any claim that supports his agenda, and present it as his authentic—unfiltered by political correctness or the opaque tact of an establishment politician—judgment, which to many of his supporters is just as credible if not more so, than any hard evidence that contradicts him (Montgomery 2017).[6]

Perhaps a defining moment in this alignment was when Kellyanne Conway referred to the "alternative facts" that allegedly informed Trump's perceptions of the size of his inauguration party (Strong 2017). Trump's team thus enlisted relativism as his defence, and the host of Meet the Press came down on the side of empirical evidence and objective truth, represented by his on-air reply to Conway that would remain the general position of the Left-wing critique of "post-truth" Trumpism: "Alternative facts are not facts. They're falsehoods" (Bradner 2017). During the COVID-19 pandemic, anti-Communist paranoia was marshalled again in a different way by some on the far-Right, to associate the virus and protective measures against it with Communist takeover (Rooke 2020; Stone 2020; Media Matters Staff 2020). The Left has aligned strongly with the scientific community, the data coming from organizations like the WHO, and the suggestions coming from figures like Dr. Anthony Fauci. Since his campaign leading up to his presidency, Trump has capitalized on white anxieties about becoming a minority in America. Illegal immigrants were his initial primary Other to defend society from, and the construction of a wall along the US/Mexico border would be the symbol of that defence (Donovan and Redlawsk 2018).

Once the #BlackLivesMatter protests started up very strongly after George Floyd was killed by a police officer, Trump focused on the disruption of rioting and the illegality of looting, and suddenly the protesters became framed as

Others who were endangering "normal" society (Sherfinski 2020). He threatened to declare Antifa a terrorist organization, attempting to transfer to them and to the protesters in general some of the friend-enemy legacy of the War on Terror (Haberman and Savage 2020). Armed far-Right militias and counter-protestors showed up at #BlackLivesMatter rallies (Okoren 2020). The police used rubber bullets, tear gas, and excessive force and violence against protestors (Amnesty International 2020). In one instance, to get a photo shoot in front of a church, peaceful protestors were tear gassed to clear a pathway for Trump and photographers (Rogers 2020). Trump's authoritarian tactics escalated to having unidentified federal agents abduct protestors off the streets (Levinson et al. 2020). The President framed it as a question of escalating force until the problem was taken care of. His rhetoric was of protecting society from random violence and chaos, of ensuring order.

During the Trump era the Left identified a few Others at different times. Most consistently, it was white nationalists. After a protestor punched white nationalist Richard Spencer in the face on camera, debate would abound about whether it is "okay to punch a Nazi" (Stack 2017). During the COVID-19 pandemic, some voices on social media started adopting a kind of joking Social Darwinist language, to say people who ignore the advice from scientists will be naturally weeded out because they are not intelligent enough to survive. Similarly, social media abounded with voiced happiness or humour at prominent conservatives against social distancing or mask wearing contracting the virus. Black Nationalist views were promoted by an armed African American militia called the Not Fucking Around Coalition (NFAC), notably the desire to have the United States politically and financially support a separate black nation, either Texas, or elsewhere (Goldberg 2020). During the #BlackLivesMatter protests in the summer of 2020, the NFAC became a public presence, and began showing up to counteract far-Right groups who counter-protested #BlackLivesMatter rallies, such as the Kentucky "Three Percenters" (Zengernews 2020).

Around this same period, fantasies about beheading grew in popular political discourse. In February of 2017, a Jesus statue in Indianapolis was beheaded twice (Holcombe 2017). In May of 2017, Kathy Griffin posed for photos with a fake Trump head, bloodied and decapitated (Romano 2017). In May of 2020, the Trump campaign released an advertisement with doctored footage from *Star Wars*. Trump's head superimposed on Yoda's body, he proceeded to decapitate two enemy soldiers, with media logos for CNN and NBC respectively superimposed over their heads (Coleman 2020). During the 2020 #BlackLivesMatter protests, when statues of historical figures were being torn down, two Christopher Columbus statues were beheaded. In June, a Christopher Columbus statue in Boston was beheaded (Dwyer 2020) and on July 4, a Christopher Columbus statue in Connecticut (Owens 2020). About a week later, a statue of Jesus was beheaded outside a Florida Catholic church (Associated Press 2020).

Considering the above, it might not be coincidence that in zombie films, beheading is often taken up as one of the ways to effectively kill a zombie. Casting the political Other under zombie metaphors has also come in vogue, picking up speed in 2020. In 2010, bestselling author Jason Mattera's book *Obama Zombies: How the Liberal Machine Brainwashed My Generation* was published (Mattera 2010). In 2015, Ted Nugent published a blog post titled "Liberal Zombies' Toxic Logic" that begins:

> The Zombie Apocalypse has arrived. They're here, present and very dangerous to the American experience.
>
> Instead of eating our brains, the current crop of zombies wants to destroy America with poison logic and turn this wonderful country into just another failed turd-world nation.
>
> (Nugent 2015)

Several videos posted to YouTube use the zombie metaphor to refer to left-wing protestors, with titles such as "Zombified Anti-Trump Protestor goes NUTS!" and "Leftist Zombies Claw at SCOTUS Doors," etc. An essay in *The Guardian* from 2019 refers to conservatism as "The Zombie Party" (Beckett 2019). Economist Paul Krugman (2020) has recently referred to empty conservative economic mythologies using the zombie metaphor. On a blog post from April of 2020 called "Ahhh! The Liberal Zombies are Everywhere!" the author— "Mr. Erickson"—says: "There is no known cure for zombie liberalism." Below this sentence is a meme of a cartoon doctor pointing to the words "Liberalism is a MENTAL DISEASE!"

Notes

1 The field of sociology harmonized with the trend. To gain legitimacy as a "social science," sociology allied with professional medicine to help doctors ensure patient compliance, and to increase the foothold of sociology in the University (White 2017). Talcott Parsons, by far the dominant sociologist theorist of the 1950s, articulated the notion of "the sick role," a set of unwritten rights and obligations that were associated with a person being "truly" sick and taking appropriate action. Being in the sick role meant, among other things, actively trying to get better, and this included seeing a physician and complying with the physician (Parsons 1951).
2 This is reflected in the overwhelmingly honorific representation of doctors in film during medicine's "Golden Age" (Malmsheimer 1988; Dans 2000).
3 Especially since the rise of the internet, consumers have more access to medical knowledge and have become more knowledgeable about health, illness, and medicine. Part of the demand for greater collaboration in the relationship between provider and consumer is due to this narrowing of the gap in knowledge.
4 Going rogue or defying the bureaucracy was still a common trope in popular films, as in *The Verdict* (1982), where the lawyer we were rooting for wins a medical malpractice case by cajoling the jury to stand up to institutions (Dans 2000).
5 The 1985 authoritarian Biff character was modelled after Donald Trump (Stuart 2015).

6 At the same time, the alt-Right has started to specifically embrace the "classics" of the Western canon—the thought of writers from ancient Greece and Rome (Zuckerberg 2018). Despite this curious uptake of the classics by the alt-Right, the larger schism is between an identity politics of the Right combined with rejection of science, and an identity politics of the Left combined with an embrace of science.

References

Agar, J. (2012). *Science in the Twentieth Century and Beyond*. Malden, MA: Polity.

Amnesty International. (2020, August 4). USA: The World is Watching: Mass Violations by U.S. Police of Black Lives Matter Protesters' Rights. Retrieved from *Amnesty International*: https://www.amnesty.org/en/documents/amr51/2807/2020/en/.

Armelagos, G. J., & Harper, K. N. (2016). Emerging Infectious Diseases, Urbanization, and Globalization in the Time of Global Warming. *The New Blackwell Companion to Medical Sociology*, Chichester: Wiley, 291–311. doi:10.1002/9781444314786.ch13.

Associated Press. (2020, July 17). Jesus Statue Beheaded at Catholic Church in South Florida. Retrieved from *AP News*: https://apnews.com/c6f626d09dbf183d6bed915314e333c5.

Beck, U. (1992). *Risk Society: Towards a New Modernity*. New Delhi: SAGE.

Beckett, A. (2019, May 28). 'A Zombie Party': The Deepening Crisis of Conservatism. Retrieved from *The Guardian*: https://www.theguardian.com/politics/2019/may/28/a-zombie-party-the-deepening-crisis-of-conservatism.

Bell, D. (1974). *The Coming of Post-Industrial Society*. New York: Harper Colophon Books.

Bradner, E. (2017, January 23). Conway: Trump White House Offered 'Alternative Facts' on Crowd Size. Retrieved from *CNN*: https://www.cnn.com/2017/01/22/politics/kellyanne-conway-alternative-facts/index.html.

Burston, D. (2020). Jordan Peterson and the Postmodern University. *Psychoanalysis, Politics and the Postmodern University*. London: Palgrave Macmillan, 129–156.

Campbell, J. W. (1938/2009). *Who Goes There?* New York: Rocket Ride Books.

Coleman, J. (2020, May 4). Trump Campaign Video Shows President as Yoda Decapitating Cable News Networks on Star Wars Day. Retrieved from *The Hill*: https://thehill.com/blogs/blog-briefing-room/news/495985-trump-campaign-video-shows-president-as-yoda-decapitating-cable.

Dans, P. E. (2000). *Doctors in the Movies: Boil the Water and Just Say Aah*. Bloomington, IL: Medi-Ed Press.

Donovan, T., & Redlawsk, D. (2018). Donald Trump and Right-Wing Populists in Comparative Perspective. *Journal of Elections, Public Opinion and Parties*, 28(2), 190–207. doi:10.1080/17457289.2018.1441844.

Dwyer, D. (2020, June 10). Head Removed from Christopher Columbus Statue in Boston. Retrieved from *Boston.com*: https://www.boston.com/news/local-news/2020/06/10/christopher-columbus-statue-beheaded-boston.

Ellul, J. (1954/1964). *The Technological Society*. New York: Vintage Books.

Erickson, M. (2020, April 8). Ahhh! The Liberal Zombies are Everywhere! Retrieved from *Mr. Erickson Rules!*: https://mrericksonrules.com/2020/04/08/ahhh-the-liberal-zombies-are-everywhere/.

Frayling, C. (2005). *Mad, Bad and Dangerous?: The Scientist and the Cinema*. London: Reaktion Books.

Freidson, E. (1970). *Professional Dominance*. Chicago: Aldane.

Garrett, L. (1995). *The Coming Plague: Newly Emerging Diseases in a World Out of Balance.* New York: Penguin.

Giddens, A. (1991a). *Modernity and Self-Identity.* Stanford: Stanford University Press.

Giddens, A. (1991b). *The Consequences of Modernity.* New York: John Wiley & Sons.

Goffman, E. (1963). *Stigma: Notes on the Management of Spoiled Identity.* New York: Simon and Schuster.

Goldberg, P. (2020, July 6). More Details Emerge of 'NFAC' Groups After 'We'll Take Texas' Viral Video. Retrieved from *News Thud*: https://newsthud.com/more-deta ils-emerge-on-nfac-group-after-well-take-texas-viral-video/.

Goldstein, M. S. (2000). The Growing Acceptance of Complementary and Alternative Medicine. In C. Bird, P. Conrad, & A. Fremont (Eds.), *Handbook of Medical Sociology* (5 ed.). Upper Saddle River, NJ: Prentice Hall, 284–297.

Guba, E. G., & Lincoln, Y. S. (1982). Epistemological and Methodological Bases of Naturalistic Inquiry. *ECTJ*, 30(4), 233–252. doi:10.1007/0-306-47559-6_19.

Guba, E. G., & Lincoln, Y. S. (1994). Competing Paradigms in Qualitative Research. In N. Denzin & Y. S. Lincoln (eds.), *Handbook of Qualitative Research.* Thousand Oaks, CA: Sage, 105–117.

Haberman, M., & Savage, C. (2020, May 31). Trump, Lacking Clear Authority, Says U.S. Will Declare Antifa a Terrorist Group. Retrieved from *The New York Times*: https:// www.nytimes.com/2020/05/31/us/politics/trump-antifa-terrorist-group.html.

Hendershot, C. (2001). *I Was a Cold War Monster: Horror Films, Eroticism and the Cold War Imagination.* Bowling Green, OH: Bowling Green State University Popular Press.

Holcombe, M. (2017, February 23). Statue of Jesus Christ Beheaded Twice in Two Weeks. Retrieved from *CNN*: https://www.cnn.com/2017/02/22/us/jesus-statue-behea ded-trnd/index.html.

Jamin, J. (2014). Cultural Marxism and the Radical Right. In P. Jackson, & A. She- khovtsov, *The Post-War Anglo-American Far Right.* London: Palgrave Macmillan, 84–103. doi:10.1057/9781137396211_4

Jewson, N. D. (1976). The Disappearance of the Sick-Man from Medical Cosmology, 1770–1870. *Sociology*, 10(2), 225–244. doi:10.1177/003803857601000202.

Krugman, P. (2020). *Arguing with Zombies: Economics, Politics, and the Fight for a Better Future.* New York: W. W. Norton & Company.

Levinson, J., Wilson, C., Doubek, J., & Nuyen, S. (2020, July 17). Federal Officers Use Unmarked Vehicles to Grab People in Portland, DHS Confirms. Retrieved from *NPR*: https://www.npr.org/2020/07/17/892277592/federal-officers-use-unmarked- vehicles-to-grab-protesters-in-portland.

Light, D. W. (2000). The Medical Profession and Organizational Change: From Pro- fessional Dominance to Countervailing Power. In C. Bird, P. Conrad, & A. Fremont (eds.), *Handbook of Medical Sociology* (5th ed.). Upper Saddle River, NJ: Prentice Hall, 201–216.

Light, D. W. (2004). Introduction: Ironies of Success—A New History of the American Health Care 'System'. *Journal of Health and Social Behavior*, 45, 1–24.

Light, D. W., & Hafferty, F. W. (1993). *The Changing Medical Profession: An International Perspective.* New York: Oxford University Press.

Malmsheimer, R. (1988). *Doctors Only: The Evolving Image of the American Physician.* New York: Greenwood Press.

Marcuse, H. (1964). *One-Dimensional Man: Studies in the Ideology of Advanced Industrial Society.* Boston, MA: Beacon Press.

Mattera, J. (2010). *Obama Zombies: How the Liberal Machine Brainwashed My Generation*. New York: Simon & Schuster.

Media Matters Staff. (2020, February 24). Rush Limbaugh: "The Coronavirus is an effort to get Trump." Retrieved from *Media Matters*: https://www.mediamatters.org/rush-limbaugh/rush-limbaugh-coronavirus-effort-get-trump.

McKinlay, J. B., & Arches, J. (1985). Towards the Proletarianization of Physicians. *International Journal of Health Services*, 15(2), 161–195. doi:10.2190/jbmn-c0w6-9wfq-q5a6.

McKinlay, J. B., & Stoeckle, J. D. (1988). Corporatization and the Social Transformation of Doctoring. *International Journal of Health Services*, 18(2), 191–205. doi:10.2190/yevw-6c44-ycye-cgeu.

McKinlay, J. B., & Marceau, L. D. (2002). The End of the Golden Age of Doctoring. *International Journal of Health Services*, 32(2), 379–416. doi:10.2190/jl1d-21bg-pk2n-j0kd.

Mirrlees, T. (2018). The Alt-right's Discourse on 'Cultural Marxism': A Political Instrument of Intersectional Hate. *Atlantis: Critical Studies in Gender, Culture & Social Justice*, 39(1), 49–69.

Montgomery, M. (2017). Post-truth Politics?: Authenticity, Populism and the Electoral Discourses of Donald Trump. *Journal of Language and Politics*, 16(4), 619–639.

Mooney, C. (2007). *The Republican War on Science*. New York: Basic Books.

Nugent, T. (2015, December 9). Liberal Zombies' Toxic Logic. Retrieved from *TedNugent.com*: https://www.tednugent.com/liberal-zombies-toxic-logic/.

Okoren, N. (2020, July 27). The Birth of a Militia: How an Armed Group Polices Black Lives Matter Protests. Retrieved from *The Guardian*: https://www.theguardian.com/us-news/2020/jul/27/utah-militia-armed-group-police-black-lives-matter-protests.

Otto, S. L. (2016). *The War on Science: Who's Waging it, Why it Matters, What we Can Do about it*. Minneapolis, MN: Milkweed Editions.

Owens, D. (2020, July 4). Christopher Columbus Statue in Waterbury Beheaded. Retrieved from *Hartford Courant*: https://www.courant.com/news/connecticut/hc-news-waterbury-columbus-statue-beheaded-20200704-cnxqmzryhjce5ar2kjqbyhxhnu-story.html.

Parsons, T. (1951). *The Social System*. Glencoe, IL: The Free Press.

Pluckrose, H., & Lindsay, J. (2020). *Cynical Theories: How Activist Scholarship Made Everything about Race, Gender, and Identity–and Why This Harms Everybody*. Durham, NC: Pitchstone Publishing.

Preston, R. (1994). *The Hot Zone: The Terrifying True Story of the Origins of the Ebola Virus*. New York: Anchor Books.

Preston, R. (1999, October 18 & 25). West Nile Mystery. *New Yorker*, 90–108.

Reeder, L. G. (1972). The Patient-Client as a Consumer: Some Observations on the Changing Professional-Client Relationship. *Journal of Health and Social Behavior* 13, 406–412.

Ritzer, G., & Walczak, D. (1988). Rationalization and the Deprofessionalization of Physicians. *Social Forces*, 67, 1–22. doi:10.2307/2579098.

Rogers, K. (2020, June 1). Protesters Dispersed with Tear Gas so Trump Could Pose at Church. Retrieved from *The New York Times*: https://www.nytimes.com/2020/06/01/us/politics/trump-st-johns-church-bible.html.

Romano, A. (2017, May 31). Kathy Griffin, Political Protest Art, and the Backlash over 'Beheading' Donald Trump. Retrieved from *Vox*: https://www.vox.com/culture/2017/5/31/15719118/kathy-griffin-donald-trump-beheading-feminist-art.

Rooke, M. (2020, April 18). 'Social Distancing = Communism' Over 100 Protesters Defy California's 'Stay-At-Home' Order on the Beach. Retrieved from *Chicks on the Right*: https://www.chicksonright.com/blog/2020/04/18/social-distancing-communism-over-100-protesters-defy-californias-stay-at-home-order-on-the-beach/.

Said, E. W. (1979). *Orientalism*. New York: Vintage.

Sherfinski, D. (2020, August 2). 'Law and Order': Trump Counts on Riots, Looting to Help Him Win in Suburbs. Retrieved from *The Washington Times*: https://www.washingtontimes.com/news/2020/aug/2/trump-law-and-order-campaign-sees-rioting-way-win-/.

Sontag, S. (2001). *Against Interpretation and Other Essays*. New York: Picador.

Stack, L. (2017, January 21). Attack on Alt-Right Leader Has Internet Asking: Is It O. K. to Punch a Nazi? Retrieved from *The New York Times*: https://www.nytimes.com/2017/01/21/us/politics/richard-spencer-punched-attack.html.

Starr, P. (1982). *The Social Transformation of American Medicine*. New York: Basic Books.

Stevens, R. (1971). *American Medicine and the Public Interest*. New Haven, CT: Yale University Press.

Stone, M. (2020, March 13). Pastor Claims Coronavirus is Satanic Plot to Bring Socialism to the U.S. Retrieved from *Progressive Secular Humanist*: https://www.patheos.com/blogs/progressivesecularhumanist/2020/03/pastor-claims-coronavirus-is-satanic-plot-to-bring-socialism-to-the-u-s/.

Strong, S. I. (2017). Alternative Facts and the Post-Truth Society: Meeting the Challenge. *University of Pennsylvania Law Review Online*, 165, 137–146.

Stuart, T. (2015, October 21). 'Back to the Future' Writer: Biff is Donald Trump. Retrieved from *RollingStone*: https://www.rollingstone.com/politics/politics-news/back-to-the-future-writer-biff-is-donald-trump-190408/.

Susser, M., & Susser, E. (1996a). Choosing a Future for Epidemiology: I. Eras and Paradigms. *American Journal of Public Health*, 86, 668–673. doi:10.1093/acprof:oso/9780195300666.003.0024.

Susser, M., & Susser, E. (1996b). Choosing a Future for Epidemiology: II. From Black Box to Chinese Boxes and Eco-Epidemiology. *American Journal of Public Health*, 86, 674–677. doi:10.1093/acprof:oso/9780195300666.003.0025.

Szasz, T., & Hollender, M. (1956). A Contribution to the Philosophy of Medicine: The Basic Models of the Doctor-Patient Relationship. *Archives of Internal Medicine*, 97(5), 585–592.

Timmermans, S., & Berg, M. (2003). *The Gold Standard: The Challenge of Evidence-Based Medicine and Standardization in Health Care*. Philadelphia, PA: Temple University Press.

Touraine, A. (1969/1971). *The Post-Industrial Society. Tomorrow's Social History: Classes, Conflicts and Culture in the Programmed Society*. New York: Random House.

White, K. (2017). *An Introduction to the Sociology of Health and Illness*. London: Sage.

World Health Organization. (2004, April 21). Summary of Probable SARS Cases with Onset of Illness from 1 November to 31 July 2003.

Zengernews. (2020, July 27). Militia Groups Face Off in Louisville. Retrieved from *Atlanta Daily World*: https://atlantadailyworld.com/2020/07/27/watch-militia-groups-face-off-in-louisville/.

Zuckerberg, D. (2018). *Not All Dead White Men: Classics and Misogyny in the Digital Age*. Cambridge, MA: Harvard University Press.

Chapter 3

Diseased Others films

In the past two chapters, I have outlined "authoritarian populism" and highlighted three of its "elements"—tribalism, distrust of rational elites and their institutions, and willingness for coercive violence, then described the intertwining of pandemics and authoritarian populist politics, and outlined in broad strokes a social history of science and medicine, as it relates to popular film and to elements of authoritarian populism. Before moving on to the central case studies of this book, I will complete this broad conceptual backdrop by briefly outlining the history of what I refer to as "Diseased Others films." These films constitute a subgenre that sits at the intersection of outbreak films (explained below), science fiction, and biological horror. "Diseased Others" films may include zombies, vampires, contagious madness, rabies, and many other afflictions, and these films are particularly significant nowadays for three reasons. First, these films have rocketed to extreme popularity in the twenty-first century. Second, the basic premise of such films is the quintessential cinematic distillation of the narrative fusion of pandemics and elements of authoritarian populism. Third, rising over the late decades of the twentieth century and the early decades of the twenty-first century, and skyrocketing especially in the year 2020, pandemics and authoritarian populism have become central issues in contemporary American life and politics.

The outbreak film

My concept of an "outbreak film" corresponds to films that carry an "outbreak narrative" (Schweitzer 2018; Wald 2008). Dahlia Schweitzer contends that the outbreak narrative

> reveals anxieties related to three types of increasingly ineffective boundaries: first, between the personal body and the body politic; second, between individual nations; and third, between "ordinary" people and potentially dangerous disenfranchised groups.
>
> (Schweitzer 2018, 2)

The first of these types of ineffective boundaries indicates some mixture of fear of authoritarian biopower and fear of having one's body compromised, co-opted, or violated. The second has to do with fear of globalization and immigration. The third is a fear of being a victim of violence brought on by tribal resentments. The second and third types of ineffective boundaries respectively pertain to two out of three types of outbreaks that structure these films (the types can and often do intersect). These three types are the globalization outbreak, the terrorism outbreak, and the post-apocalypse outbreak. Both of her typologies deal with issues directly related to authoritarianism and populism, especially when Diseased Others are part of the story. She suggests that the twenty-first-century rise in the popularity of zombies reflects "a larger tendency to position the elite at war against the masses" (36), and that the outbreak narrative "simplifies moral ambiguities, which allows the viewer to judge—and even despise—the 'othered'" (37)—an analysis commensurate with what Sontag (2001) wrote about science fiction films in the 1960s.

While infectious diseases that could devastate civilizations go back as far as there were civilizations to devastate, and epidemics and pandemics in literature go as far back as there was literature, American outbreak films can be traced back to 1950, with *The Killer that Stalked New York* and *Panic in the Streets*. Hollywood was nowhere close to as prolific back then, but still it is striking that no discernible outbreak films were released before 1950, nor between 1950 and the early 1960s. Even then, in the 1960s, the pace was still slow, with only a few films, e.g., *The Masque of the Red Death* (1962), *The Last Man on Earth* (1964), and *The Satan Bug* (1965). While the scarcity is striking, it is also consistent—this was the era when infectious diseases seemed all but conquered, as the "infectious disease era" gave way to the "chronic disease era."

The Diseased Others film

The *Diseased Others* trope—especially vampires and zombies—has a very long history as well, and it has carried different meanings within different cultural contexts. The figure of the modern vampire derives from Bram Stoker's (1897/1997) novel, *Dracula*, which in turn bases Dracula loosely on Vlad Dracul, more commonly referred to as "Vlad the Impaler," a Romanian ruler of the fifteenth century, well known for his rumoured bloodlust (Beresford 2008). The first American vampire film was *Dracula* (1931), starring Bela Lugosi. This gave rise to a vampire trope which was passionate and sexual, animalistic yet aristocratic, with an accent like that of Bela Lugosi. Preceding this Dracula, however, was the German film *Nosferatu* (1922), which depicted the vampire in more animalistic and monstrous, less human terms (Skal 2001). The vampires in the novella of *I Am Legend* (Matheson 1954/2007) can use basic speech, and act in a few different ways—one seductive, one slow and stupid as in the book's first film adaptation *The Last Man on Earth*, and one quite animalistic and ferocious. And very significantly, they travel in hordes, and there are many of them.[1]

The Last Man on Earth brought their caliber and complexity down substantially, limiting the vampires to something more of the slow, dumb, plodding style; this overall slowness fit in with the zombie stylings of such pre-Romero American films as *White Zombie* (1932), *Revolt of the Zombies* (1936) and *I Walked with a Zombie* (1943). These early films gained their basic model of the zombie from one of several types of zombie in Haitian voodoo: "a reanimated, mindless, soulless corpse taken from its grave to serve the master who had awakened it" (Kordas 2011, 16).[2] These early zombies, although braindead, did not appear in the partially decomposed fashion that modern zombies so often don. In 1954 and 1964, the vampires could easily be mistaken for unturned people, as the protagonist of *I Am Legend* and *The Last Man on Earth* did in his roster of killings. The combination of Matheson's vampire hordes with the slow zombie-slave motif combined in the 1964 film to create creatures who, aside from an occasionally torn garment, appeared much like "normal" people, just with limited intelligence, surfacing only at night and in groups.

During the 1960s concern over the threat of biological weapons grew, along with the anti-war movement, and domestic racial and political tensions ran very high in the later years of the decade. Against this backdrop, in 1968—often seen as a kind of turning point where the optimism of the counterculture began to falter—George A. Romero's *Night of the Living Dead* made its appearance, igniting a revolution in zombie representation. He took enormous influence from their presentation in *The Last Man on Earth*, but took away their power of speech, and added in the element of cannibalism. Now zombies *ate* people, expressing a bloodlust like the vampire but even more extreme, and their bite—like that of a vampire—would turn a person into a zombie, inaugurating the modern zombie era. Zombie cinema remained more or less exclusively within the George Romero mould for decades (Luckhurst 2015).

In the 1970s, the frequency of outbreak films sped up a little, especially with Diseased Others films. The decade included two more such Romero films—*The Crazies* (1973) and *Dawn of the Dead* (1978)—as well as David Cronenberg's *Shivers* (1976) and *Rabid* (1977), among several other films such as the bio-terrorism thriller *The Cassandra Crossing* (1976) and the first outbreak film set on a plane, *SST: Death Flight* (1977). Perhaps related to the beginning of the AIDS crisis, the 1980s had a dramatic increase in Diseased Others films, the year 1985 including both classics *Day of the Dead* and *Return of the Living Dead*. From here on, the epidemiological sands were shifting, as the threat of pandemics returned and the "chronic disease era" ended.

In the 1990s, when Ebola and emerging infectious diseases in general became popular fears, there were around twice as many outbreak films as the 1980s. *Outbreak* (1995) is one of the most famous outbreak films of the decade. The film is known for attempting to portray Ebola somewhat realistically. The protagonist, a doctor played by Dustin Hoffman, fills the role of the hero doctor who goes rogue and bucks the bureaucracy. It was released in 1995, the year after *The Hot Zone* (Preston 1994) was published, and the same year as the widely popular film *12 Monkeys* and the book *The Coming Plague* (Garrett 1995). *12 Monkeys* stars Bruce Willis, who is a prisoner sent back in time to bring back to the future a sample of the virus that wiped out most of humanity, so future scientists can devise a cure. The virus was unleashed by a terrorist, a charismatic leader played by Brad Pitt, who is manic, with monkey-like mannerisms, and is convinced that humanity deserves to be wiped out. He inspires young radical environmentalists to collaborate with him. Between the filming of the movie and its release in theatres, the Unabomber Ted Kaczynski's manifesto "Industrial Society and Its Future" was printed in *The Washington Post* (1997). The manifesto does not advocate wiping out humanity, but it does advocate a less technological lifestyle, and includes the claims that the current civilization is headed for collapse, and that many people will have to die in order for civilization to be able to reconfigure along much more environmentally and psychosocially sound lines. Then came the turning of the millennium, quickly bringing with it the popular fear of a catastrophe at the end of the year 1999 having to do with a massive malfunction of computer systems—the "Y2K bug" (Uenuma 2019). Soon came the 9/11 terrorist bombings, the subsequent anthrax letters, heightened bioterrorism fears, and Bush's "War on Terror." There were various contagions as well—West Nile Virus, SARS, swine flu, and bird flu. In the 2000s there was a concomitant explosion of Diseased Others films, which has lasted to this day, just like the threat of emerging infectious diseases (Wonser and Boyns 2016).[3]

In 2002, the film *28 Days Later* introduced the fast zombie. This zombie is reminiscent of the more animalistic type of vampire in Matheson's *I Am Legend*, even inhumanly sped up, but otherwise retains the Romero stylings, often including cannibalism. One difference is the occasional introduction of roaring—in hunger, anger, triumph, or some amalgamation. Hence, it is more predatory, more dangerous, and more menacing. In the new millennium, the fast zombie has been the staple of Diseased Others stories. The dim-witted zombie/ghoul is gone. Now zombies are more like rabid beasts in fast-forward. Both remakes of *Day of the Dead* (2008, 2018) use fast zombies. The Diseased Others of *I Am Legend* (2007) share much in common with the fast zombies—so much that at this point the "Darkseekers" in *I Am Legend* (2007) are arguably in a fuzzy, undecidable space between vampire and zombie.

Morality and Diseased Others

There is plenty of difference between various films in the combined category of Diseased Others films. There is also much difference in the way Diseased Others are portrayed, not just in terms of vampirism or zombiedom, slowness or quickness, etc., but also in terms of their moral framing, and in their relationships between humans and Diseased Others. By no means are Diseased Others universally portrayed in a negative light. For example, in the hit television series *Buffy the Vampire Slayer*, as well as in its spin-off series *Angel*, some of the vampires form very close relationships with humans, and in fact take on roles much more like superheroes than villains. They defend humanity and exhibit integrity, moral codes, and so on. Some degree of moral complexity is present in a variety of other films about vampires and zombies, for example in the *Twilight* series or *The Cured*. As a broad category, Diseased Others science fiction is very open-ended and diverse.[4]

Yet in a common subset of the genre—especially when the stories qualify as horror just as much as sci-fi—the relationships between humans and Diseased Others are staunchly antagonistic. In this subset, a major—if not the only—relationship between the infected and the "normal" is the real or perceived threat to "normal" people of the Diseased Others, through contracting their illness or being killed by them. It is similarly common for "normal" people in these films to take measures to do away with the Diseased Others, through curing them, killing them, or a combination. My sense is that this basic set-up really captures that part of the cultural unconscious where pandemics and authoritarian populism meet. In this book I am concerned with the history of this subset of Diseased Others films, and so when I refer to "Diseased Others films," above and below, the reader should assume I am referring to this subset.

That said, Diseased Others films (the subset I am focusing on) do not categorically support authoritarian populism. They do suggest that within a large enough segment of American culture, many people at least feel some affinity toward elements of it, if not explicitly support it. But this should be read as a kind of baseline. The basic binary Diseased Others outbreak narrative is a template within which much can be asserted, complicated, or contested. For me, the ones that are particularly interesting within these Diseased Others films, test or outright subvert the friend-enemy binary. If my assumption is that Diseased Others films carry metaphorical elements of authoritarian populism, then Diseased Others films that subvert the friend-enemy binary also complicate if not subvert elements of authoritarian populism. The Diseased Others trope indicates a cultural preoccupation with elements of authoritarian populism, and as mentioned, the very existence of such a preoccupation indicates some amount of at least flirting with authoritarian populist inclinations, in some critical mass of the larger culture. Films where moral elements are introduced that challenge the friend-enemy binary suggest there are also trends in the larger culture that are more nuanced, more compassionate, more complicated, etc. If popular culture is flooded with films containing morally simplistic if not morally liquidated us-vs.-them violence, it should be read as a warning.

Notes

1   Technically these *I Am Legend* stories feature vampires, not zombies. Yet these vampires are dim-witted, animalistic, and travel in hordes, much closer to modern zombies than to the character of Count Dracula or the vampires from *Twilight*. Thus, Matheson's story might be considered the true mother of the modern zombie.

2 As for other types of Haitian zombie, not carried over into American horror lore: "A zombie could be a soul stolen from a living person by a magician to be used to bring luck or to heal illness. A zombie could also be a dead person who had willingly, at the time of death, given his or her body to the Vodou gods to use as a receptacle" (Kordas 2011, 16).

3 Admittedly, some of this has to do with the increase in the sheer volumes of films produced in the late twentieth century going into the twenty-first century, especially with the rise of independent film production companies—some tied to the majors, some not. Regardless, the extent of the uptick—especially in Diseased Others films— is so dramatic that it becomes difficult to count them all. It is also difficult to count them because of the confusing judgment calls one makes about at what point on the low end of popularity and budget does a film no longer deserve to be counted. For instance, a 30-minute home video made by a couple of high school students that never played in a theatre would not count, but what about a 90-minute video made by a handful of film students that played in a very small number of independent theatres? Then there is the blurring of the distinctions between television series and films in our era of Netflix and "binge-watching." A 2-part TV miniseries should probably make the cut, but should one include full television series like *The Walking Dead*? Regardless of the fuzzy boundaries of "Diseased Others films," the zombie craze has undoubtedly been enormous in the twenty-first century. There are, of course, a variety of films that feature pandemics, but not Diseased Others, *Contagion* (2011) perhaps being the most famous example.

4 The borders of the Diseased Others subgenre are too complex to be certain. There are stories that involve extra-terrestrials who kill and create copies of people, such as in *Invasion of the Body Snatchers*. In these films, the doppelgangers operate according to an "outbreak narrative," much like the spread of contagion (Wald 2008). Hence in applying a definition of this terrain, I cannot draw solid boundaries around it. There are films about contagions that make people primitive and homicidal, but do not transform them per se or make them "undead" or "living dead." For example, this is the case in George Romero's *The Crazies* (1973, remade in 2010). Some stories, however, fit right in the centre and really typify the genre. *I Am Legend* and *Day of the Dead* are by no means supposed to be the quintessential films of the genre, that therefore accurately represent all other films of the Diseased Others genre. They clearly fit, but I could have made different choices.

References

Beresford, M. (2008). *From Demons to Dracula: The Creation of the Modern Vampire Myth*. London: Reaktion Books.

Garrett, L. (1995). *The Coming Plague: Newly Emerging Diseases in a World Out of Balance*. New York: Penguin.

Kordas, A. (2011). New South, New Immigrants, New Women, New Zombies. In C. Moreman & C. Rushton (eds.), *Race, Oppression, and the Zombie: Essays on Cross-Cultural Appropriations of the Caribbean Tradition*. Jefferson, NC: McFarland.

Luckhurst, R. (2015). *Zombies: A Cultural History*. London: Reaktion Books.

Matheson, R. (1954/2007). *I Am Legend*. New York: Tor.

Preston, R. (1994). *The Hot Zone: The Terrifying True Story of the Origins of the Ebola Virus*. New York: Anchor Books.

Schweitzer, D. (2018). *Going Viral: Zombies, Viruses, and the End of the World*. New Brunswick, NJ: Rutgers University Press.

Skal, D. J. (2001). *The Monster Show: A Cultural History of Horror*. London: Macmillan.

Sontag, S. (2001). *Against Interpretation and Other Essays*. New York: Picador.

Stoker, B. (1897/1997). *Dracula*. Peterborough, ON: Broadview Press.

Uenuma, F. (2019, December 30). 20 Years Later, the Y2K Bug Seems Like a Joke–Because Those Behind the Scenes Took it Seriously. Retrieved from *Time*: https://time.com/5752129/y2k-bug-history/.

Wald, P. (2008). *Contagious: Cultures, Carriers, and the Outbreak Narrative*. Durham, NC: Duke University Press.

Washington Post. (1997). The Unabomber Trial: The Manifesto. Retrieved from *Washingtonpost.com*: https://www.washingtonpost.com/wp-srv/national/longterm/unabomber/manifesto.text.htm.

Wonser, R., & Boyns, D. (2016). Between the Living and the Undead: How Zombie Cinema Reflects the Social Construction of Risk, the Anxious Self, and Disease Pandemic. *The Sociological Quarterly*, 57(4), 628–653. doi:10.1111/tsq.12150.

Part 2

Chapter 4

Case study I

I Am Legend

I Am Legend (1954)

It was only a few years after the United States dropped atomic bombs on Hiroshima and Nagasaki. Atomic military power was new, and the shadow was threatening. Despite the fact that it was the United States who deployed it, the newfound capacity fueled a stance that the United States must possess the best weaponry, lest it fall behind and become vulnerable to a more powerful Communist rival. After proof that the Soviets had atomic weaponry in 1949, the United States developed the far more destructive hydrogen bomb, first testing it in 1952. In other words, enter the Cold War arms race. Much funding went into science in service of the military (Agar 2012). The Korean War, a clash between the Communist North and the capitalist South, raged in the early part of the decade, from 1950 to 1953. Many Americans feared the far-Left, while many others feared the far-Right, who were moved by a moral panic spearheaded by senator Joseph McCarthy about the far-Left infiltrating American society (Schwartz 2003).

As discussed in Chapter 2, the 1950s were an era of reactionary conformity, paranoia about Communism (including McCarthyism/the second "Red Scare") and racial tensions between blacks and whites (Jancovich 1996). Alien invasion was a common sci-fi trope of the times. "Films of the 1950s fed the persistent dark fantasy of a malevolent communist threat armed with the atomic bomb and evil intent that would invade and annihilate or enslave America" (Nimmo and Combs 1990, 119). *Invasion of the Body Snatchers* (1956) is the quintessential example. Its allegorical force simultaneously embodied anti-Communism and anti-conformism. It condensated conservative and liberal themes and displaced them onto extraterrestrials (Nimmo and Combs 1990; Jancovich 1996).

Matheson's *I Am Legend* (1954) is similar, albeit involving terrestrial double-invasion: the virus invades the body and the ill invade the population. Cold War anxieties about Communism and apocalypse have also been interpreted in the story (Wald 2008). The year 1954 was the beginning of the American Civil Rights movement. Specifically, it was the year of *Brown vs. Board of Education*, when the Supreme Court ruled against segregation in schools. Also that year, the US

Immigration and Naturalization Service began Operation Wetback, to find and deport undocumented immigrants from Mexico (Adams, Bell, and Griffin 2007). And the racial metaphor was—although perhaps not ostensibly dominant—explicit in Matheson's book (Patterson 2005). In 1955, just one year after *I Am Legend*'s publication, 14-year-old African American Emmett Till would be kidnapped and murdered for "talking fresh" to a white woman (his murderers would not be sentenced), and Rosa Parks would refuse to cede her bus seat to a white passenger, sparking a bus boycott in Montgomery, Alabama (Schwartz 2003). While racial tensions ran high, partisan politics were not polarized. In other words, the racial element of tribalism was clear, and there was a political tribalism in the form of anti-Communism, but there was not a left/right partisan political polarization. The *partisan* divide would take root by 1972 (the year after *The Omega Man*), after which time it would steadily increase (Mason 2018).

Matheson's *I Am Legend* is a landmark novella in the history of vampires and zombies in that it was the first popular story to medicalize the affliction. It was written during an era where the fear of nuclear annihilation was pressing, science was a national priority and much public money was poured into it, and medicine and doctoring were in their Golden Ages, doctors having considerable respect and authority while scientists came up with win after win, developing cures and vaccines so prolifically that the leading medical causes of death shifted from contagion to chronic illness. In 1952, "for many Americans the development of a vaccine for polio [...] was the most important event of the year" (Schwartz 2003, 136). The vaccine would prove successful and be widely administered later, starting in 1954.

In outline, the story goes as follows. Robert Neville is a medical scientist living alone in a suburban house, after a killer virus turned everyone left into vampires. He is immune and believes himself to be the only living human. His wife and daughter were among those who turned vampire. He spends his days killing vampires, his nights hiding in his house. He is also working toward finding a cure. Eventually he comes across an unturned woman (Ruth). He brings her back to his home against her will. They talk, and develop romantic feelings. Against her will, he tests her to see if she is infected. She is in fact infected, and knocks him out when he finds out. She leaves him a note of explanation, saying she was a spy from a colony of infected but unturned people (which I call "survivors"), who keep the illness dormant through medication. She includes a sample pill with the note. She insists her affections for him were genuine and encourages him to flee for his safety. He does not. Survivors come to his home to capture him. They take him and imprison him. Ruth visits him as he is locked up and gives him more pills, allowing him to commit suicide rather than be killed by the survivors.

In this novel of 1954, the origins of the pandemic are undetermined. The question is briefly raised, but there is no clear conclusion. It takes place in one of Robert's memories: Robert and his partner Virginia ponder possible origins to the disease. Their speculations do not identify scientific expertise as culpable.

They mention the issue of germs, but the topic of germ warfare is broached as "the bombings," and the conversation is concluded by referencing "war." In other words, to the extent that science is implicated as to blame for the pandemic, speculative blame is directed more at war than at medicine and technology. Yet in the last analysis the origin is unknown.

Robert is ambivalent about the infected. He frequently curses them to himself as "bastards," and fantasizes thoughts such as "Someday I'll knock a stake right through his goddamn chest. I'll make a foot long for him, a special one with ribbons on it, the bastard" (8).[1] Yet he wrestles with his conscience. For example, in a scene where he kills an infected woman, he struggles with a sense of identification with her: "Usually he felt a twinge when he realized that, but for some affliction he didn't understand, these people were the same as he" (28). He also struggles with feelings of care for her: "All right, she's suffering, he argued with himself, but she's one of them and she'd gladly kill me if she got the chance. You've got to look at it that way, it's the only way" (28–29).

He also repeatedly wrestles with sexual attraction to the infected women, suggesting some identification with them as human. For example: "It was the women who made it so difficult [...] All the knowledge in those books couldn't put out the fires in him; all the words of centuries couldn't end the wordless, mindless craving of the flesh" (7–8).[2] In one scene, carrying one of these women, he wrestles down sexual impulses as well as an explicitly moral internal voice of care and moral self-condemnation regarding his potentially predatory desire. Here, his relationship to morality is shown to be conflicted. He disowns his own moral voice. The description is that he is "beginning to suspect his mind of harboring an alien. Once he might have termed it conscience. Now it was only an annoyance. *Morality, after all, had fallen with society. He was his own ethic.*"[3] Despite his framing of himself in an amoral light, he continues to hold himself accountable to this "alien," his conscience, at the same time that he is cautious against his sexual impulses overcoming him. Regarding the woman in the scene, "he wouldn't let himself pass the afternoon near her" (49–50).

Robert's ambivalence—and its relevance to tribalism—is perhaps most memorably expressed in a sardonic and ambivalent internal dialogue, where he directly connects treatment of the infected in general to Othering. Most of it is expounding on the idea that vampires are a "minority" who suffer "prejudice." He even mentions that vampires have "no means of support, no means for proper education," and do not have voting rights. His train of thought is satirical, but genuinely relevant, and closes with conceding to a challenge (from himself): "but would you let your sister marry one?" Yet his concession to his own prejudice suggests playfulness: "You got me there, buddy, you got me there." It is a jovial and ambivalent expression of self-condemnation, lacking identification or any clear moral foundation. Humour aside, his back and forth between versions of himself indicates both an acknowledgment of the humanity of the infected, and the personal rejection of them based on their difference (20–21).

Robert's ambivalence is also present in his partial humanization of Ben Cortman, an old friend whose relationship with Robert changed drastically post-infection. In one of his meditations on Ben, Robert notes Ben's similar appearances before and after infection. "But there was a beard on his face now [...] That was the only real difference" (53). Elsewhere he compares Ben to a comedian. "That was who Ben Cortman was—a hideously malignant Oliver Hardy buffeted and long-suffered" (55). He also humanizes Ben when hunting him, approaching it as "a relaxing hobby," imagining Ben "knew he was singled out for capture. He felt, further, that Cortman relished the peril of it" (107).

Robert makes progress but never succeeds at devising a cure. Robert's attempt to conquer the disease through science fails, or at least, he dies before he could succeed. The medication of the survivors is something of a success for science, although it does not actually overcome the pandemic. Maybe Robert could have found a cure if the survivors had not captured him. His demise is due to a militarized colony, tightly coordinated, violent, and effective. Robert's ambivalence surfaces dramatically in relation to the survivors. When they arrive outside his home and he witnesses them killing the infected, he morally condemns the survivors for their excessive infliction of harmful violence. He cares for the infected, whereas the survivors are "like gangsters" and "cruel," practising "black and brutal slaughtering" and "methodical butchery." When the survivors kill Ben, Robert "almost felt the bullets in his own flesh" (146–148). The only survivor we learn anything about is Ruth, who both facilitates his suicide and is "a ranking officer in the new society" (157), a designation with a distinctly militarized tone. The survivors are scientifically advanced enough to devise medication that keeps the disease dormant. This is a real but only partial victory for science. The survivors are still vampires, just unturned.

Ruth is ambivalent when it comes to Robert versus the survivors. In the note she leaves when she knocks him out and escapes, she warns Robert to flee; the survivors will come kill him. She seems to care for him, yet she identifies with the survivors and—loyally—does not morally condemn them for their violence. Despite her loyalty to them, her leaving of the note was an act of subversion. As a whole, the note and the act of leaving it are ambivalent.

> I know now that you were just as much forced into your situation as we were forced into ours. We are infected. But you already know that. What you don't understand is that we're going to stay alive. We've found a way to do that and we're going to set up society again slowly but surely. We're going to do away with all those wretched creatures whom death has cheated. And, even though I pray otherwise, we may decide to kill you and those like you.
>
> (143)

While she continues to identify with the survivors, she cares for Robert. He morally condemns survivors for killing without care; Ruth morally condemns him for killing without care. When she comes to visit him after he has been captured, this duality is directly voiced. Robert says he has only killed to survive, to which Ruth replies "That's exactly why we're killing." "Did you see their faces when they ... they killed?" Robert says. Ruth challenges him right back. "Did you ever see your face," she says, "when you killed?" The central debate here between Robert and Ruth—the pivot of legitimate moral condemnation—surrounds the issue of cruelty; not only of lacking care but also of enjoying killing. As in the leaving of the note, in Ruth's visit she displays ambivalence: loyalty to the survivors, caring for Robert, and some subversion via giving him pills. And Robert's moral identity hinges here on his status within the discourse surrounding care and harm. As he kills himself, he is willing to adopt—or at least not reject—an identity as he imagined himself through the eyes of the Others, as a killer. Robert cares for the survivors, and he accepts being Othered and morally condemned.

> To them he was some terrible scourge they had never seen, a scourge even worse than the disease they had come to live with. He was an invisible specter who had left for evidence of his existence the bloodless bodies of their loved ones. And he understood what they felt and did not hate them [...] He knew he did not belong to them; he knew that, like the vampires, he was anathema and black terror to be destroyed [...] A new terror born in death, a new superstition entering the unassailable fortress of forever.
> I am legend.
>
> (160)

The Last Man on Earth (1964)

Matheson wrote a full screenplay adaptation of *I Am Legend* called "The Night Creatures" for a production company called "Hammer." The script was rejected due to having profane material—vomiting, the word "damn," etc.—that would not get past the censors (Matheson and Dawidziak 2012). The script that became *The Last Man on Earth* has a fake name/disguise (Logan Swanson) for Matheson signed onto it, but he claims to have had no part in writing it and that he did not like the script.[4] Despite his distaste for the watered-down film rendition of 1964, *The Last Man on Earth* stayed close to Matheson's novel. The film was released only two years after the Cuban Missile Crisis, when Cold War fears about nuclear annihilation seemed more likely than not to be fulfilled.

By the mid-1960s, the Civil Rights movement reached its full force, and much turbulence surrounded it. Martin Luther King's famous "I Have a Dream" speech was given at the March on Washington in 1963. The March was led by King and attended by 200,000 people (twice the population of Washington, D.C.). King's message of non-violence and racial integration was embraced by the Kennedy administration, which helped organize the march. At the same time, Malcolm X had considerable popularity and influence, and carried a more militant, revolutionary message, rejecting King's support for nonviolence and integration (Maga 2003). White-on-black violence was both prevalent and protested, such as in the famous 1964 KKK killing of Mississippi civil rights activists James Chaney, Andrew Goodman and Michael Schwerner (Adams, Bell, and Griffin 2007). The Civil Rights Act was signed by President Johnson that year as well. A pro-segregationist populist movement led by George Wallace had moderate success during the 1960s, Wallace being elected as a governor in Alabama in 1962, and running for president against Nixon and Humphrey in 1968 (Judis 2016).

Also in 1963, a vaccine for measles was invented. The illness had been quite a scourge in the years prior. According to the CDC:

> In the decade before 1963 when a vaccine became available, nearly all children got measles by the time they were 15 years of age. It is estimated 3 to 4 million people in the United States were infected each year. Also each year, among reported cases, an estimated 400 to 500 people died, 48,000 were hospitalized, and 1,000 suffered encephalitis (swelling of the brain) from measles.
>
> (Centers for Disease Control and Prevention 2018)

The Last Man on Earth is a relatively faithful rendering of Matheson's original novel, although Matheson specifically rejected this version, as mentioned above. Its estimated budget was $300,000; its box office revenue is not publicly available. It was directed by Ubaldo Ragona and Sidney Salkow, produced by Robert L. Lippert and Associated Producers, Inc. and Produzioni La Regina, and written by William F. Leicester. It starred Vincent Price as the male protagonist, with Franca Bettoia as the white female lead.

The story runs as follows: Robert Morgan is a medical scientist, alone after a killer virus turned everyone left into vampires. He is immune and believes himself to be the only healthy living human. His wife and daughter were among those who turned vampire. Neither science nor war is identified—nor even hypothesized—as responsible for the disease. There is no discussion of the origins of the pandemic. He spends his days killing the infected/vampires, his nights hiding at home. Robert experiments, looking to find a cure, conquer the virus with his scientific expertise. He finds a healthy woman (Ruth). He suspects she is infected. He wants to try to cure her. She declines, but he tries anyway, against her will. With Ruth, his cure—his scientific expertise—finally works. Ruth reveals she is a spy from a colony of infected but healthy/unturned people (which I call "survivors"), who keep the virus dormant through injections. She encourages him to flee. He refuses. Survivors chase him into a church and kill him.

The film begins with a number of images of the city, showing many buildings and roads, with no human activity, and then we begin to see dead bodies littering the sidewalks. Then we cut to Robert in bed. His alarm goes off, and his voiceover says: "Another day to live through. Better get started." Here, as is the case for a substantial part of the film, Robert's demeanour is tired and depressive, and his voiceovers generally corroborate this, as well as that life has become meaningless for him. For most of the film Robert makes no statements indicating moral consideration for the infected. His voiceover complains about his role, but not for moral reasons. He complains of monotony: "How many more of these [stakes] will I have to make before they're all destroyed? [...] How many of them still exist? How long will I have to keep up this search?" Two key aspects of this are: (a) Robert is sick of doing the same thing over and over again, and is feeling more than a little existential emptiness about it, and (b) Robert's complaints of monotony do not indicate the infected maintain humanity.

Regarding (a), Robert continues to don a kind of "proper" attire for a middle-aged middle-class American man, even though it is three years since the pandemic hit and everyone else died or became vampires. He keeps his hair neat with product, wears a sport coat, slacks, dress shoes, undershirt, buttoned down shirt (tucked in, of course), and sweater vest. He lives in the same suburban home that was his when his wife and daughter (and the rest of humanity) were still alive. He drinks out of china teacups. He is essentially the last vestige of modernity, which he now clings to in a way that is arguably objectively absurd, although on the other hand, if he were to let go of the old ways, what would be left for him? This is really his paradoxical situation. On the one hand, he clings to his identity as an upstanding, modern American middle-class man, part of a way of life that he single-handedly is keeping alive. He fends off the hordes who threaten to burst into his home and disrupt his order and dignity, qualities that are all but annihilated in the new, infected world. To note, the infected display quite literally a kind of herd conformity. They have little to no agency. They are an aggressive mass of automatons seeking to absorb Robert's individuality into their fold. On the other hand, he is modernity outliving itself, discovering itself as aimless, tired, and meaningless in a context of alienation and isolation.

Regarding (b), the infected are outside the sphere of Robert's moral consideration. His identification does not include them. In a later scene, he describes his numbness toward the infected with Ruth: "Hear that? That's Ben Cortman. He was my friend [...] He was like a kid brother [...] When I find him I'll drive a stake through him just like all the others." His divisive identification goes far enough that his loyalty to individuals does not cross over once they cross over. Ruth confesses to Robert survivors exist, indicating they morally condemn him for his killing. Ruth is ambivalent. She identifies with survivors but cares for Robert. When describing the situation, she shifts between "we" and "they" pronouns. For example she says "You can't join us. You're a monster to them." She suggests he should run away because they will come for him to kill him that very night. Robert reflects "Your new society sounds charming." Robert's sarcastic quip about the new society sounding "charming" implies moral condemnation of them for their readiness to execute him.

The survivors (other than Ruth) make their first appearance arriving on military vehicles at Robert's home to kill him. When they get there, they spear or gun down every vampire they can find. They are tightly coordinated, dressed in black, and—at least in the scenes they are depicted in—relatively speechless, with the exception of brief injunctions or communications to facilitate violence. For example, a survivor yells "up there!" when he spots Ben on the roof of a house, and "Get him! Get him!" when the survivors locate Robert. When chasing Robert and hunting him with spears, they move in an almost synchronized way.

Robert exhibits a new ambivalence. After he is impaled by a thrown spear, he first yells divisively "You're freaks! All of you!" and "I'm a man! The last man." This is Robert's clearest declaration of denotative identification[5] as an uninfected human when he classifies himself as "a man! The last man." "Man" is here associated with normality, in contrast to the infected "freaks." Robert's insults indicate condemnation of survivors for being abnormal, and lack of identification with them. But then as Ruth sits with him, his last words are a repeating "they were afraid of me." His repeating "they were afraid of me" suggests something different from condemnation, but it is not clear what.

As the film closes, Ruth has the cure in her blood. It is unstated whether she will tell the survivors and advocate for them to produce more of the cure. Rationality may—or may not—eventually win out over the disease. The efficacy is there in principle, but technically the jury is out on the surrounding context of human decision. It is possible, for instance, that the new, militarized society is too rigid for Ruth to feel safe informing them about it. The film ends ambiguously, with the possibility but not the assurance that the cure will be distributed.

The Omega Man (1971)

More vaccines for infectious disease were invented in the late 1960s; the mumps vaccine in 1967 and the rubella vaccine in 1969. In 1971, the year of *The Omega Man*'s release, the measles, mumps and rubella vaccine (MMR) was created (Immunization Action Coalition 2020). As discussed in earlier chapters, Susser and Susser (1996) have characterized this time period following World War II and extending through the next several decades as the "chronic disease era," a change from the preceding "infectious disease era." The years spanning 1954–1971 (from Matheson's *I Am Legend* novel to *The Omega Man*) may be understood as belonging to this period. Interestingly, after the apocalypse, the plague in *The Omega Man* acts more like a combination of chronic disease (the infected, who possess full power of speech, are distinguished by chronic skin and eye conditions) and *emotional* contagion (the hypnotic power of Matthias' voice carries the contagion of groupthink).

The years 1954–1971 of course contain *the 1960s*,[6] well-discussed as an age of unrest and social change in many aspects of American culture. In the late

1960s and early 1970s, racial tensions between blacks and whites ran high. The following are a few expository landmarks. Malcolm X and Martin Luther King, Jr. were assassinated, in 1965 and 1968 respectively. In the late 1960s and early 1970s there was the rise of the Black Power movement and the Black Panther Party, the assassination of several of the latter, the imprisonment of their founder Huey P. Newton, the kidnapping of co-founder Bobby Seale. Charles Manson, attempting to ignite apocalyptic race war, convinced followers—"The Manson Family"—to murder nine people in 1969. He was imprisoned in 1971.

Generally speaking, the optimism about social change the counterculture displayed in the early to middle years of the 1960s floundered going into the 1970s. The counterculture continued on, more militant *and* more disillusioned (Hamilton 2006). The economic blossoming in post-war America shifted to a long downturn. Political culture shifted Right. The "me generation" came to fruition. Disaster films became popular. Charlton Heston rose to become a sci-fi and action star, often playing cynical individualist antiheroes (Haas, Christensen, and Haas 2015). *The Omega Man* was one such instance.

This film departs much from Matheson's 1954 novel as well as the 1964 film. It earned $8,720,000 at the United States box office. It was directed by Boris Sagal, produced by Walter Seltzer and Warner Brothers, and written by married partners John Corrington and Joyce H. Corrington. It starred Charlton Heston as the white male protagonist, and Rosalind Cash as the black female lead.

To sum up the plot: Robert Neville is a medical scientist (who used to work for the military), alone in a city apartment. A killer virus turned the surviving infected locals into a blue-skinned, white-eyed cult who avoid sunlight. Robert is immune, believing himself to be the only living healthy human. He spends his days killing infected members and enjoying civilization's remnants, his nights hiding at home. They view him as evil because he is uninfected, healthy, uses modern machinery, and because he kills them. Eventually he finds a healthy woman (Lisa) and chases her unsuccessfully. The infected capture him and sentence him to death. A healthy man (Dutch) and the woman he saw (Lisa) rescue him. They take him to a small colony of healthy people (which here I call "survivors"). One of them (Richie) is ill. They ask Robert to try and cure him. Robert cures him with a serum made from his own blood, and becomes romantically involved with Lisa. Robert and the survivors plan to move away and bring Robert's cure so they can all be immune. Richie goes to the leader of the infected (Matthias) to attempt peace, but he is killed. Getting supplies for the move, Lisa encounters the infected and becomes ill (one of them). Using her, infected members enter Robert's home and abduct and kill him. Dutch and the other survivors find him the next morning. Dutch is able to get a bottle of cure off him. The survivors take ill Lisa into their car and leave.

Matheson says his 1954 Robert Neville was not a monster, just a person trying to survive. Joyce Carrington, the co-screenwriter for *The Omega Man*, gives a more complex picture. She says of her Neville: "The cold scientist, the killer, and yet the compassionate person who was willing to sacrifice himself and through his blood save humanity" ("Introduction by Co-Stars" 2007). Yet in a brief documentary filmed on the set of the film, Charlton Heston—who played Neville—describes Neville without the heroism and altruism, "his prime concern being his own survival, defense, I suppose the ultimate extension of man as a killer ape" ("The Last Man Alive" 2007). Anthropologist Ashley Montegue, reflecting in conversation with Heston in the documentary, offered an interpretation that this survivor mentality was reflective of a general cultural condition in modernity, of "the psychology of the survivor."[7]

Certainly, Robert is alone in his situation, at least until he is discovered by the survivors' colony. From the start of the film, we are given a variety of far-back images showing the large, uninhabited buildings and streets of Los Angeles, at times with a tiny Robert walking or driving along them. Clearly, he is small and alone in these images, but it is not a tortured aloneness. He is too jaded for that. Robert's aloneness is dripping with meaninglessness. It is absurd and sardonic. This aspect of Robert's isolation is driven home by other cues, for instance, when we first meet him he is cruising down the post-apocalyptic streets in a red convertible, wearing aviator sunglasses, seemingly unbothered. He pops some slow jazz into the car stereo and we see him with the wind in his hair, the relaxing music playing. When he spots a silhouette in a window, he immediately halts the car, takes out a machine gun and fires at the figure behind the window. Then he just keeps driving. It is all very casual.

Similarly, when he encounters dead bodies his attitude is casual amusement. For instance, once his red convertible gets a flat tyre, he finds his way to a used car dealership. There, he pretends to be conversing with a dead body still sitting in a chair, assumedly the chair whoever it was died in. Entertaining himself, he pretends to be unhappy with the high price the dead body is selling the car for. "Cheating bastard" he says, and he drives off briskly, out of the already broken storefront window.

Being the chief medical scientist of the film, and often the lone protagonist against the infected, Robert's significance reaches beyond himself, to modernity in general. He is the last bastion of modernity, by default the spokesperson for "the users of the wheel"—as Matthias puts it—as a monolith. His apartment is decorated very densely with pieces of art and other objects that exhibit a bourgeois aesthetic sensibility, as well as a respect (to put it lightly) for the high arts and Euro-American history. The collection includes stained glass, carved pillars, claw-foot furniture, statues, tall candles in tall candle holders, golden chalices, paintings, and so on. One—if not the—centrepiece of the apartment is a table set up with a chessboard, with a bust of Caesar positioned in a chair on one side as Robert's imaginary opponent. His indulgences reveal him to be something of a bourgeois hedonist; for example, in an early scene of him alone in his apartment we see him indulging in whiskey drunk from a tumbler and donning a green velvet sport coat over a shirt with large white ruffles.

Yet we can tell he doesn't really enjoy anything. And this protection of and reverence for modernity is paired with a deep cynicism about it. Nothing is sacred to Robert. Pouring himself a drink of hard liquor at his fancy in-apart-ment bar, for instance, he offers some to Caesar. When there is predictably no response (the camera just shows the bust sitting there for a second) Robert casually calls the bust of Caesar a "miserable schmuck." Robert's jadedness is his most immediate character trait. As modernity incarnate, Robert portrays a modern world still going, but deeply troubled and dejected.

Enlightenment values of rationality and scientific progress came under much open scrutiny by many during the 1960s which continued into the 1970s. Often the protest was of the values and culture associated with scientific rationality and "the technological society" (Ellul 1954/1964). At the same time, many others enthusiastically celebrated scientific achievements, which were considerable during the decade. About the contrast, historian of science and Jon Agar says: "The point to grasp is that these two interpretations of science provoked each other" (Agar 2012, 414).

Heston and Montegue also discuss Neville's scientism in a way that lends some legitimacy to the anti-technological slant of Matthias and The Family, which in the film is presented both sympathetically (The Family are correct to blame the apocalypse on modern technology) and vilifying (The Family are diseased, brainwashed and reactionary):

HESTON: Over in the laboratory section of Neville's nest we can see how much of his life and how much of the civilization of which he was the end product was spent in simply the pursuit of naked truth. What would they call that machine, for example?

MONTEGUE: Well, that is [...] capable of analyzing from 9 to 12 or even more different substances in the blood simultaneously and in a few minutes giving you the exact characteristics of each of those substances.

HESTON: But it can't tell you the proportion of passion in the blood.

MONTEGUE: No, no I'm afraid that this is a human trait.

("The Last Man Alive" 2007)

Here Heston and Montegue refer to the other side of the "technological society" that came under first with the 1960s counterculture. It was not only the fact that science is destructive; scientific reason also ascends at the expense of meaning, values, and human connection. The technological society is an alienated and dehumanized society. In these terms, Robert's cynicism is given an explicit referent when he goes to an abandoned (of course) Movie Theater to watch the film *Woodstock*. His attitude is sardonic and dismissive. He bitterly speaks to double over the voice of a man on the film who talks specifically about his own personal transformation at Woodstock, how he recognized how important human connection is. Possibly the definitive event of the '60s counterculture in America, Robert is there after-the-fact, sarcastically driving home the fact that the festival is now very much in the past, and that the high hopes of the era are now revealed to be quaint and ignorant. Again here, society speaks through Robert. In a pessimistic, dark, early 1970s frame, he channels the bitterness of a society in the wake of crushed 1960s dreams, and synchs with the harshness that would continue into the 1970s.

Much turmoil of the late 1960s surrounded the Vietnam War, which had—for a variety of reasons—struck down national confidence and trust in the military (King and Karabell 2003). In light of the way screenwriter Joyce Carrington describes *The Omega Man*, the new emphasis on biological warfare in 1971 can be understood at least partly in relation to the historical context. She says:

> [I]t just didn't feel right to do vampires. I have a PhD in chemistry. So germ warfare—chemical warfare (this was 30 years ago)—was on my mind as a way you could wipe out civilization. So we used that theme instead of vampires.
>
> ("Introduction by Co-Stars" 2007)

Her explanation that germ warfare was on her mind due to her education aside, the time period was marked by greater public concern over the possibility (Guillemin 2006). The Vietnam War era saw growing concern about the dangers of the United States' biological weapons programme (which ended in 1971–1973), as well as the use and human side-effects of military herbicide Agent Orange (Hamilton 2006). *The Omega Man*'s combination of science and military in a symbol of apocalypse was certainly in line with the rejection of modernity and anti-militarism that blossomed in the late 1960s.

Matthias is the head villain in the story, and the most outspoken opponent of science, including modern medicine. Despite his status of villainy, in the story he is clearly not wrong about the destructiveness of modern technology. And this is how it is framed—in terms of modern technology, not medical science in particular, not war in particular, but in their intersection as elements of modernity. Science and war are both to blame for the apocalypse. We learn this through Neville's memories, particularly through a newscast reporting germ warfare, martial law, and so on. We are also privy to sounds and sights of explosions. It is not Robert who describes this culpability however. The central enemy from the infected, the leader Matthias, is the one who calls out accurately (if also globally and superstitiously) the source of the pandemic. Humanity and its ruthless progress, its hunger for technological power and weaponry caused it. In a scene from Robert's memories, he is sitting at a desk in a lab coat, his name "COLONEL ROBERT NEVILLE" (in all capital letters) on an identifying block on his desk, with Matthias giving a newscast on television, with a televangelist flare:

MATTHIAS: Now the question is survival. Is this the end of technological man? Is this the conclusion of all our yesterdays? The boasts of our fabled science? The superhuman conquests of space and time? The age of the wheel? We were warned of judgment. Well, here it is. Here. Now. In the form of billions of microscopic bacilli. This is the end.

Matthias does not mention war per se as the cause of humanity's downfall. He blames modern technology. In one scene, one of Matthias' followers (Brother Zachary) eagerly indicates to Matthias he wants to use modern weaponry to kill Robert. Matthias forbids it: "He will be destroyed Brother, he will. But not by guns, not by machines, not by the evil forbidden things, the tools that destroyed the world." Matthias' view of scientific expertise is that it is both dangerous and ineffective. On the one hand science produced "tools that destroyed the world," yet on the other hand it is impotent and hubristic.

The primary rivalry in the film revolves around Robert as embodying medical science and modernity, and Matthias as anti-science and anti-modern. Robert argues for Matthias and his infected to be cured, Matthias argues for Robert to be killed. On both sides, the argument is that the Other group should be eradicated in its Otherness or removed from society, whether through killing, curing, banishment, or whatever other unarticulated means. Matthias dramatically expresses his desire to be rid of Robert because of Robert's non-infected status in a scene where Robert is ostensibly placed on trial after being captured by the infected. Matthias speaks from a podium in a church, to an audience of infected who sit in the pews watching him: "Do you see him as we were before the punishment, before we gained grace? Do you see lying there the last of scientists, of bankers, of businessmen, the users of the wheel?" Matthias thus condemns Robert for his Othered status as uninfected, and associated with this by his connection to modern technology, degrading the world with his existence. He asks if Robert is "of the family" and "of the sacred society," to both of which the audience respond "no" in a unified voice. "Then what is he?" Matthias asks. The voice of the audience replies: "evil." Matthias says "He is part of the dead. He has no place here. He has the stink of oil, electrical circuitry about him. He is obsolete." Pointing a finger at Robert, Matthias continues; "You are discarded. You are the refuse of the past." Because of Robert's status as uninfected and modern, Matthias and the audience together identify and condemn Robert not just as Other, but in moral terms, as an evil to be done away with. The final ruling on Robert is that he be sentenced to death.

The following scene contains Matthias' and Robert's most extensive conversation, where they trade condemnations back and forth. The exchange opens with a brief discourse on Robert's identity, as well as the value (or lack thereof) of science. Matthias initially indicates some lack of clarity surrounding Robert's title, denotatively identifying him ambiguously with both medicine and the military: "Mr. Neville, or doctor or colonel, whatever it was they called you." Robert replies definitively and crassly: "I'm a scientist. What the hell are you?" Matthias is not impressed, and asserts his anti-science worldview. "Definition of a scientist," he says, "a man who understood nothing until there was nothing left to understand."

Overall, neither indicates moral recognition for the other side or identification with them. Because Robert's condemnations of Matthias contain the moral argument that Matthias should be helping the infected be cured, there is arguably a shadow of recognition for the infected in Robert's words. For example, at one point, Robert says "Look, why don't you quit these bloody games, throw away those Halloween costumes and get these people organized, damn it. Or are you already too far gone? [...] [W]hy don't you try finding a cure?" Yet when he argues this, his words never contain a clear moral rationale. He obviously condemns Matthias in particular for his lack of appropriate and effective action.

Implicitly, however, Robert is arguing for the liberation of the infected from Matthias' despotism. Beyond the need to stay out of the sunlight, and the odd slowness with which the Diseased Others move and speak, their primary symptom is susceptibility to the hypnotic power of Matthias' voice, thus following his authority with a cult-like loyalty. Robert's use of the term "organized" is pertinent here within a discourse of liberty (e.g. the "organization" of the working class in unions or under party leadership to struggle against the oppression of the capitalist class); otherwise it is something of a non sequitur. The logic is a little confused, because Matthias' power is deeply intertwined with the disease. Suggesting that Matthias lead his people to liberation from the disease is simultaneously suggesting that Matthias lead his people to liberation from his own leadership. This will not fly with Matthias. But even worse, it is a suggestion that Matthias and his people have some sort of incorrect, "diseased" status. Since Matthias frames their condition as a new race of people, rather than an illness, it is actually a badge of honour. Considering this, Robert's suggestion of finding a cure is—for Matthias—the suggestion of a kind of genocide—to wipe out Matthias' race through biophysical conversion. Matthias makes this even simpler by denying the possibility of a cure: "There was no cure, and there is no cure." It is unspoken here, but implicitly we understand that Matthias is defensively avoiding seeking a cure.

Matthias continues: "But the family has found its way. We can bear it. The only burden left is you." Matthias indicates Robert in particular should be done away with. At the trial, he had claimed Robert was "refuse of the past," and associated Robert—and by extension the uninfected in general—as representing a morally inferior race that should be eliminated. Hence the genocidal impulse is on both sides. Now, he further morally condemns Robert as "the angel of death," because of his killing of the infected. Yet what his moral basis for condemning Robert's killing consists of is unspecified.

Next, addressing a small number of his underlings, Matthias says that Robert has confessed to "everything," meaning "murder, use of forbidden tools, practice of proscribed rites, he admits science, medicine, weapons, machinery, electricity." As he did in the trial scene, Matthias proceeds to talk about "punishment." Here Matthias displays again the moral of sanctity for his condemnation of Robert. And in divisive identification, Matthias is clear that the disease left visible "marks" on the infected, and that it was a punishment for modernity. This time, language such as "punishment," "forbidden," and "proscribed" indicates further that Robert's moral transgression was against a higher authority. Matthias implies that modern civilization harboured "evil" and "dangerous" things that were worthy of moral condemnation, and that condemnation had manifested through some higher force that left "marks" of differentiation on the infected.[8] Why those things were "dangerous" has been shown earlier, through flashbacks about apocalyptic biological warfare. Why they have the status of "evil" exactly is unclear, other than their status of degradation. Robert calls Matthias and his people "barbarians," once again dividing their group from his, and positing his own as the superior group.

The similarity in Robert's and Matthias' tribal stances is strongly implied in this pivotal exchange. Later on, it is explicitly called out by Richie, who indicates he can connect with both sides. While he indicates compassion for the infected, Richie sees them as incorrect overall, in that they truly are sick, not simply different. Richie identifies with Robert and the other survivors. Richie's proposed solution is for Robert to cure the infected. Richie urges Robert to give the serum to the infected, not just survivors. Richie attempts to build Robert's caring for the infected, and identification with them: "Hey man, they're humans! I mean they're sick, you know." Robert says he will not cure them because they are "homicidal maniacs" and "vermin," in both cases, indicating their difference from the uninfected, and their group's inferior status. Richie challenges Robert: "Okay then. If you don't want to cure them then kill them." Robert defects: "No need. They're half dead right now." In this statement, Robert is yet again denigrating them, explicitly framing them as outside of his consideration. Yet he might be revealing a hint of compassion for the infected. His words ring with detachment, but at the same time, he may be changing his stance from wishing for the infected to be eradicated (through killing or curing), to a "live and let live" position. He still sees them as an inferior race, but now he is aiming for a kind of segregation, rather than genocide. He just wants the two groups to leave each other alone, and he will just tend to those who are uninfected or at least unturned, leaving the infected to whatever their fate may be.

Robert's refusal receives Richie's condemnation. His injunction to "kill them or cure them" is ostensibly a plea of instrumentality to do away with the plague through whatever method, but morally it is also a challenge to choose a relation of either care or harm. Richie's grounds of condemnation of Robert are moral ones yet he articulates this condemnation with a specific focus on defining Robert as an Other—he calls him "a hostile" and says, "you just don't belong." Robert holds onto a position of resigned detachment. He sarcastically quips: "Nice of you to let me hang around." Finally, Richie says: "At times you scare me more than Matthias does." This is the most direct statement of the film, directly associating Robert's tribalism with Matthias' tribalism, directly pointing out the murkiness of the morality of the situation, directly leading us to ambivalence, or at least to entertaining it. Robert just laughs and walks away—a refusal, but not a meaningful rebuttal.

Later, Richie sneaks out to tell Matthias about the serum, leaving Robert a note that he is "going to find out who's right, you or me." Richie shows recognition of both sides, and he attempts to build Matthias' identification with Robert. In Richie's introduction of Robert's plans to Matthias (e.g. the word "help"), he implies his own motives are caring ones, and insinuates that Robert's desire to cure is similarly born out of a caring orientation. He appeals to Matthias that he and Robert should communicate to work together, that Robert can help return the infected. "Listen," he says, "he's got a serum for what's wrong with you. And if you could just talk to him, get with him, then everybody could be …" "Yes? Everybody could be what?" "Everyone … well … everybody could be *normal* again." The word "normal" is given quite an emphasis. Richie's reticence to say it, and his verbal emphasis once he finally does, is added to by a rapidly zooming in camera angle. It is as if the *truth* has finally come out. Here Richie is not off to a great start. He has already indicated that Matthias' illness is something wrong with him, and that Matthias is not normal. By extension, of course, this frames all of the infected as abnormal, and belonging to a diseased (or at least "wrong") race. Matthias rejects Richie's notion of normality, framing the illness as a change, but not with value ascribed: "You mean we could be as we were before? […] And that's what Neville thinks we want?"

Matthias refuses to see Richie's plea as a genuine offer of help. Instead, Matthias convinces himself that Robert sent Richie as a trick, to try and get the infected to submit to racial conversion. He frames Robert as dishonest rather than caring and condemns both Robert and Richie—both in a moral sense and in the sense that they are Other. He condemns Robert under the assumptive accusation that Robert is lying and manipulating. In his rejection of Richie's offer, he uses Othering language—"He sent you, to offer us something from *his world*"[9]—and he condemns Richie somewhat ambiguously—"You have been damned, Richard. Don't you see that? Don't you?"—although presumably because of Richie's physical and/or moral identification with Robert's group (the uninfected), and his use of the word "damned" suggests—with more than a hint of religiosity—the accusation that Richie has been tainted and degraded. Richie's execution drives home the point that in the end Robert was right, not Richie. Robert was right at least as far as his general stance of non-communication and assuming conflict to be inevitable. It is useless to try and make peace with Matthias and his clan, as implied by Robert's designation of them as "homicidal maniacs" in his debate with Richie.

Generally speaking, both sides—Robert and the survivors vis-à-vis Matthias and "the family"—are determined not to listen to the other. With the notable exception of Richie's initial ill state and Lisa's conversion near the end of the film, Robert and the survivors are not charmed by Matthias either. Yet none of them provide a compelling defence of modernity, other than appreciating Robert's capacity to use science to devise a cure. In one telling scene, Robert informs the survivors that the cure works, and he tells them they will all go far away into a place civilization hasn't touched. Dutch, in his excitement, says it will be just like a new Garden of Eden, "only this time we won't trust no friggin' snake!" The Garden of Eden reference indicates a blissful world without civilization, in effect agreeing with Matthias in large measure that the growth in humanity's technical capacities was overstepping its rightful place, and was an arrogant mistake.

Military violence throughout the film is important for facilitating the absconding of the survivors with the cure at the closing of the film, although somewhat indirectly. The survivors enter the film via Dutch and Lisa, who use (among other things) guns and explosives to save Robert from execution. In several scenes throughout the film, Robert also uses military weaponry against the infected, which in retrospect allows him to survive long enough to devise a successful cure. Robert is killed, but his cure makes it out with Dutch and the gang. What exactly they will do with it remains to be seen, but presumably it will at least work to protect the small colony of unturned survivors, who are now on a pilgrimage to begin a new "Garden of Eden" era of total separation if not segregation between themselves and the infected.

I Am Legend (2007)

Moving to 2007,[10] it was between the 9/11 bombings and Obama's election (the country's first black president). During the "war on terror" [white] racial anxieties were directed to Arabs, Muslims, and South Asians, exacerbating racializing tendencies that were already happening (Cainkar and Selod 2018). A wave of strong conservatism accompanied the Bush presidency, as well as publicized willingness of the military to torture, dehumanize, and brutalize (real or suspected) enemies—inspiring concerned debate. While many were appalled at knowledge of torture or photos from Guantanamo Bay, many supported military excesses. White nationalist militias were on the rise domestically (Keller 2009). As evidenced by Obama's election, much of the country was ready to see black men in positions of central power and influence. Yet Bonilla-Silva and Dietrich (2011) caution this was not due to America being truly "post-racial"; rather it was an expression of white America's growing colour-blind racism. Surrounding the turn of the millennium, disaster films boomed again, as they had in the early 1970s. Several blockbusters featured Will Smith battling alien Others (Independence Day, Men in Black, Men in Black 2). Starting around 2003, zombie films have boomed (Wonser and Boyns 2016).

In I Am Legend (2007), the plague has returned to the character of an infectious disease; it is a genetically altered form of measles virus intended to cure cancer. And it is now solely the fault of medical science rather than the military. Director Francis Lawrence provides no indication that the choice to move from biological warfare to lethal consequences of cancer cure as the cause of the virus had anything to do with critique of the medical or scientific establishment. When discussing the decision in an interview, he said:

These horrible viruses can pop up out of nowhere, it's not just bio-terrorism. It can be a change in the environment that brings an unseasonable grain to the area which attracts an animal with a disease and something is born and spreads.

(Turek 2007)

Two sides to this statement are: (a) in terms of infectious disease and its treatment, by 2007 we had graduated beyond the "chronic disease era," with threats from a host of deadly pathogens that we did not have treatment for. First there was the AIDS crisis starting in the 1980s, and then there had been several outbreaks of diseases such as Swine Flu, Bird Flu, West Nile Virus, and Ebola; (b) the description is not systemic. Lawrence frames the issue in terms of general unpredictability rather than collective human folly. Neville's status as a doctor fighting the plague with science, and failing to stop it before it overtook civilization, is further described by Will Smith in personalized terms rather than institutional. It was not medical science that was unable to protect humanity; it was Robert Neville. Smith says: "I loved the idea of Robert Neville in this position and to have to try to survive after he was the one who couldn't save humankind" (Warner Brothers 2012).

The focus on Neville *himself* is further echoed in director Francis Lawrence's description, which contains no indication of themes of morality or intergroup relations with the infected:

The heart of the story for me is really—it's about hope. What's interesting to me is this idea of you've got a man who has somehow survived the disappearance of humankind and he's had and seen and experienced so much loss [...] It's really a struggle of how do you find the will to live? [...] I guess what first appealed to me about the story was the idea of a man surviving alone in an urban environment. I've always been fascinated about that idea, and I had read Richard Matheson's novel, and so it's just something for years I've really been interested in.

(Warner Brothers 2012)

The description is about the struggles of Neville *alone*.

This rendition returns closer to Matheson's original than the 1971 rendition (e.g., the infected are animalistic rather than cult-like), but retains some remnants of the latter (e.g., Neville has an evident penchant for rifles and fast driving). This time, Robert Neville is a medical scientist and (former) lieutenant colonel living alone with a dog in a city apartment, after a killer virus has turned the surviving population into vampire-zombie-like creatures (which here I call "the infected"). Robert was immune, and holds out only a small hope that he may not be the only living human. His wife and daughter died in a helicopter crash during the chaos of the outbreak. He keeps trying to devise a cure; sometimes this involves capturing and experimenting on the infected.

After he has to kill his recently-turned dog, he goes on a late-night murder-suicide rampage. An uninfected woman (Anna) saves his life, brings him back to his home and fixes up his wounded leg. Anna travels with a boy (Ethan), the two headed toward a colony of surviving humans. She tries to convince Robert to believe in God and to come with her to the colony. Robert declines. Robert's home is attacked by the infected, who evidently followed Anna's car back to Robert's home the previous night. Robert extracts blood from a recovering infected he had recently experimented on, evidently with success. He gives the vial to Anna, tells Anna and Ethan to hide, and saves them by suicide-bombing the infected in his basement laboratory. Anna delivers the vial to the survivors' colony.

The very first scene frames scientific expertise as to blame for the pandemic. It was created out of attempts to cure cancer using a kind of bioengineering: "the measles virus," Dr. Alice Krippin explains in a television interview, "was engineered at a genetic level to be helpful rather than harmful." War and the military have no relation. After the TV interview clip, the next scene begins with the words "THREE YEARS LATER" superimposed on the first of a short series of images of post-apocalyptic New York City. The images mostly contain tall buildings and big streets populated by stopped cars and natural overgrowth, otherwise empty other than a couple of birds here and there. Finally, we see one moving car, from an aerial view. The lone car is very small from the height of the image, and we see it moving in a straight line down the street, past the abandoned cars and buildings. The contrast of the massive, empty city, against the comparatively tiny Robert, is a recurring visual theme throughout the film. Through these angles it is driven home how small and alone Robert is, and how his tiny person is consumed by the seemingly endless landscape of unoccupied buildings and roads.

The next image is a close-up from inside the car on Robert's rifle, which he takes from his side and lays across his lap, and the camera pans up and we see him driving, donning a leather jacket and concerned look. The appearance of Robert's rifle has us associate him with guns from his first moment onscreen. The playing up of Robert's militarism—like his smallness and aloneness—is reinforced visually all throughout the film. For instance, in his flashbacks and on the picture of himself from a magazine on his refrigerator he is shown in military uniform, when wandering around town he always keeps a rifle with him (very visible to the audience), he sleeps next to a handgun if not clutching a rifle, his hair is in a very close buzz cut, his pants have a cargo pocket, his biceps are articulated, he frequently dons a brown canvas courier bag, and in a daily radio address that he uses to call out to any potential surviving humans he includes his military title when introducing himself. Though Robert is a medical scientist, his identification as military has a more prominent place in the film. His scientist identity is mostly just reinforced when he is in his basement laboratory. There and only there he wears a lab coat and glasses.

New York City as the site as disaster necessarily rings with 9/11 overtones in 2007, just 6 years after the infamous bombing of the Twin Towers, when terrorists hijacked planes to collide with the buildings. Also, very significantly, one of Robert's flashbacks contains a metaphor for the event. It is the moment when he loses his family, and it is also the last moment, chronologically, contained in his flashbacks within the film. In this particular scene, Robert is waving goodbye to his wife and daughter, who are being taken away to safety on a helicopter. As they are taking off, Darkseekers and military personnel begin unexpectedly squaring off in chaotic fashion. Quickly, everything falls apart. And most significantly, Darkseekers leap up to a helicopter near the one containing Robert's wife and daughter, causing it to spin out of control. In its spin, we see that the hijacked copter is going to crash into the one with Robert's family inside.

Robert's home is secretly a fortress. In the earlier scenes of the film, we discover this via the sliding industrial metal shutters that he closes inside behind all of his windows. Later on, when the Darkseekers attack, we see the full extent of it. Not only has he rigged the outside with explosives, he has guns strategically placed at the bottom of the staircase, which in a key moment probably saves his life (and by extension, Anna's and Ethan's). Even in his lab, there is a barrier of [presumably] plexi-glass, which holds off the Darkseekers for a few minutes before Robert's final, fateful, heroic self-sacrifice.

For most of the film, Robert expresses no compassion for the infected. Generally, when he kills them it is in self-defense, or as part of failed non-consenting medical trials in which he tests various possible cures. Yet he expresses no regret about killing or otherwise harming them. In a video journal entry, he describes the infected in an alienated, medicalized fashion, specifically voicing how separate they are from normal healthy humans. His language is primarily technical and medicalized. He refers to the Darkseekers as "infected hosts," and suggesting that an "infected male" exposing himself to sunlight may indicate "decreased brain function," "ignor[ance of] their basic survival instincts," and "social de-evolution." He ends the report with "Typical human behavior is now entirely absent," a direct statement pointing to a clear and important difference between humans and Darkseekers.

Robert is strongly identified with and loyal to humanity. One clear expression of this is when he repeats back to Anna verbatim the words he originally spoke to his now deceased wife on the night that she died, as we witness earlier in the film in one of Robert's dream/flashbacks: "I'm not leaving. This is ground zero. This is my site. I'm not gonna let this happen. I can still fix this." This mantra also conveys Robert's denotative military identification and militaristic loyalty, especially within the second two sentences where he uses the term "ground zero"—associating the disease outbreak with nuclear war—and "my site"—connoting an official stationing and his loyalty to maintaining that station.

Robert's divisive identification against the infected is also exhibited when he shows Anna what is going on in his laboratory. "That's heavily sedated," he tells her, "Don't worry, it's safe." This informs Anna that it is safe for *Anna*, but shows no regard for the infected woman. Anna asks if Robert thinks a serum he is administering will "cure her." Of course, her reference to the Darkseeker as "her" indicates the sedated infected woman possesses sexual traits, thus opening up the possibility of empathy or bridging. Robert answers her question first with "no, this will almost certainly kill it," indicating the infected woman as an object with his use of "it" instead of a gendered pronoun. Quickly, he refocuses on the science rather than on the infected woman's life: "but it's possible by drastically reducing the body temperature I can increase the compound's effectiveness." Anna asks if all of the infected headshots in Robert's wall of photos died, and he answers "yes" in a very factual, emotionless tone. She says "my God," expressing astonishment at the number that died. Robert responds not by referring to her astonishment, but instead shifting to a broad focus on morally condemning humanity as responsible: "God didn't do this, we did." He does not, however, indicate exactly what he means by "this"; he does not clearly articulate what humanity is responsible for, other than unavoidably implying the larger post-apocalyptic context. Which part of the context is morally objectionable, and why, is left open. His response acts correctively to Anna's referencing of God, rather than expressing emotional engagement with her expression of shock and hinted recognition by extension. Yet Anna's expressed recognition for the infected stops at this hinting.

Robert does eventually create a cure, and hence presumably saves humanity. However, his method is a combination of medical and military techniques. When Robert, Anna, and Ethan are cornered by the infected in Robert's basement laboratory, Robert yells "I can save you! I can help!" and so on, at them (the infected). His words suggest compassion, selfish pleading, or some combination. We cannot know for sure.

He gives to Anna a vial of blood from a healing infected woman (the one she saw earlier), and uses a grenade to kill the mob of infected in his basement laboratory, sacrificing himself in the process, allowing Anna and Ethan to survive and deliver the vial to the survivors' colony. Robert's combined medical and military background saves the world, or at least makes saving the world possible. Robert saves the world with a syringe and a grenade. It is when Anna and Ethan actually make it to the survivors' colony that humanity's salvation is finally secured. When they come to the survivors' colony, we observe that it is surrounded by a massive wall, and has military men at the gates. Evidently here too, the meeting of medical and military power is central to saving the world. Delivering the vial of blood to this militarized colony officially inaugurates the beginning of humanity's recuperation.

In the final scene, Anna's character gives a voiceover. In her summation, there is no indication of her earlier hinted recognition of the Diseased Others. She makes no mention of them, and her description of Robert is idolizing,

never mentioning him killing the infected or fatally experimenting on them
without consent. Anna's framing of Robert as martyr indicates his strong identification with his in-group, that is, humanity. During the voiceover, we see a bird's
eye view of the survivors' colony, which is surrounded by a massive wall.

ANNA'S VOICEOVER: In 2009 a deadly virus burned through our civilization,
    pushing humankind to the edge of extinction. Doctor Robert Neville
    dedicated his life to the discovery of a cure and the restoration of
    humanity. On September 9, 2012, at approximately 8:49pm, he dis-
    covered that cure. And at 8:52 he gave his life to defend it. We are his
    legacy. This is his legend. Light up the darkness.

Combined summary

Broadly, the moral trajectory across renditions of the story appears to be of
liquidation of recognition for the Other. Condemnation, bridging, division,
and ambivalence all become less pronounced; there is a simplification of intergroup relations to a purer and more taken-for-granted friend-enemy model.
Bridging identification is notable in 1954 and 1971, less so in 1964, and never
directly stated in 2007. It occupies a central place in the dramatic plot twist and
moral identity crisis of 1954, and is raised—albeit futilely—by Richie in 1971,
in protest against the divisive identifications of both Robert and Matthias.

   Divisive identification is the primary mode of identification in all versions of
the story—as the plot hinges upon the in-group/out-group division between
the healthy and the infected—although, like bridging, it is most prominently
articulated in the 1954 novel and 1971 film. In 1964 it is present and brought
into crisis in the final scenes, less so than the 1954 novel and more vaguely, but
following a similar plot twist. In 2007 it is almost never directly stated, it is just
obvious and implicit at once.

   Overall, condemnation follows a similar pattern to the divisive and bridging
modes of identification, in that it figures prominently in 1954 and 1971, less
prominently in 1964, and is never directly stated in 2007. Regarding its specific
modes, condemnation for moral transgressions is the only mode of condemnation in 1954 (barring Robert's aggressive and profane thoughts, which are more
expressive and amoral than declarative judgments). Both modes are present in
1964 and 1971. In 2007, all we have is a vague hint at self-condemnation ("God
didn't do this Anna, we did").

   Denotative identification is marginal until 2007, when Robert's military
identity is prominent and repeatedly emphasized. This is particularly interesting
in the context of declines in form of identification that concern intergroup
relations. In their place—if it is not too strong to claim replacement—the one
form of identification that emphasizes self-definition is raised in prominence.
And the peculiarity of the military identity is that *loyalty* and *authority* are more

honoured than in prior renditions, even if playing minor roles. In 1971 these elements were emphasized within Matthias' cult, but his cult was clearly presented as pathological. True, Robert is a little extreme, and we view him as "losing his mind" in some sense, especially considering his "post" that he is so committed to no longer effectively exists under the scope of the apocalypse. Yet Robert is our hero and protagonist and so his positive clinging to these values still grants them a positive spin. This is the first time that Robert shows anything like patriotic duty; and significantly, it turns out that without his commitment humanity would not have been saved.

In 1954 and 1964, killing survivors marked Robert as condemnable in the eyes of survivors. Ruth expresses this in both versions. Robert and survivors generally accepted the killing of the infected as necessary, yet Robert questions the survivors' excesses. In 1954, Robert's internal monologues reveal he still struggles with his conscience regarding the infected. In 1964, Robert's voice-overs do not reveal such a struggle. In both versions, when survivors come to get Robert, he is alarmed by their massacre of the infected. In 1954 there is an extended meditation on it, Robert's condemnation of them made explicit. In the 1964 scene Robert appears shocked, but the voiceover is inoperative by that point in the film, hence not articulating any condemnation. In 1954 and 1964, the major dramatic twist of the story relies on Robert's and Ruth's ambivalence; and for Robert, the upending of his "moral identity" (Blasi 1984). The twist is marked more profoundly in the book. In 1954, Robert's final moments explicitly contain bridging regarding survivors, and the capacity to see himself as a dangerous and condemnable Other. In 1964 Robert's "they were afraid of me" croaks indicate a change of perspective, but they do not articulate the same level or clarity of bridging and self-condemnation that punctuated the end of the 1954 novella. In 1954, Robert has glimpses of bridging identification with Others. In 1964 (and after) there is no such identification. In 1954 and 1964, the survivors seek Robert's execution without knowing his situation and motives (that he can cure them and that his killing of survivors was done out of ignorance rather than malice). Each side attacks one another from positions of ignorance (Robert's ignorance of the survivors' health, the survivors' ignorance of Robert's medical agenda and of his ignorance about their health). In 1954 and 1964, one might read some degree of absolution for one or both sides due to ignorance.

In 1971, ignorance is no longer to blame, providing no hypothetical absolution. Robert knows from the beginning that the infected possess speech and reason, and so his routine killing of them is not due to his ignorance of their humanity. When Richie goes as peacemaker to talk with Matthias and tries to convince him that Robert is not bad and will cure him, Matthias acutely rejects the idea, hearing the argument but disregarding it. The ambivalence of 1954 and 1964 changes further in 1971. There is no longer a dramatic moral twist as in the earlier versions. Now, Matthias and Robert both condemn one another through the entirety of the film, neither considering the other one's side as potentially legitimate, neither one being moved to bridging or recognition. Richie's debates with Robert and Matthias emphasize that the refusal of each to work together is unnecessary, and that the two are somewhat alike. However, neither Robert nor Matthias are moved by Richie's arguments. Neither side shows acknowledgement or insight into the other's position.

In 2007, no moral questions are raised regarding killing the infected, capturing them, or experimenting on them without consent. Robert does not bridge with them and gives them no recognition. The one possible moment of moral questioning is in the scene where Robert shows Anna his laboratory, and she uses a gendered pronoun for the unconscious infected woman, asks if all of Robert's infected patients died, and says "my God" at Robert's affirmative answer regarding their deaths. This is a subtle moment in the film, however, hardly an overall moral framing or a dramatic twist. It is simply a passing scene, with the moral challenge occurring through pronouns and hints, not explicit articulation.

The Otherness of the infected is more severe over time, and in tandem, the moral distance between Humans and Others is more severe over time. In 1964, Diseased Others looked fairly "normal," albeit with exaggerated slowness and simplicity. In 1971, Others had different eyes and skin, cult-like groupthink, black robes, and active rejection of modernity's remnants. In 2007, Others have strange skin, no hair, no speech, monstrous voices, and so on (they are also computer animated). Those who are different appear increasingly strange and predatory.

It appears that the lack of speech, and strong abnormality in 2007 directly coincided with the shrinking of the focus to be squarely on the protagonist. In other words, when the Diseased Others became less human, issues of intergroup moralities receded. Note that over this same period of time (1971–2007), when for *I Am Legend* the infected become less human, for America political divisions between left and right sharpened, and the racial composition of the parties split increasingly on the left/right axis, the two cleavages (political and racial) dovetailing (Mason 2018).

Another example: In an early, sardonic scene of *The Omega Man*, Charlton Heston watches a film of Woodstock and recites along with a speaker in the film a comment about the importance of living in a friendly and intimate culture. In 2007, Will Smith recites some lines over the movie *Shrek*, which are less of a cultural statement and more of a discussion between two characters about the question of loneliness and sticking together. The themes are related of course, but the cultural critique from 1971 is dropped in favour of a much more personalized and decontextualized refrain. Lawrence says of the *Shrek* recital scene that it is about *family*:

> The idea of "Shrek" for us was that there's something nice about a guy who has lost his family—it's not nice—but there's something nice about the experience of coming downstairs to find a child in front of the TV and "Shrek" is on. If you think about it, the last time he has seen that image was when his daughter was alive.
>
> (Turek 2007)

In a more recent interview, Lawrence (Cotter 2018) describes wishing his 2007 version were more like the original novella. His description of why the 2007 rendition strayed centres on the precariousness of securing audience satisfaction. He describes the 1954 ending as "nihilistic," but this is not to decry it. Overall, his statements indicate that much of his creative autonomy was hampered by the felt need to cater to the predicted audience. Hence much of the "meaning" of the film was manufactured for others, rather than being purely an artistic expression of the author(s).

> We could have literally made the book, which I would have been much happier with, but you know when you're spending that much money you're panicking that you're making this weird little kind of art film about a guy alone with a dog in New York and you're trying to you know sort of create that spectacle.
>
> (Cotter 2018)

Perhaps most starkly representing this issue, there was an alternate ending filmed in 2007, which was closer to the complexity of the original book, but it was rejected in favour of the simpler narrative. Lawrence says of the alternate version:

> [I]t's the better ending. I mean, it's the more philosophical version of the end, but in terms of story math we're doing everything you're not sup-posed to do, right? The hero doesn't find the cure, right? They drive off into the unknown and the creatures you've been saying are the bad ones the whole time you learn actually have humanity and aren't the bad ones—the hero's the bad one. And so you've basically turned everything on its head. We tested it twice and it got wildly rejected, wildly rejected, which is why we came out with the other one.
>
> (Cotter 2018)

The upshot here is that the "more philosophical" ending, which would have provided a dramatic twist as in 1954 and 1964, which would have framed the story in moral ambivalence rather than the simple humans-vs.-Others narrative, was rejected not due to the artistic vision or preferred narratives of the writers or directors, but rather due to the calculation of audience preferences en masse.

The changes in moral framing are further evidenced by the changes in the meaning of Robert's "legend"-ary status. In 1954, the words "I am legend" mark his final thoughts during suicide, meditating on the fact that he has become a monster to the survivors, and will be remembered as such. 1964, Ruth mouths the term "legend" in emphasizing that Robert was well-known by the survivors as a dangerous killer. In 1971, the term is not used. However, Dutch indicated having admiring awareness of Robert's former research, while to the infected Robert is known as an evil killer. In 2007, Robert was a celebrity scientist before the apocalypse—revealed by his appearance on a magazine cover on his refrigerator and the mentioning of his name on one of his mealtime replayed television news shows and by Anna saying "you are *the* Robert Neville, aren't you?"—and moving forward, his "legend" is very positive, as indicated by Anna's use of the term in her voice-over at the end of the film, describing him as a martyr who found the cure for humanity. Hence Robert's "legend" moves through the renditions of the film along with the fading ambivalence and bridging identification. In 1954, Robert's legacy is only negative. In 1964, it is articulated only as negative, but positivity becomes possible (he cures Anna and potential future cure is then in her blood). In 1971, it is both positive and negative. In 2007, it is only positive. These narrative assessments of him move along with a general trend between the versions of declining bridging and ambivalence, with a shrinking of Robert's (and the story's) moral framework toward "us"-versus-"them."

The following is a concise summation regarding medical science and the military. In 1954, war is suspect for blame, and so is medical science, although to a lesser degree. Yet in both cases, it is only in a passing conversation, no proof is presented, and the protagonist in the story specifically discards the hypothesis as at best impossible to determine. Science does not save humanity, but it does succeed to some degree. Military violence is at least partly responsible for the failure to devise a full cure, as Robert must die before any completion of his studies and experiments. In 1964, there is no focus of blame for the pandemic for either military or science. Medical science is successful in the conclusion although we do not know for certain if humanity is saved, as military violence might stand in the way of humanity's salvation. In 1971, the military and science are to blame for the pandemic, yet science is emphasized. For the conclusion, medical science is quite successful without struggle. It will *presumably* save the survivors; saving humanity does not appear an immediate goal. Military violence is also instrumental for paving the way to the somewhat happy ending. In 2007, medical science is to blame for the pandemic. The military is innocent. Military violence and medical science combine to save humanity.

The various renditions of *I Am Legend* are heterogeneous in likely impactful ways that make a strict comparison impossible. There are quite a number of grey areas, how to interpret "germ warfare," for example; many of the scientific gains of the 1950s were in service of the military. The 1954 version is the only novel, the other three are films. Also, in 1964 the origin of the pandemic is not addressed. This is perhaps less an indication of a narrative touting neutrality, and more an indication of origins simply not figuring into the script. Overall, there are multiple progressions to track, and most of them are not unidirectional over time.

Yet even with the above caveats in mind, four notable trajectories still stand out regarding the medical science and military. One is the trajectory of the impact of military violence on the conclusion of the story. The trend is from negative to positive. Science is implicated as clearly culpable in the origin of the pandemic in 1971 and 2007, entirely to blame in 2007. Prior to this its influence on the origin was unclear. Yet science's power to provide a solution increases across the renditions. Science is increasingly believed to cause problems *and* to solve them. And the military is increasingly believed to solve problems, its overall portrayal increasing in positivity across the renditions.

Notes

1 The quote is in reference to his old friend—now one of the infected—Ben.
2 In the novel, Robert's attraction to the infected women and his moral struggles against his erotic and exploitive impulses toward them are strong and recurring elements. This topic deserves its own analysis separate from the issue of his attitude toward the infected "in general." For the sake of brevity, and because gender themes have been already analyzed at length elsewhere (Pulliam and Fonseca 2016; Ransom 2018), I leave this discussion outside the scope of this book and refer the reader to the aforementioned volumes.
3 Emphasis added.
4 He similarly disliked *The Omega Man* and feels negatively about adaptations of his story that are not true to the novella.
5 In an earlier extended flashback sequence, Robert identifies himself with science in contradistinction to those people touting "alarmist" ideas.
6 Some historians, such as Arthur Marwick (2005, 2011), refer to "the long sixties," which extends from the late 1950s to the mid-1970s.
7 Reviewers such as Roger Ebert declined to comment on the film's particular treatment of moral complexity of intergroup relations, instead focusing on Neville as being normal and The Family (Matthias' group) as being infected and deranged (Ebert 1971; Thompson 1971; Kelly 1971).
8 The precise "marks" appear to be bluish-white eyes. When Matthias instructs his underlings to show Robert the marks, they remove their sunglasses to reveal their very pale blue eyes.
9 Emphasis added.
10 The 2007 film was wildly successful, but reviewers tended to be unimpressed, describing it in relatively shallow terms.

References

Adams, M., Bell, L. A., & Griffin, P. (2007). History of Racism and Immigration Time Line: Key Events in the Struggle for Racial Equality in the United States. In *Teaching for Diversity and Social Justice*. New York: Routledge.

Agar, J. (2012). *Science in the Twentieth Century and Beyond*. Malden, MA: Polity.

Blasi, A. (1984). Moral Identity: Its Role in Moral Functioning. In W. M. Kurtines & J. J. Gewirtz (eds.), *Morality, Moral Behavior, and Moral Development*. New York: Wiley, 128–139.

Bonilla-Silva, E., & Dietrich, D. (2011). The Sweet Enchantment of Color-Blind Racism in Obamerica. *The ANNALS of the American Academy of Political and Social Science*, 634(1), 190–206. doi:10.1177/0002716210389702.

Cainkar, L., & Selod, S. (2018). Review of Race Scholarship and the War on Terror. *Sociology of Race and Ethnicity*, 4(2), 165–177. doi:10.1177/2332649218762808.

Centers for Disease Control and Prevention. (2018). Measles History. Retrieved from https://www.cdc.gov/measles/about/history.html.

Cotter, P. (2018). I Am Legend Director Reveals the Movie He Wishes He'd Made. Retrieved from *Screenrant*: https://screenrant.com/i-am-legend-ending-approach/.

Ebert, R. (1971). The Omega Man Movie Review and Film Summary. Retrieved from *RogerEbert.com*: https://www.rogerebert.com/reviews/the-omega-man-1971.

Ellul, J. (1954/1964). *The Technological Society*. New York: Vintage Books.

Guillemin, J. (2006). Scientists and the History of Biological Weapons: A Brief Historical Overview of the Development of Biological Weapons in the Twentieth Century. *EMBO Reports*, 7(1S), S45–S49. doi:10.1038/sj.embor.7400689.

Haas, E., Christensen, T., & Haas, P. J. (2015). *Projecting Politics: Political Messages in American Films*. New York: Routledge.

Hamilton, N. A. (2006). *The 1970s*. New York: Facts on File.

Immunization Action Coalition. (2020). Vaccine Timeline: Historic Dates and Events Related to Vaccines and Immunization. Retrieved from *Immunization Action Coalition*: https://www.immunize.org/timeline/

Introduction by Co-Stars Eric Laneuville and Paul Koslo and Screenwriter Joyce H. Carrington. (2007). *The Omega Man* [DVD]. United States: Warner Brothers.

Jancovich, M. (1996). *Rational Fears: American Horror in the 1950s*. Manchester: Manchester University Press.

Judis, J. B. (2016). *The Populist Explosion: How the Great Recession Transformed American and European Politics*. New York: Columbia Global Reports.

Keller, L. (2009). The Second Wave: Around the Country, Evidence Accumulates of a Return of the Militias and the Larger Antigovernment 'Patriot' Movement. Retrieved from *Southern Poverty Law Center*: https://www.splcenter.org/20090731/second-wave-return-militias.

Kelly, K. (1971, August 26). Theater/Arts: 'Omega Man': Film Review. *Boston Globe*.

King, D. C., & Karabell, Z. (2003). *The Generation of Trust: Public Confidence in the US Military since Vietnam*. Washington, D.C.: American Enterprise Institute.

Maga, T. (2003). *The 1960s*. New York: Facts on File.

Marwick, A. (2005). The Cultural Revolution of the Long Sixties: Voices of Reaction, Protest, and Permeation. *The International History Review*, 27(4), 780–806. doi:10.1080/07075332.2005.9641080.

Marwick, A. (2011). *The Sixties: Cultural Revolution in Britain, France, Italy, and the United States, c. 1958–c. 1974*. London: A&C Black.

Mason, L. (2018). *Uncivil Agreement: How Politics Became our Identity*. Chicago, IL: University of Chicago Press.

Matheson, R. (1954/2007). *I Am Legend*. New York: Tor.

Matheson, R., & Dawidziak, M. (2012). *Richard Matheson's Censored and Unproduced I Am Legend Screenplay*. Washington, D.C.: Edge Book.

Nimmo, D. D., & Combs, J. E. (1990). *Mediated Political Realities*. London: Longman Publishing Group.

Patterson, K. D. (2005). Echoes of Dracula: Racial Politics and the Failure of Segregated Spaces in Richard Matheson's I Am Legend. *Journal of Dracula Studies*, 7, 19–26.

Pulliam, J. M., & Fonseca, A. J. (2016). *Richard Matheson's Monsters: Gender in the Stories, Scripts, Novels, and Twilight Zone Episodes*. Lanham, MD: Rowman & Littlefield.

Ransom, A. J. (2018). *I Am Legend as American Myth: Race and Masculinity in the Novel and its Film Adaptations*. Jefferson, NC: McFarland.

Schwartz, R. A. (2003). *The 1950s*. New York: Facts on File.

Susser, M., & Susser, E. (1996). Choosing a Future for Epidemiology: I. Eras and Paradigms. *American Journal of Public Health*, 86, 668–673. doi:10.1093/acprof:oso/9780195300666.003.0024.

The Last Man Alive. (2007). Special feature: *The Omega Man* [DVD]. United States: Warner Brothers.

Thompson, H. (1971, August 14). Screen: All Alone in L.A.: Charlton Heston Stars in 'The Omega Man'. *New York Times*.

Turek, R. (2007). An Exclusive Interview with Francis Lawrence. Retrieved from *Comingsoon.net*: https://www.comingsoon.net/horror/news/708425-an-exclusive-interview-with-francis-lawrence.

Wald, P. (2008). *Contagious: Cultures, Carriers, and the Outbreak Narrative*. Durham, NC: Duke University Press.

Warner Brothers. (2012). I Am Legend: Creating a Legend. Retrieved from YouTube: https://www.youtube.com/watch?v=fyZ4Qf4V2q4.

Wonser, R., & Boyns, D. (2016). Between the Living and the Undead: How Zombie Cinema Reflects the Social Construction of Risk, the Anxious Self, and Disease Pandemic. *The Sociological Quarterly*, 57(4), 628–653. doi:10.1111/tsq.12150.

Chapter 5

Case study II
Day of the Dead

Day of the Dead (1985)

> *Day of the Dead* really grew out of that '80s [...] giving up on everything: government, the military, faith in financial systems; and everything was just starting to look [like] a house of cards.
>
> (Romero, from "The Many Days of Day of the Dead," 2003)

In 1979, President Jimmy Carter gave his famous "malaise speech" identifying a "crisis of confidence" in America. The country was suffering from an energy crisis, and continued economic woes including problems with unemployment and inflation. The late 1970s into the 1980s was the era in which Stuart Hall coined the term "authoritarian populism" to refer to Thatcherism in Britain and by extension its cousin Reaganism in the United States (Hall et al. 2013; Hall 1980). Neoliberalism, immigration restrictions, and cracking down on crime were combined together—Reagan was especially energized in the "war on drugs" (Woodger and Burg 2006). In 1986—the year following *Day of the Dead*—the Immigration Reform and Control Act would be passed, criminalizing the employment of undocumented immigrants and building up the Border Patrol (Bell, Adams, and Griffin 2007).

As discussed in Chapter 3, the 1980s also marked the beginning of the end of the "chronic disease era," with the first known cases of AIDS documented in 1981 (Woodger and Burg 2006). The chronic disease era had emerged after World War II, at the end of the "infectious disease era," during which time the science of epidemiology was focused on the study, treatment, and prevention of infectious diseases such as polio and tuberculosis. Owing to multiple factors including the development of vaccines for a variety of contagions, epidemiology switched to a "chronic disease paradigm" in the post-World War II era, as non-contagious, long-lasting conditions such as cancer and heart disease became the main focus. During the chronic disease era in the United States, there was a widespread popular assumption that the dangers of deadly pathogens were a thing of the past, as medical science had essentially overcome the threat. HIV/AIDS provided a shattering blow to that idea (Susser and Susser 1996).

The resumption of the fear of deadly infectious disease came along with particularly scapegoated populations—AIDS became associated with people of colour, with gay men, and with intravenous drug users. All three of these populations were already Othered by straight white America overall, but now the association of Them with a deadly plague was added in. As Sontag (1989) notes in *AIDS and its Metaphors*, this blaming of a subpopulation as morally "polluted/polluting" is typical for the "plague metaphor," even going back to ancient times. Perhaps not unrelated, the 1980s had an uptick in Diseased Others films starting mid-decade. The uptick was strong enough that the 1980s would close with more Diseased Others films released than in all previous decades (Schweitzer 2018; Russell 2014).

Day of the Dead (1985) is the third and final instalment of Romero's initial trilogy of zombie films. It was both written and directed by George Romero, and produced by Richard P. Rubinstein, Dead Films Inc., Laurel Entertainment Inc., and Laurel-Day Inc. It starred Lori Cardille as the white female protagonist. The film is actually a substantially scaled down version of an original (unpublished) screenplay by George Romero that never made it to production. Like the case of Matheson's "The Night Creatures" script, the reason has something to do with being too extreme. Twenty years separate the incidents of course, and the ways that concern around obscenity influenced the non-use of the original screenplays vary accordingly. In Matheson's case, he simply included too much for the censors to permit. In Romero's case, he combined a high level of obscenity with an extravagant script that would require high production costs. A trade-off had to be made. With Romero's typical and desired level of obscenity, the film would go beyond the limits of "R" and would have to be unrated. This was fine with Romero, but the production company refused to put an exorbitant amount of money into an unrated film, as in general unrated films brought in comparatively little financial returns in comparison with R-rated films. The company would be willing to pay for the film to be made, provided Romero toned it down to R level. But Romero considered the very profane nature of his films to be essential, and so he let go of the old script. The version that became the actual film was hurriedly drafted in just the two weeks prior to filming. It contained several of the same characters as the old script but was considerably toned down from its original epic "Ben Hur with zombies" form (Karr and Nicotero 2014; "The Many Days" 2003). In the end it cost $3,500,000 to make. It earned $5,804,262 in the domestic box office, so the modest budget seems warranted. Now, however, the movie is a cult classic.

Despite having to scale down and rewrite the entire film, Romero has indicated that *Day* carries through the meanings that he had intended in the original script. Romero explains that he intended *Day of the Dead* to capture the times. In his words:

[I]t came out of what I was perceiving at the time as a disintegration of values, of trust—trust in institutions, trust in government—and so I think that it all added basically to the patina of the film. And that's really what this film is about, the loss of community [...] [Ev]en in a small group of people they can't pull it together. They can't work together. You know it's sort of like the Congress today. Basically, all I lost were some action sequences that are absolutely unnecessary to make the point of the film. People often say to me "don't you wish you could have made that" and I say "you know what? I made the film that I wanted to make, because I took the essence of what was in it and just reduced it down and I think all to the good. I think it turned out better."

("The Many Days" 2003)

He was specifically trying to be timely, and part of this was to depict what he saw as a 1980s "disintegration of values," and "loss of community." The latter issue has been given empirical support by the work of Robert Putnam (2001): throughout the second half of the twentieth century, "social capital" and civic engagement declined in America overall. As far as meanings that Romero intended, then, he felt the film rendered them faithfully. The team on site to film was small, and several of them knew one another from working together on prior Romero films. Perhaps partly due to this fact, Romero's intended metaphors for 1980s America stayed intact to his satisfaction—even despite the drastic, last minute overhaul.

Yet Romero's intended metaphoric message generally missed reviewers, who—staying on the surface—characterized the film as having too much dialogue, and of course plenty of gore. "Blood and guts pour across the screen" reported one reviewer (Geduld 1985). Roger Ebert (1985) claimed that "the real drama in the film gets lost" in all the arguing between Sarah and Rhodes.[1] Another viewer reports "there are enough spilled guts and severed limbs to satisfy the bloodthirstiest fan. But these moments tend to be clustered together, and a lot of the film is devoted to windy argument" (Maslin 1985).

Odd as it may seem, George Romero's *Day of the Dead* is very rich in metaphor and social commentary. The remakes have considerably less depth, but are still rich enough, and as can be expected, they preserve, modify, and discard various themes from the original 1985 rendition. Being so rich, it is also complex, and scenes tend to combine various elements relevant to this book, to such an extent that the following exposition is the longest in this book, and it is not entirely sequential. And yet even despite this richness and complexity, some overall trends stand out, which will become clear by the end of the chapter.

Before digging deep, here is the story in outline: The world has been overrun by zombies. A small group of scientists, technicians, and military personnel have been stationed in an underground compound to facilitate the scientists' work toward finding a medical solution to combat the zombie apocalypse. For this, the military capture zombies one by one for the scientists to experiment on and learn from. One of the scientists—Dr. Logan—has been conducting surgical experiments on the zombies, and training one of them—"Bub"—to regain human characteristics and to follow his orders. Another scientist—Sarah—continues to search for a cure for the disease that turns people into zombies. Rhodes has assumed a commanding role among the group, and the military and scientific factions are increasingly agitated with one another. The technicians mostly keep to themselves and avoid conflict. When Rhodes discovers Logan has been conducting surgical experiments on recently deceased military personnel, Rhodes kills Logan and officially severs cooperation with the scientists, and starts killing them. After having his arm bitten and then severed, Sarah's traumatized military boyfriend Miguel escapes outside and lets a crowd of zombies simultaneously eat him and enter into the compound. The military men become panicked and the zombies kill them off one by one. Bub, having broken free of his restraints, discovers Logan's dead body and shoots Rhodes, who is then torn apart by zombies. Sarah and the technicians escape in a helicopter to a tropical island.

There is no explanation given for the origin of the disease. Science and the military are both effectively neutral on that account, or to put it put differently: they are not worth mentioning. Regarding the possibility of a solution, the situation is just as empty. Military violence is mildly helpful, but only in the sense that it is necessary for self-defense. Logan's experiments are somewhat successful, but the story is littered with skepticism about the value of science. In the end, neither military nor science offers any real solution. Escape is the closest thing. Throughout the film, care and ambivalence are both notably lacking, although they might be inferred in a few cases, associated with forms of identification or moral injunctions. Their relative absence is made up for by an over-riding *instrumentality*. Most courses of action, deliberations, and philosophies represented in the film point toward this as a kind of ubiquitous "last word."

The film opens to an extended silent shot of Sarah sitting on the floor in a barren room, against a white stone wall, alone, head down, looking like she has given up hope, exhausted and potentially asleep. This sense of emptiness and hopelessness is underscored in other textures throughout the film. For instance, soon after we find Sarah and Miguel visiting a city street, in hopes of finding human life. We are given many shots of the street, which feature dead bodies, trash, dead palm trees, abandoned cars, unexpected animals (a large tarantula, a crocodile) and of course zombies. Miguel yells into his megaphone: "Hello! Hello! Is anyone there?!" His voice echoes, driving home a sense of nothingness and aloneness. There is no human answer. Only zombies hear him and begin to collect and slump toward him and Sarah. The main location of the film is an underground facility that in many sections is littered with rock, appearing more like a cave than a building. In the large meeting room, as well as in the more cave-like areas, loud voices echo, underscoring again and again the sense of emptiness and desolation.

Returning from the visit to investigate the city, John, Billy, Sarah and Miguel arrive in a helicopter outside the underground facility. We learn very quickly that Miguel is on edge, by his reluctance to exit the helicopter, and by his hostile and fatalistic words toward Sarah. He says yes, she is stronger than everyone else, but that it doesn't matter because the whole operation is falling apart anyway. He is petulant like a recalcitrant child, and emotionally unstable. After Miguel leaves the helicopter, John and Sarah stand outside it and talk. Following a brief disagreement with Sarah over where to leave the helicopter, John echoes some of Miguel's fatalism, but without the emotional desperation. "If you've got an alternative to what we're doing we'd be happy to listen to it," Sarah tells him. Of course, her comment is meant as more of a rhetorical challenge. She is suggesting that there is no alternative. John retorts that he does in fact have an alternative: fly the helicopter to a deserted island and "spend what time we got left soaking up some sunshine."

"You could do that, couldn't you? With all that's going on you could do that without a second thought," Sarah challenges him again. Although in the form of a question, Sarah's words suggest moral disapproval of John's attitude. Sarah poses the issue as one of conscience and connectedness—that trying to fix the situation means acting in accordance with a caring moral sensibility, being impacted by what is happening, and being invested meaningfully in some form of the greater good. If John *could* just leave and go to a deserted island and enjoy himself it means he is disconnected, uncaring, and amoral.

John simply replies that yes, he could, "even if all of this wasn't happening." His response dodges the moral implications of Sarah's challenge, in a way that is a little unclear. If it is not nonsense, then John is proposing an alternate set of values—that defecting from active participation in society and enjoying a simple, secluded life is always attractive and reasonable to him, and even more so under current circumstances. He might also be suggesting that society is gone, so any moral compulsion there would be to continue working for the greater good is gone with it; there is no greater good left to serve. In any case, his response indicates that he embraces an amoral and even detached stance, and it also indicates that he does not share Sarah's moral framework regarding this choice. He is not without conscience; he just does not see this issue as a matter of conscience.

We will later find out that John is correct from the beginning, at least in a predictive sense—science will not save them, that they may need to make a quick escape in the helicopter, and that a deserted island would be a good destination. And as the film progresses, we discover gradually that these exchanges between them frame the story. In a later scene, when Sarah visits John and Billy at their living quarters ("The Ritz"), John gives the same message, but at greater length and with clearer disdain for the gathering of scientific knowledge. According to John there is an enormous amount of written records kept in the bunker, of many different kinds, well beyond what specifically pertains to the issue at hand—the zombie apocalypse. From his description, the facility doubles as a kind of storage facility for general archives on human civilization before the outbreak. But according to John, the record-keeping is pointless. "This is a great big 14-mile tombstone! With an epitaph on it that nobody gonna bother to read," he says. He yells the word "tombstone," and the hopelessness of the word is driven home as it echoes throughout the caverns. Comparing Sarah's "charts and graphs and records" to the archives already down there, John suggests they are and will be just as pointless.

He continues to voice skepticism not just at the current project, but the scientific search for knowledge in general. He says she will never figure out how to stop the virus, "just like they never figured out why the stars are where they're at. It ain't mankind's job to figure that stuff out." Instead, he advocates starting society over again, with a neo-primitivist slant: "Start fresh, get some babies, and teach them, Sarah. Teach them never to come over here and dig these records out." He goes on to suggest that maybe (probably) the zombie apocalypse is a punishment from God, for humanity's scientific hubris.

John is perhaps the "voice of wisdom" throughout the film, almost to the point of qualifying as a spiritual leader. He is generally calm if not philosophical, his actions are deliberate and at times one step ahead of everyone else. He is on the cusp of total amorality, if not already there, yet he is still compassionate—especially when it comes to Sarah. In his predictions he is always right, one way or another. He is also the most reasoned mouthpiece for the "giving up on everything" spirit of the 1980s that Romero wanted to represent in the film. Others express forms of hopelessness or nihilism about the project at many points, but when they do it tends to be out of frustration or desperation. John's nihilism, on the other hand, is always clear-headed, and closer to sage wisdom. Sarah is the protagonist, but John is the hero.

Besides the zombies, Rhodes is the lead villain of the story. He is problematic because he is despotic, and willing to kill other people if they test him and disobey him. Although he is positioned as the key villain in the film, most of his assessments—and they tend to be pessimistic—turn out to be correct. He is almost as right as John. Hence it is not altogether clear from the film what we are to make of his positions and attitudes. We have to denounce them in the first instance, but we cannot entirely refute them in the last. He is also, of course, stationed in the facility to facilitate the research of the scientists; so, although he seems to be their primary obstacle, his position is not altogether oppositional to the scientists—at least not in principle. While he is a loose cannon and a terrible person, his role is a little ambivalent, and we can even be somewhat sympathetic to him, despite his obvious villainy.

Rhodes is very pessimistic about the scientific research in the facility. He can be sadistic and ruthless, but he has a more pronounced moral orientation than John. This is not to say that he is compassionate. He is far from it. He is moral, but uncaring. His moral position is a combination of rigid belief in the necessity of obedience to (his) authority, and intense tribal loyalty to his military men in contrast to the scientists, technicians, and zombies. At times his loyalty to the military feels blurred together with a tendency toward calculating self-interest. By the end of the film, his self-interest eclipses his loyalties, but through most of the film, his selfishness, loyalty, and authoritarianism all blend together.

Our protagonist Sarah openly disagrees with his dominating approach, and frequently disobeys his orders. In one scene, their differences come to a head when Sarah gets up to leave the meeting hall without being dismissed. Rhodes tells her to "sit down or so help me God I'll have you shot." Sarah continues to stand, and Rhodes orders Steel, one of his military men to shoot her. At first Steel plays it off as a joke. "Bang! You're Dead!" he says and then laughs. Rhodes reasserts his authority: "Shoot that woman or you're dead. You think I'm fucking around, Steel? You're Wrong." Rhodes begins to count to five, and when he reaches five, he will shoot Steel and Sarah both if Steel defects. Steel waits, nervously. John tries to convince Sarah to sit down, but Sarah doesn't listen. Steel's turning the command into a joke, and then stalling, show ambivalence on his part toward shooting Sarah, indicating some form of (unvoiced) compassion for her, rather than seeing her purely as a member of an outside group (scientists as opposed to military). It is an inter- esting moment because Steel generally comes across as the roughest and toughest of Rhodes' military underlings and possibly even as Rhodes' most loyal officer. He will ultimately follow Rhodes' command, but drags his metaphorical heels until the last second. When Rhodes reaches five, Steel reluctantly acquiesces and aims his gun at Sarah. Just as Steel is about to shoot her, John makes motions to pull out his own gun—presumably to shoot Steel before Steel shoots Sarah—and Sarah immediately puts her hand out, jumps forward a little and yells "No!" She walks back to her chair, pulls it out, slams it down on the floor, and sits in it.

We learn later that Sarah's basic faith in humanity leads her to doubt that she was in actual physical danger during the confrontation.[2] "He wouldn't have done it," she says to John, "I can't believe he would have done it." Her moral compass speaks here. John replies: "No, he wouldn't have done it. He would have had Steel do it." "He can't be that inhuman," she says. Her feelings and predictions about Rhodes aside, she implies here that having her shot would display some kind of basic lack of empathy on Rhodes' part. Actually letting Steel follow through and shoot her would be an amoral (never mind immoral) act, coming from a place of sadism or psychopathic detachment. "No, he's human. That's what scares me, you know," says John, and he continues to explain that Rhodes' primary reason for not killing the scientists and techni- cians is that they individually provide some selfish, instrumental advantage for him when alive. Sarah says: "Maybe if we tried working together, we could ease some of the tensions! We're all pulling in different directions." She is still arguing for a humanitarian solution, for a kind of bridging and cooperation between everyone, rather than maintaining social divisions. And casually, walking away, John replies: "Well that's the trouble with the world, Sarah darling. People got different ideas concerning what they want out of life."

John here has delivered a concise pessimistic philosophy not only about Rhodes, but of human nature. Sarah sees people—and by extension Rhodes—as basically moral and caring at their core. John sees selfishness and lack of caring as normal, predictable human features. And difference between people is inevitable, destined to lead to conflict. He may not like it, but he accepts it. For John, as for Sarah, Rhodes is not the exception; he is the rule, albeit a notably inflamed version. But for Sarah, being somehow normally human means not killing other people for small acts of disobedience, whereas for John, being normally human means being ruthlessly self-interested and prone to conflict, in the last analysis.

Sarah characteristically displays or advocates bridging between identity groups. Not only is she interested in preserving the peace and encouraging cooperation generally, but in the tribal scenario of the film, she implicitly seeks bridging across group divisions. Sarah's character is in a kind of bridging position from the start of the film, since she is romantically involved with Miguel, one of the military. Hence, she already has a strong sense of loyalty and caring for someone in the other group, and has intrinsic desires to bridge between factions. That said, her focus on caring or compassion, and her optimism about human nature, are not explained by this fact alone. Sarah truly is the humanitarian of the story.

Her relationship with Miguel is not without difficulties. Miguel is deteriorating emotionally and psychologically. Early in the film, Sarah argues for him to be pulled off active duty. "He's close to the breaking point and that's dangerous for all of us."

SARAH: I want him pulled off active duty for a while until we can evaluate his condition.
RHODES: Can't spare him.
SARAH: He's over the edge. He's turning into Jell-o! [...] Miguel is seriously disturbed. He's close to the breaking point and that's dangerous for all of us. He can't handle any more stress right now.

Rhodes ignores Sarah's *care*-infused warnings, and opts to keep Miguel around. This is a mistake, as Miguel is ineffective at zombie-catching (his primary work responsibility), and just further deteriorates emotionally. In another large meeting, Sarah argues for bridging between groups very clearly when she says to Rhodes "We need each other. Can't we just get along?!" Rhodes just digs his heels in, and sticks to a divisive discourse. He says "You need us [...] I'm not so sure we need you at all [...] I'm not even sure [...] just what the hell it is my men are risking their asses for." Notice the different use of pronouns; Sarah says "we" when referring to her position vis-à-vis that of Rhodes, while Rhodes sticks to "I," "you" and "my." Rhodes statement is important in another sense as well. As synecdoche, he is saying that the scientific establishment needs the military to protect it, but the military establishment does not need medical science. Violence is necessary and science is a luxury—perhaps even a parasite. Sarah eventually condemns Rhodes for being uncaring when she says "We're talking about a man's life here, you son of a bitch!" Rhodes again dodges her moral discourse, and just makes off-colour jokes in response. By the end of the film, Miguel's deterioration and the mismanagement of his condition will prove to be fatal for the assignment at the bunker.

Let's return to the scene where Rhodes threatens to shoot Steel and Sarah. Ted participates in this interaction too, and exhibits a different sort of moral orientation—one more political in tone. "Goddamn it you can't shove us around like this! Since when did this become a military operation?" he says. In fact, this is just one of several moments in the film where Ted voices disagreement with Rhodes' dictatorial style, condemning him for being oppressive and unfair. Basically, his arguments tend toward a language of human rights against oppressive authority. Rhodes characteristically, brushes the challenge aside with the retort "Since I took over. Steel? Shoot that woman."

After Sarah sits back down in her chair, Rhodes and Ted resume their disagreement. First Rhodes frames the incident in terms of solidifying his authority within the facility, and his obedience to authority outside the facility. Overall, he insists that everyone had to adhere rigidly to the rules and hierarchy, and that he is at the top of the pyramid while they are down in the bunker. He says "Anybody else have any questions about the way things are gonna run around here from now on? [...] I'm not down in this cave for my health; I'm down here on orders!" Rhodes here makes it clear that his attempt at total control is supported by his own belief in authority—it is not just a lust for power. He condemns Sarah and anyone else who disobeys him. Rhodes believes orders must be followed, especially considering the war-like situation of the humans against the zombies.

Ted challenges both of Rhodes' appeals: "Your orders are to facilitate the job of this scientific team [...] and we don't have to be subjected to your tyranny." Ted's language "we don't have to be subjected" and "tyranny" rings of liberal values and political protest. He emphasizes human rights, and speaks out for liberty against oppressive authority; yet in doing so he still appeals to the fair rule of law, which he now claims Rhodes is testing, and even disobeying. Orders should be followed, in service to human rights, not in an oppressive military dictatorship. Ted's comment also very clearly divides the scientists from the military, the latter embodied in Rhodes; "we" against "your."

Rhodes continues with the tribal language, not only narrating the groups as separate, but including their death counts in the separation: "Who's being subjected to what, Fisher? You've lost one man [...] We've lost five!" He continues "Where does it say we got to keep those dumb fucks next door to where we sleep?! Where does it say we should do any one thing but shoot the mothers in the head?!" Here Rhodes engages again with the question of obedience to authority of orders coming from outside the compound. Instead of addressing Ted's liberal political discourse directly, he shifts the focus to what he sees as unnecessary tolerance toward the zombies, foisted upon the military by the scientists. He implies that the scientists have started acting outside of the parameters of their arrangement, have started a leg of their operation that escapes the purposes set by the outside authorities. In other words, he avoids the liberal discourse, and instead focuses on the differences between groups (military, scientists, and zombies), insists they should have no moral relation to the zombies, and accuses the scientists of disobedience.

Ted also gets a word in following the second disagreement between Sarah and Rhodes explained above. After Sarah's unsuccessful bid to get Rhodes to take Miguel off of active duty, she debriefs with Ted about the interaction. Ted tells her "You better watch yourself. I mean physically watch yourself." Here again, Sarah is optimistic about people, and advocates building bridges: "Don't worry, it's not going to come to that. We've just got to pound some logic into their heads." Ted says that would be "impossible," pessimistically indicating that their tribal divisions are insurmountable, and that bridging is not always a viable option.

Ted's cynicism and defection from bridging is evident again when Dr. Logan presents his progress with Bub—his partially domesticated zombie—to Ted and Sarah. Behind a one-way mirror, Ted and Sarah observe Logan training Bub, reintroducing the zombie to objects people use: a shaving razor, a toothbrush, and a book (*Salem's Lot* by Stephen King). Bub picks the razor up off the table and puts it to his face. He then picks up the book and opens it. Ted is unimpressed. "What's he trying to prove?" he says to Sarah. "I saw one of those things sitting in a car in D.C. trying to drive down Independence Avenue. It didn't make me want to be its friend." Ted has no intention of finding common ground with anyone from the zombie population. But Sarah is amazed that Bub doesn't react to Logan as if Logan is his prey; that Bub is bridging with humanity through Logan. The fact that she is willing to recognize this bridging suggests that she is also willing to entertain functional relationships between zombies and humans. She is not in principle against it; she just doesn't seek it out either. She does not, for example, talk about seeking cooperation with the zombies, the way she advocates for cooperation between the military and the scientists.

Logan's bridging with zombies, on the other hand, is more extreme. The zombie trainee "Bub" is named after Logan's father, and in one scene Logan even [successfully] coaxes Bub to speak the words "hello Aunt Alicia" into a telephone receiver. This strong humanization of the zombies does not translate into compassion, however. Logan's bridging is instead typically accompanied with an argument for the instrumental benefit to humans of training the zombies to obey human commands. Basically, because they are so similar to us, we can control them. There is no moral overlay. Logan even explicitly explains "civilized" behaviour in terms of operant conditioning and lies. He displays a bridging identification with zombies, but ultimately it is a manipulative one, not a caring or moral one. Explaining his approach to Sarah and Ted:

They are us! They are the extensions of us. They are the same animal, simply functioning less perfectly. They can be fooled, you see? They can be tricked into being good little girls and boys the same way we were tricked into it in promise of some reward to come. They have to be rewarded. Reward is the key. I'm convinced of that now.

In an earlier interaction with Sarah in his lab, Logan displays his self-interested, instrumental bridging orientation again when he explains his research:

The brain is the engine, Sarah! The motor that drives them! [...] Now I've severed all the vital organs in this one. There's nothing left of the corpse but brain and limbs! And still it functions. Look Sarah, look. See it wants me! It wants food, but it has no stomach, it can take no nourishment from what it ingests. It's working on instinct! On deep dark primordial instinct! [...] It still has motor function! Probably still has powers of deliberation. It can be domesticated Sarah, don't you see? It can be conditioned to behave, the way we want it to behave.

Sarah voices skepticism at Logan's methods. She urges him to work on "something more practical." Being a scientist herself, this is not a wholesale indictment of their experiments, much less of medical science. Yet as he soon expresses during a group meeting, Logan is also skeptical of Sarah's approach. Both of them assess that the other's methods are too slow and unreliable. In the end, perhaps they are both correct in their skepticism of the other, because neither one of them pulls through before the whole operation collapses in on itself. As a whole, these skepticisms and this grand failure constitute an indictment of their attempts. As synecdoche, the implication is that science cannot and will not solve humanity's problems.

Logan's instrumental attitude toward the zombies is further displayed when he explains to Sarah about one of the corpses, "It was too unruly, I couldn't handle it; I had to destroy it. We can still get information from it." Not only was he content to "destroy" the zombie based upon its unruliness, but he uses no gendered pronouns. He refers to the zombie as "it" several times. Showing her a different specimen—one that is not "destroyed" per se, but still operational enough for him to experiment with—Logan explains that it is the body of the former military commander, from before Rhodes took over. "This is Major Cooper. I needed him, Sarah! He's helping us more now than he ever did when he was alive."

Sarah emphatically questions—almost condemns—Logan on the experimentation on Major Cooper's corpse, but her orientation to the zombies is not a caring or otherwise moral one either. Her reason for caution is her concern that the military ("they") will react by doing something (perhaps punishing, perhaps taking revenge) to the scientists ("us"). Her reasoning is self-interested, and divides between the scientists and the military. Logan, not surprisingly, responds to that concern about the military's possible reaction. There is no stated consideration that the hypothetical reaction of the military might have some legitimate morality associated with it.

Logan's bridging and Rhodes' tribalism are brought into direct contrast when Rhodes wanders into Logan's room for training Bub. The partially domesticated zombie reveals his military roots when he salutes Rhodes, unprompted. Bub, of course, is supposed to be acting on very base instinct and lingering memories, so his salute is ostensibly something of a pre-programmed reaction, rather than one with a moral or interpersonal relevance. Yet the gesture is a communication from zombie to human, which erodes the division between them some, and just as significant, the gesture is a sign of respect, kinship with Rhodes through mutual belonging to the military, and arguably even—in the deference to authority that such a gesture signifies—a support to Rhodes' moral emphasis on (his own) authority. Rhodes, who is an outspoken advocate of tribalism, is now faced with a gesture from a zombie that signifies bridging in multiple ways.

Logan's orientation is very connective. He invites Rhodes to "Return the salute and see what he does." Rhodes refuses the offer to participate, and refers to Bub as a "pile of walking pus." Notice that his refusal contains a description of Bub that makes him sound entirely grotesque, without consciousness, and even without any form of sentience or resemblance to a living, breathing animal. He dramatically focuses on the difference between humans and zombies, reinforcing tribal sentiments. And he refuses to take part in Logan's experiment, keeping his tribal distance by extension—the military man will not join with the scientist. Logan then reaffirms connections. "How are we going to set an example for them if we behave barbarically ourselves?" he says. Logan's statement recognizes a distinction between humans and zombies here, but also implies relatedness in the sense that "we" provide a socializing context for the zombies. In addition, his pronouns "we" and "ourselves" here make no distinction between scientists and military.

Next, Logan hands Bub an unloaded gun to see what he will do. Bub points the gun at Rhodes and pulls the trigger. This action again bridges between zombies and humans, but whereas in the salute the threat to Rhodes was mutual recognition, in the pointing of the gun the threat is of potential physical violence, and perhaps even more importantly for Rhodes, it is an action that signifies subverting his authority. Bub pulls the trigger, repeatedly, driving home the threatening bridging metaphor.

In the next scene, in the conference hall, Rhodes is furious. He says "What the fuck is wrong with you people?! They're dead! They're fucking dead and you want to teach them tricks?" In this framing, Rhodes again emphasizes the differences between groups. The zombies are dead, first of all, and to Rhodes this means they should remain outside the moral and even communicative orbit of the humans. Second, they are being taught "tricks," which is what you do with a pet or a circus animal. He generalizes from this to question the efficacy of the scientific experiments in general. "Is this your progress? Is this the shit that's supposed to knock our socks off?"

Logan responds to Rhodes with affirmations of the instrumental benefits of training the zombies using rewards and punishments: "They have to be rewarded, captain. Why else will they do what we want them to do?" Even more directly expressing the nihilism behind his bridging orientation, he says "Civility must be rewarded, captain. If it isn't rewarded, there's no use for it. There's just no use for it at all." This is a very general statement. He is not just talking about zombie psychology; he is also talking about people by extension. He suggests people are not guided by moral sentiment other than to the degree that they are conditioned to do so, *and* that there is no intrinsic moral value to civilized behaviour. The only reason to engage in it is to attain instrumental rewards.

Logan and Rhodes differ concerning identification styles. Logan's bridging identification contrasts with Rhodes' divisive identification concerning zombies. Rhodes' condemnation of Logan—and the other scientists by association—is doubtless somewhat for failing to deliver enough meaningful success, and as synecdoche, medical scientific research is implicated as suspect and as failing to deliver. But Rhodes' condemnation of Logan is also for bridging with zombies, which violates the sanctity of humanity, especially that part of humanity that is of Rhodes' in-group: the military.

Throughout the film, the value of scientific research is questioned many times. Ted, although a member of the scientific team, is pessimistic. When he expresses his attitudes about Logan's experiments (he never says anything about Sarah's work), Ted tends to be dejected or sardonic. He mutters things like "It's no good. It's no fucking good" in reference to Logan's attempts to get Bub to eat "beef treats," and "What's he trying to prove?" when he and Sarah observe Logan and Bub through the one-way mirror. The most vocal detractors of the scientists' work are John and Rhodes. In the main consultation hall, Rhodes frequently voices impatience and skepticism that the scientists—and by extension medical science in general—are doing anything worthwhile. An example from earlier was in the debate between Rhodes and Sarah about Miguel.

In a later meeting, Rhodes says to Sarah that the scientists have only given the military "a mouthful of Greek salad: formulas, equations—a lot of fancy terms that don't mean a thing." Here Rhodes' protest includes an anti-intellectual element. Soon after, in a verbal jockeying match with Logan, he slams his hand loudly on Logan's table, punctuating with the gesture his first word as he bursts out with:

> I'm running this monkey farm now Frankenstein, and I want to know what the fuck you're doing with my time!! If we're just jerking off here— I'm gonna have my men blow the piss out of those precious specimens of yours! [...] And we're gonna get the hell out of here, and leave you and your highfalutin asshole friends to rot in this stinking sewer! Is that food enough for ya?!

Clearly Rhodes is asserting power here. But this is not all he is doing. His imaginary/threatened scenario shows the scientists as useless and pretentious ("highfalutin") and the military as practical and effective. Once again as synecdoche, Rhodes displays anti-intellectualism and anti-science, instead supporting the use of violence for the defence of one's own tribal group. While science receives most of the direct contestation here and in the rest of the film, Logan directly voices here skepticism at military violence as an effective solution to the zombie apocalypse: "Where will you go, Captain? You can destroy my specimens, but what about the millions more that are waiting to greet you outside? You really think you can 'blow the piss out of' them? All of them?" This challenge is based not on morality, but on the instrumental failure of Rhodes' envisioned scenario. The logic that wins is amoral self-interest. Logan's response effectively shuts down the argument.

Things start to really fall apart when a zombie that the military attempt to capture gets temporarily free, uses the opportunity to kill one of the military, and bites Miguel's arm. It is not entirely Miguel's fault that the zombie initially got loose of its restraints, but Miguel's incapacity to do anything helpful in the situation is clearly at least partially responsible for how bad the situation gets. Miguel runs off. Sarah, Billy, and John chase him down and knock him out. Sarah chops off his arm to save his life. Rhodes and some of his men show up with guns, Billy and John have guns ready. Rhodes and Steel argue for Miguel to be killed lest he turn into a zombie. The situation is somewhat reversed from Sarah and Rhodes' earlier discussion about Miguel. Now that he is bitten, Rhodes evidently no longer considers him within the circle of his loyalties—he is effectively a zombie now. He argues Miguel is a threat, and would have him killed or at least cast out. Caring Sarah wants to keep Miguel close by and try to help him until and unless he turns, in which case "I'll shoot him myself." Steel threatens that he is about to shoot Miguel, and that Sarah should get out of the way if she doesn't want him to shoot her in the process.

John pulls his gun up and aims at the men, and everyone pulls out their guns in rapid succession. John says "We get to make this a habit, man, pointing guns at each other you know." Steel replies instead "We just lost two men 'cause of [Miguel]." "Well, that kind of evens the odds between us then." John's statements are characteristically detached and amoral. They make a habit of pointing guns at one another—but is that good or bad, according to John? Instead of any explicit moral statement here, John declares a tribal alignment—the technicians and the scientists are one group, the military is the other. Steel is emphatic that "We've got to blast him, captain!" but Rhodes uncocks and lowers his gun, makes a few more references indicating utter disdain for the zombies and tribal separateness from the technicians and scientists, and informs them that the military will no longer help them, instead they will kill every zombie in the bunker the following day. Rhodes accepts Sarah's answer to take responsibility herself for Miguel if and when he turns, provided Sarah, Billy, and John truly keep him away from the rest of the military.

Rhodes' reasoning characteristically displays a calculating rather than typically "moral" thread, but does display division again, that "me and my men" will no longer help the rest of the humans, and that he will soon lead a killing spree of the zombies. John exhibits the same divisiveness when he talks of "the odds between us" being evened, splitting Rhodes and the military against everyone else (John included in the latter camp).

Sarah and Billy explore Logan's workspace and are repulsed—Sarah especially. When Billy quips "[What] the hell has he been doing down here, slaughtering cattle?" Sarah sardonically replies "In his mind that's probably not far from the truth." The implication is that Logan's bridging (train zombies like living people, use human bodies like any dead material) verges on—or simply includes—sociopathy. In some sense, zombies are elevated to the level of humans, but in another sense humans are treated just as inhumanly as zombies. Logan makes no moral distinctions, but this is not because he *respects* all life; it is because he sees all life as amoral, as something to be *used*. Looking around Logan's workroom, Sarah and Billy find another example of Logan's sociopathic bridging, in the form of the severed head of one of the military men, still exhibiting signs of life, hooked up to wires. Emoting, Sarah wants to shoot it (no explanation is given) but Billy stops her—for reasons of their own interest, not of compassion for the living head, or moral prohibition against killing it. "No Sarah, don't!" he warns. "It'd just bring out Rhodes and the men! Leave it be." He then adds "I'm beginning to think we should take that helicopter before somebody else does."

Rhodes is the most critical of Logan's style of compassion-free bridging. Logan's final transgression that motivates Rhodes to condemn and kill him violates two tribal moral guideposts of Rhodes'. The transgression is feeding the remains of recently deceased military personnel to Bub. Rhodes' tribal morality is violated on at least the following two accounts: (a) Logan's actions bridge when Rhodes wants tribalism, thus violating the sanctity of group separation—he treats human bodies with the same lack of reverence as zombie bodies (and perhaps very literally "like cattle"), while he interacts with Bub as if Bub were a young person; and (b) this lack of reverence is applied to Rhodes' military tribe, so stoking his heated sense of loyalty. One might further suspect that, because such acts were going on behind Rhodes' back, (c) Logan has further violated Rhodes' sense that his (Rhodes') authority must be obeyed. Logan's last words are a plea for communication from a scientist: "You must listen to me Captain." Rhodes responds by refusing, and by offering the power of violence instead: "Listen to this," he says, as he fills Logan full of bullets. And right after, once again expressing his tribal loyalties, he yells: "Those are my men in there!" The most disturbing thing to Rhodes seems to be that something demeaning (and gruesome) is happening to *his own tribe*.

Soon after, Rhodes and his military entourage, towing Sarah and Ted, confront John and Billy (again). A brief exchange about the killing of Logan ensues, and Rhodes displays again his sharp distinction between "my men" and the other people in the bunker, another expression of his persistent tribalism.

He refers to Ted dehumanizingly as "this scum," and threatens to kill him unless John flies "me, my men, you, that's it" away in the helicopter.

Not surprisingly, Ted and Rhodes view the killing of Logan differently. Ted the scientist claims it was amoral—"in cold blood"—and so worthy of wariness as well as condemnation (as the term "cold blood" tends to carry distinctly negative connotations) for Rhodes to kill Logan the scientist. Rhodes, on the other hand, explains it as execution due to what Logan was doing, and how it in turn defined his character. He was "a butcher," violating the bridge between human and non-human by casually cutting up humans—from the military, of course—and feeding them to the zombie Bub. Rhodes casually executes Ted in front of everyone, however, which lends more credibility to Ted's assessment of Rhodes' killing "in cold blood." Some combination of the following may be interpreted: (a) Rhodes' moral sense is rapidly eroding, (b) Rhodes' tribal morality extends only to his military men, and (c) Rhodes' relationship to violence is instrumental and strategic, not moral. Option (c) is a little suspect, however, due to Rhodes' killing of Logan, who was operating only on dead people, hence not posing a physical threat to Rhodes and the other living military personnel. When John refuses Rhodes' demand, Rhodes immediately shoots Ted in the head, and Sarah yells out. John's refusal "You'll never get me to do that, Rhodes" likely signifies some combination of internalized moral rules and caring for Sarah, Billy, and possibly Miguel (whom they are protecting in their trailer—the entrance to "The Ritz"). Of course, his actual motivations here are never articulated. Sarah's yell more directly indicates caring for Ted.

As it turns out, Rhodes and Steel are correct about the threat that Miguel poses, but for the reasons Sarah originally articulated. Not long after the exchange, Miguel opens the main gate to let a zombie crowd in. He lies down pushing a button to let him and a collection of zombies descend into the bunker while the zombies tear him apart. When actually running for their lives from the mob of zombies, Rhodes ends his loyalty to the other military men, driving off in a golf cart and abandoning them. Soon after, Bub finds Rhodes and shoots him, avenging Logan's execution. Basically, everything falls apart, the operation was a failure, and morality is eclipsed by nihilism, neutrality, and instrumentality.

When Billy, Sarah, and John finally do escape to the helicopter, Billy shoots a zombie in order to save John's life. But rather than narrate the save in moral terms, he explains it in self-interested terms: "Come on Johnny! [I'm] counting on you to fly us to the Promised Land!" It is tempting to speculate that there is an unspoken understanding between them of their mutual loyalty, but it is impossible to know, much less to measure vis-à-vis Billy's stated motivating self-interest.

By the end, *all* of the skepticism voiced over the course of the film is proven justified. The project fails. The disease is not conquered. The zombies are too much for the military to fight. Most of the human characters die. The solution—if one could call it that—is just to escape to a deserted island. The philosophy of defection, and the suggestion for this escape, comes neither from the scientists nor the military personnel, but from John and Billy, the technicians. Military violence deserves a small modicum of credit, however, because John, Billy, and Sarah would not be able to escape without the use of gun violence. On another level, despite Rhodes' despotism and reactivity, he turns out to be correct in his overall pessimism. The scientists do not make useful progress, yet their operation results in a steady stream of military casualties.

Sarah—more or less the protagonist—exhibits possible signs of care via emotional reactions that might signify compassion. She explicitly advocates bridging identification and cooperation between the scientists and the military, but she is the only one to push in this direction. She indicates small steps in the direction of bridging with zombies. Ted is resigned to a divisive identification vis-à-vis both the military and the zombies, and also argues in political language for anti-authoritarian, pro-human rights convictions, i.e. for liberty and fairness. Logan is bridging between humans and zombies to an extreme degree—even mimicking a parent-child dynamic, but without a moral of care. His reasoning is only instrumental, which manifests fatally for him via his wholly manipulative and degrading attitude toward human bodies.

In the end it is John's philosophy of resignation and detachment which proves to be the wisest. For him, the operation was always hopeless, people are unavoidably self-interested, and groups are unavoidably prone to conflict. He tends to defend Sarah, although he never offers a moral reason why. Regardless, he, like her, tends to insinuate some caring. Still, from the beginning he advocates giving up and simply escaping as the only sensible option, and in the end, this proves to be true.

Day of the Dead (2008)

This rendition strays considerably from Romero's 1985 film. The budget for the film was an estimated $18,000,000, and it only made back $301,771 internationally (presumably the domestic earnings were less, as they tend to be). It was directed by Steve Miner, written by Jeffrey Reddick, and produced by James Glenn Dudelson, Robert Franklin Dudelson, Randall Emmett, George Furla, Millennium Films and Emmett/Furla Films. It starred Mena Suvari as the white female protagonist.

This is the plot: A virus has broken out and the town within which it is happening has been put under military quarantine. Sarah, a Corporal in the military, works under Lieutenant Rhodes to enforce the quarantine. A young, new, and naïve member of the military named Bud is paired up with Sarah. Stopping by Sarah's home, Sarah finds her brother Trevor and his girlfriend Nina taking negligent care of Sarah and Trevor's sick mother. Sarah takes their mother to the hospital. There, waiting for emergency care, the waiting area is overflowing with people who are similarly sick. Another military person, Salazar, is on duty there. Rhodes introduces Sarah to medical scientist Doctor

Logan, who is studying the disease. Eventually everyone who is sick at the hospital turns into a zombie at the same time. Rhodes is overtaken and killed. Sarah, Bud, Salazar, and Logan are cornered in a storage room. Bud gets bitten. The group escapes in a vehicle, although Logan absconds with the vehicle that was supposed to be for everyone. Driving away from the hospital, Sarah hears her brother on the radio calling for help. She takes Bud and Salazar with her to the radio station to pick up Trevor and Nina. By now Bud has turned into a zombie, but he is not attacking the group. They keep him with them under Sarah's continued insistence. They go to a shack that is actually an underground military facility. There they discover Logan, and the truth that the virus came from a botched secret attempt at developing a bio-weapon. Sarah, Trevor, and Nina are able to escape by sending fire from missiles through the facility, incinerating all the zombies there. Driving, the three of them hear a radio broadcast saying the military quarantine is effective and the threat is contained.

The theme of family loyalty is highlighted throughout the film in an ambivalent way. Family loyalties are placed in unresolved positions of rivalry with other moral concerns. This starts very early on in the film, in the scene where we first encounter Rhodes, and then Sarah. In the scene, traffic is stopped before a military blockade. People are frustrated, and one man, who we learn is a father with a sick child, becomes particularly belligerent:

DAD: This is bullshit, bullshit. You can't do this. We're in America. Who gave the order for this exercise?
RHODES: Sir my orders are to keep this road sealed off for the next 24 hours. You can take your son to the hospital in town [...] I understand, but...
DAD: Not unless you have kids you don't fucking understand!

The scene pits the morality of family loyalty against the morality of civic engagement, this time the latter framed in an impersonal light, as obeying orders from elites, orders ostensibly designed to protect the welfare of the larger population, but implemented in an oppressive way. The father exhibits moralities of care and loyalty, and adopts some political language that suggests a concern for defending liberty, e.g., "You can't do this. We're in America." Sarah is finally able to talk the father down; it turns out she is an old family friend. Soon Sarah's ambivalence is given voice. After convincing the father to turn the car around, Sarah expresses some misgiving to Rhodes: "Did I just tell them the truth?" Is Sarah complicit in an act of deception? Is it possible they will not in fact get the treatment they need at the facility she directed them to? Rhodes, the mouthpiece of the bureaucracy, will not satisfy her with an answer. His only response is "Corporal, your orders are to keep this shithole town—excuse me—your shithole town sealed off. Now do it." Rhodes emphasizes authority and Sarah complies. The film does not impart a clear position on this contest here.

Similarly, the film does not indicate a clear position in the several scenes throughout the film where Trevor and Sarah argue about family loyalty and care, trading condemnations concerning being present and taking responsibility. These quarrels start from the first scene they share, surrounding the condition and care of their mother. Sarah's reason for not being around is that she has been paying heed to the larger society's needs through her military post. Her actions embody choices between loyalty vis-à-vis authority and fairness in civic participation. Trevor is unsatisfied. No clear answer is given to the moral quandary. Later on, while in the car with Salazar and Bud, their disagreement flares up again, surrounding failed joint plans from years before to open a bike shop. There is still no resolution in the film, nor is there a clear message we are supposed to take from the exchange about which one of them is right.

When the people in the emergency room turn en masse into zombies, Sarah, Bud, and Logan run to find a room to hide in. While going inside Logan pushes Bud out of the way, almost getting him killed by the zombies. Sarah rescues Bud from the hallway, and Bud condemns Logan for the action: "The hell was that? You almost got me killed!" Logan plays dumb: "What do you mean? What are you talking about?" Clearly Bud is right. Yet it is unstated in the actual verbal exchange exactly what the moral grounds for Bud's condemnation of Logan are. Both people seek self-preservation, and are willing to muster some form of aggressiveness to support it. But to the extent that Bud's questioning of Logan goes beyond self-preservation to imply a moral condemnation, it is left vague. By process of elimination, one can surmise it has to do with some combination of care, fairness, and loyalty. Logan's unconvincing playing-dumb response reveals he cannot be trusted. Whatever Bud's reasons, we side with him.

This difference between their moral characters is emphasized again when the group finally battle their way through the zombies in the hospital parking lot, to make their escape. While he is about to get into a car and drive off, Logan is approached by a woman begging for his help. He speaks as if he will help her, and approaches her, but then pushes her backward when he reaches her; the backward push sends her crashing into a zombie, who promptly devours her. Logan gets into the car while the zombie is preoccupied with her, and drives away by himself, leaving Salazar, Sarah, and Bud behind. Bud expresses moral condemnation of Logan again, still without clarification as to the grounds, although again by process of elimination, one can surmise it has to do with some combination of care, fairness, and loyalty: "What a dick!"

Initially, when Sarah, Salazar, and Bud escape the hospital in a vehicle, Sarah drives around the zombies in the road. Salazar and Sarah have a brief moral debate about this, revolving around the question of identification—which mode should be assumed.

SALAZAR: What you dodging them for? Run they ass over!
SARAH: They're still somebody!
SALAZAR: Not anymore.

"Somebody" of course refers to the *human* in their *humanoid* status. Things change once Sarah hears Trevor on the radio in the car. Her *personal loyalty breaks* through her bridging identification. She turns around the car very fast, to head to the radio station and rescue Trevor, and on the way she runs freely over zombies. Salazar appreciates it, as he exclaims "Ooh shit! That's what I'm talking about! Run the[ir] ass[es] over! Now you['re] driving!" During this time, Trevor, at the radio station, has spotted his mother (actually a zombie) outside, alone on the sidewalk. He runs to try to let her in. Nina runs after him, telling him to wait. Trevor and Nina having made it to the front door, Trevor's zombie mom runs toward them. But Sarah and company arrive just then, and Sarah barrels through Trevor's mom in the army car. Trevor becomes upset. Sarah tries to comfort him by calling attention to their difference from their zombie mother, to give voice to divisive identification. She says "Trevor, it wasn't her, not anymore." We agree with Sarah. Trevor's zombie mom would have killed and eaten him, so wherever the line is between human us and non-human them, she is on the other side.

These issues—are zombies people too?—are raised most persistently through the figure of Bud. His status (how human is he?), his relation to the human group, and the moral implications of his condition are contested in several ways. Salazar and Sarah take opposing positions from the moment Bud is bitten, Salazar wanting to shoot and kill Bud right then, Sarah arguing for Salazar to hold off, presumably out of care or loyalty. The latter obliges, and treats Bud as a full human until he turns. From then on, Salazar's identification regarding Bud is divisive; he views him as a zombie, and variously toys with him and advocates getting rid of him. The toying is mocking Bud by playfully harping on human qualities as perverse remnants; he vacillates between making jokes about Bud being attracted to Sarah still, and ordering Bud around like a soldier.[3] Sarah's identification with Bud is bridging, as she advocates keeping him around, and emphasizes his still human qualities in this relation. "They seem to retain some part of themselves before they were infected," she says. Salazar's framing is different: "Must have retained his hormones because he definitely remembers who you are. I guess that also means you remember who's boss, huh bitch?" In calling attention to sexual attraction and pecking order, he insinuates that Bud has retained an animalistic—i.e. subhuman—part of himself. When the group make it to the shack (which is also an underground bunker) to hide out, Sarah snaps at Salazar to leave Bud alone, indicating she has some compassion for Bud, and morally condemning Salazar's taunting.

Bud's identification is split, manifesting at different times as aligned with the zombies or aligned with the humans. In other words, he is ambivalent in zombie form. In the shack, Bud—tied down—yells out repeatedly when he hears the zombies outside, which draws their attention. It is as if he is being held captive by the humans, and the zombies hear his cries and come to the rescue. His actions display a divisive identification. Sarah tries to get him to stop but he does not listen, and the zombies invade the shack. Yet later on, in some combination of bridging identification and compassion, Bud saves Sarah's life by shooting a gun at the zombie head doctor, who is otherwise about to attack Sarah. Bud's shooting distracts the doctor long enough for Sarah to escape. Zombie Bud acts on *loyalty*, but overall, his loyalty is split and he is ambivalent.

When the group runs into Logan again in the underground compound, Logan's problematic character is emphasized again. He is dishonest and self-centred to the point of being hazardous to others. He was somehow involved with "Project Wildfire," and was hoping to destroy the evidence, but the rest of the group found him, and the evidence, before he could finish.

When questioned about the nature of the virus and its origins, Logan is at first evasive. But when threatened at gunpoint by military persons Sarah and Salazar, Logan's truth comes out. Project wildfire was a government run operation staffed by "a few select scientists studying biochemical agents." They engineered a virus that was "designed to paralyze enemy troops by shutting down their neural system for 6–7 hours." His explanation indicates a desire to show mercy to the "enemy" out-group when at war, perhaps due to bridging identification and some form of moral recognition. "We didn't think it would mutate. Come on, this would have allowed us to capture people without killing them. It was intended to save lives."

The exact moral rationale is unstated, but either way, the aim of mercy toward the wartime out-group combined with the reality of the zombification of the real-time in-group (humanity) receives condemnation from Salazar, who quips sarcastically: "Hell of a job, Doc." There are no signs of support for the aim of project wildfire from anyone else in the group. The inclusion in Salazar's comment of the shorthand title "Doc" is telling here, in that it implicitly calls into question the prowess that might attach to Logan as a medical scientist. Via synecdoche, medical science itself is called into question. This particular engineered project of lessening harm toward an out-group was a disastrous failure, certainly on a practical level, and perhaps on a moral level. And of course, the elites (Logan included) cannot be trusted. Arguably even worse, the lead scientist on the project, Dr. Engle, speaks like a mad scientist on a video that Trevor found: "I'll die here, like the pharaohs. My legacy. Beautiful weapon. My weapon."

The contest between science and the military really begins in this scene, in a couple of ways. First, the personalities in the different roles (scientist and military) differ considerably. On one hand, there is the madness of Dr. Engle and the mild and reluctant assistance Logan gives to the gun-carrying group when he is not lying, cheating, or just generally screwing them over in narrow self-interest. On the other hand, there is the effective, take-charge heroism of Sarah and Salazar, the military characters still alive. Second, science is enlisted to develop for the military a bioweapon. But the operation goes terribly wrong. While the *collaboration* of medical science and the military created the disease—and hence both are responsible for the outbreak—science's culpability is emphasized. Scientists actually created the plague, not military personnel. Instead of control through killing, they would gain control through medically-induced paralysis. A movement of trying to transfer some exercise of power from military methods to scientific methods was the context that birthed the zombie virus.

Nina's open hostility (Nina is aligned with the military at this point, and carries a gun, which she appears eager to use) and Salazar's derisiveness toward Logan are the first direct expressions of the superiority of the military over the scientist. Logan's modest contribution is explaining the context. He offers no positive suggestions or tangible assistance. Discussing a zombie in a lab coat who escaped into the airshaft, he says: "That's Doctor Engle. He was the best man on the team. If they do retain something of what they were, we are so screwed." Note that here again the prowess of the lead scientist (Dr. Engle) makes him all the more threatening.

Sarah wants to find a way out. Logan says the only hypothetical way out is where the zombies can be heard yelling. In other words, they are screwed. But Salazar, both saving the group and striking repartee points against Logan, says "I thought scientists were supposed to be smart. Here. Follow me. Dumb asshole." Note that his first sentence doubles in potential meaning in the following way. Under Salazar's quip, Logan is not smart, and this is new evidence against the assumption that Logan must be smart because he is a scientist. But where is Salazar's intended emphasis? Is he saying that Logan is the exception, being unintelligent when scientists are smart? Or is he saying that Logan is an indication that scientists, as a group, are not smart? Because the emphasis is unstated, both meanings come through. Salazar then walks away from the group, implicitly signalling for people to follow him down a hallway. Salazar explains that missiles used to be kept in facilities like the one they are in during the Cold War. A zombie comes out of the ceiling and takes out Logan quietly. Nina says: "Hey! What happened to Fuckface?" His loss is slightly confusing, but nobody really cares. Salazar, of the military, will clearly be helpful. Logan, the scientist, is useless to the group. Via synecdoche, the use of the "I thought scientists were supposed to be smart" exchange to punctuate Salazar's moment of helpful guidance toward the group's escape, suggests that the knowledge of professional scientists is less helpful—in ways that really matter—than the knowledge of the lay public. To defeat the outbreak, the military leads the charge very helpfully and is successful, with science (lay scientific knowledge) providing mild help.

Ultimately the disease is overcome in two ways, and both point to the military as responsible for the success, science playing a very small part. In the first instance, Sarah and the others are able to kill all of the zombies in the underground facility through essentially bombing all of them. Her idea to light up the propulsion tanks arguably relies on scientific inventiveness—this is the one credit to science for overcoming the zombies. In the second instance, Sarah, Trevor, and Nina hear a radio broadcast as they drive. The voice on the radio indicates that the virus has been "contained." Presumably this means, at least, that the only zombies are within the bounds of the military quarantine. It could mean that all of the zombies have been killed. There is no mention of a cure.

The 2008 release did not carry enough respect to gain reviews or interviews in the way the 1985—or even the 2018—rendition did. However, in something akin to a collective interview, several of the cast and crew reflected upon the movie while watching it all the way through, and this was included as a "special feature" on the DVD release. Screenwriter Jeffrey Reddick explained that his original script was closer to Romero's original, but that through the entire process, they collectively moved further away from it. This openness to the collective process, to changes introduced by others, was a key and conscious part of the style of director Steve Miner. As far as the domesticated zombie character Bub/Bud, the difference from the original was always intentional by Jeffrey Reddick.

> [I]n the original film, Bub was actually just kind of a zombie piece of meat that this scientist kept around, and in this movie we wanted him to be a person, who when he evolves has some of the same characteristics of Bub in the original and I think Stark did a great job. I think when you see him in zombie mode you see a lot of nods to that.
>
> ("Commentary Provided" 2008)

Stark Sands, who played Bud, describes the role as "not just a zombie, but kind of one of the heroes as well." In comparing the *Day* of 1985 with that of 2008, Wetmore has identified the 2008 version as more reactionary and conservative. In 1985, we had crumbling faith in all institutions, and any morality other than calculating self-interest; the military were villains and the scientists were ineffective and deluded. In 2008 the military stands out heroically;[4] Reddick describes: "I wanted to keep the military motif but I didn't want them to be bad [...] So go military!"[5] In addition, government conspiracy is behind the outbreak. In effect, despite the severe drop in "windy" dialogue between 1985 and 2008, there is some social commentary still in the latter: a post-9/11, pro-military, anti-government, reactionary libertarian rap.

Day of the Dead: Bloodline (2018)

In 2018, the political and moral framing is even more stripped down. As one reviewer put it: "the social commentary that coursed underneath '*Day of the Dead*' is largely lacking here" (Tallerico 2018). This specifically narrow film arrives at a time of strong political polarization in the country, and racial tension. With Black Lives Matter such a strong presence in recent years, with Islamophobia high in the country in the middle of omnipresent terrorist threats and the recent specifically prominent threats from ISIS, with white nationalism edging into explicit mainstream discourse, with the deportation of undocumented immigrants from Latin America and Trump's promise to "build a wall" to keep them from coming in, with inflammatory and divisive Facebook posts and the added spread of fake news pushed from an effective Russian cultural sabotage campaign, etc., the past few years have been particularly charged with racial resentments and political polarization or tribalism. Infectious disease continues to be threatening, as 2014 witnessed the largest Ebola outbreak in history, in Liberia, Sierra Leone and Guinea. Real progress has been made in the treatment and prevention of HIV, however, with antiviral medication Truvada reducing rates of infection (U.S. Department of Health and Human Services 2019).

This rendition is closer to the original than was the 2008 version. While Romero's film felt like it had something to say about control and the government (even if Roger Ebert notoriously didn't think it succeeded in saying it), "'*Bloodline*' can't figure out its message" (Tallerico 2018). The way that cast and crew describe the film, it appears that "social commentary"—at least in terms of politics and institutions—was really not their take on the story. Instead, we have a drama about individual personalities and attachments. Johnathan Schaech, who plays Max (the 2018 rendition of Bub), says of the difference:

> Yeah, those underlying social issues were something that Romero was big on. It's a fun story on the outside, but it was really dealing with the horrible parts of the people that were living. Those people aren't dealing with the things in life that are most important. So we deal with the dead because we look back on our lives and all of our sins. There's a line that runs between that and this film. It's more of a ramped-up version of a Romero film because it's got more gadgets and stuff like that.
>
> (Hawkins 2018)

The budget was $10,000,000, which is not much, and like the 2008 version, it was a flop at the box office. It was written by Mark Tonderai and Lars Jacobson, directed by Hèctor Hernández Vicens, and produced by Christa Campbell, Robert Franklin Dudelson, Saban Capital Group, Campbell Grobman Films and Millennium Films. It starred Sophie Skelton as the white female protagonist.

Here is the plot: Zoe, a medical student, is plagued by a man named Max who keeps coming in to get his blood taken by Zoe for tests. He has an abnormal quantity of antibodies in his blood. During a keg party in the medical school, Max encounters Zoe alone in the morgue, insists they are connected and were meant to be together, and attempts to rape her. While on top of her, a body of a man who had died from a disease presenting like H1N1 rises up behind him, as a zombie, and attacks Max. Upstairs at the party, Zoe's teacher has also become a zombie. Soon the whole party is filled with zombies eating people. Zoe narrowly escapes through a window. The story fast forwards, and we meet Zoe stationed in a military outpost, with the job of studying the zombie virus. Her love interest is Baca, a military person and the brother of the commanding officer at the facility, Miguel. A young girl has become ill, and Zoe is able to go with Baca and some others to get medical supplies from her old school, so that she can treat the young girl Lilly. At the school, Max, now part zombie, discovers Zoe is with the group, so he latches onto one of the vehicles to be transported back to the facility with Zoe, undetected. Max eventually finds Zoe and continues to insist that they are somehow fated together. Military people shoot Max, but Zoe convinces them to keep him alive so she can study him to develop a vaccine. She knows he has great immunities in his blood, and is only part zombie (he can speak, and he does not bite her). She is able to develop a vaccine. Max opens the gate to the outpost, and the facility is bombarded by zombies. They are barely fended off, after killing Miguel and other key military characters. Zoe kills Max. Baca has been bitten, but Zoe cures him. The outpost is now immune to the zombie virus.

The post-apocalypse is not shown here as an era of wastelands. There is no footage in the entire film of abandoned streets.[6] The film opens with news footage and chaos in downtown city streets. The chaos, of course, is zombies chasing, catching, killing, and tearing open and eating people. Then, after a couple of scenes from inside a medical facility pre-apocalypse, we jump to the inside of a military outpost in an otherwise rural setting. Most of the film takes place within this outpost, in spaces with lots of grey steel, reminiscent of a factory, warehouse or garage. The outpost contains a protected outdoor area as well, as the entire facility seems to be contained within the larger circumference of a tall chain-link fence.

There is no explanation given for the origin of the disease, other than that it shares much in common with H1N1. Science and the military are effectively neutral on that account. Yet Zoe, notably the medical scientist in the story, is responsible for the plan to go back to her medical school and get supplies, which is how Max finds her and follows the team back to the compound, kills a woman and lets in the horde of zombies who kill many more, threatening the entire outpost. The axis around which the vast majority of moral language and decisions revolve is that of personal loyalties. For instance, when Zoe, Baca, and others are en route to gather supplies, one of the vehicles breaks down. Frank says they should turn back because it is taking too long to fix the vehicle. Zoe protests that Lilly needs the medicine immediately. Frank gives a utilitarian (greatest good for the greatest number) argument ("I just don't see the math in risking eight lives for one!"), which might be understood as a combination of morality and self-interest. Zoe appeals to family ties and self-interest (one's *own* family) as the rationale not to turn back ("What if Lilly was your kid? Your sick one in the bunker. Because if we don't succeed, it could be.").

Effectively, Zoe gets the last word. Her statement about family is met with a short moment of (pregnant) silence, and then the group hears zombie screams and turn guns toward the woods. They know it is "rotters." Lucy gets the car fixed. The car starts just in time. The group continues on, as Zoe wants. After getting the supplies and losing Frank to the zombies, they return to camp and Frank's death is underscored by his wife Elle finding out, becoming very upset and directing blame at Zoe: "This is all on you! It was your idea to go out there!"

Even Max is motivated by personal loyalty and self-interest. Despite being infected with the virus—and hence severely limited mentally—he discovers Sarah's scent on a dropped cloth at the overrun hospital, and subsequently follows Sarah back to the camp by holding onto the bottom of one of the army vehicles. It is his obsession with her—not his predatory zombie instincts—that presumably propel him to do this (as he says later: "I came for you"). When Zoe encounters the infected Max, she knows for sure it is him when he shows her the self-inflicted scar of her name on his arm. "Max," she says, "You recognize me? How are you still alive?" He holds her up and yells at her but he doesn't eat her, indicating his feelings for her are stronger than his new zombie instincts, which evidently proves to Sarah that he is not in fact a full zombie. When Baca, Alfonz, and Lucy arrive and they shoot Max a couple times, she yells for them to stop.

ZOE: Don't kill him! He's not a rotter!
ALFONZ: Zoe get out of the fucking way!
ZOE: Trust me! We need to catch him alive!
ALFONZ: Bullshit! He's one of them!
ZOE: No! He's not! His name is Max! He was a patient of mine! Baca he's the breakthrough I've been searching for!

Zoe argues, "Don't kill him! He's not a rotter!" Alfonz responds, "Bullshit! He's one of them!" In the first instance of this brief disagreement, Zoe argues for the group not to kill Max because she believes he is not "one of them," which indicates by extension that if he were a full zombie it would be fine to kill him. She yells for the group to "Trust me!" emphasizing that their loyalty to her should convince them to accept her assessment of the situation and do as she says. And Zoe, as protagonist, as well as having more information than the others, is the one we identify with. Yet quickly, after this negotiation about how to categorize Max, Zoe reveals a different order of reasoning which is in fact *not* based upon identifying with him or caring about him. While on the surface she is bridging and defending a half-zombie she once knew and perhaps retains some loyalty or compassion for, her reason why it matters is not out of concern for *his* welfare. She argues not to kill him because he will be instrumentally useful to her and to them: "Baca he's the breakthrough I've been searching for!" Zoe's "breakthrough" is not entirely about self-interest, since— as we will soon learn—she wants to create a vaccine. Yet that is one step removed from the moment when she speaks, and her words indicate Max as a specimen to be used, rather than anything about the people who might be saved. More, the people she wants to save with her vaccine—again, as we will soon learn—are the uninfected. She has no interest in trying to cure or otherwise help the already infected.

Once Max is chained up, Miguel questions keeping him alive: "What the hell? Are you all fucking crazy? Why didn't you kill it?" Note Miguel's lack of a gendered pronoun. He refers to Max as "it," suggesting that Max is sub-human to the point of being just an object. Again, Zoe explains that Max is still at least partly human rather than zombie, and emphasizes, "I need him for my research," rather than having care for him or bridging to identify with his human side. Zoe further makes it clear that "I'm not talking about a cure for being a rotter. I'm talking about a vaccine for the rest of us." She is not looking to help the already-turned. She intends to vaccinate those who are not yet infected. She will protect "us," or whoever is *not* a zombie. Miguel is unconvinced on all accounts: "This is all a bunch of bullshit. Shoot it."

The Miguel of 2018 can be compared to the Rhodes of 1985. In the older version, Rhodes had plausible reasons that went beyond his person, even if overstated and translated into despotic actions. Joseph Pilato, the actor who played him, also found himself sympathizing with Rhodes' position. Pilato says: "I found myself agreeing with Rhodes all the time—I mean, shoot those mother-fuckers in the head. Keeping them around is ridiculous" (Martin 1985). In 2018, Miguel at times offers shadows of Rhodes' earlier reasoning, but his need to control is now psychologized, and hence in comparison with 1985, more an issue of personality and less of philosophy. Like Elle, Miguel blames Zoe for Frank's death, and in fact his original warning was for Zoe's expedition not to happen because it was too risky. This is the one sense in which Miguel has something of a reasonable perspective. Yet when he blames Zoe, whatever rationale he has is eclipsed by the rivalry between him and Zoe for Baca's loyalty. His hatred of Zoe is *personal*. In contrast to Pilato, Jeff Gum (the actor who played 2018's Miguel) says: "Miguel doesn't want the world pieced back together because he thrives on power. And he sees Zoe as a threat to the existence of that power" ("Day of the Dead: Bloodline—Reviving Horror" 2018).[7] Screenwriter Mark Tonderai also describes the clash between Zoe and Miguel as a personality issue first: "With two different personalities and mentalities of how to view the world, of course personalities will clash" ("Day of the Dead: Bloodline—Reviving Horror" 2018).

Miguel is won over by an argument from Elle: "Miguel wait," she says, "If there's a chance Zoe can do it, we should let her try. This vaccine could have saved Frank." She connects Zoe's purpose now in a positive way to hypothetically saving her dead husband after he was bitten. Evidently the plea based on family loyalty is convincing enough to Miguel. Later, Zoe plays into Max's romantic attachment to her in order to trick him into being docile for her to take his blood sample. "Just relax Max. You want me, right? Here I am, your Zoe. That's right. I know you came all this way just for me. You like feeling my touch?" She takes Max's blood while he licks her face.

Zoe walks away with the blood, delivering an agonistic look to Max. This duality—Zoe's need for Max in a self-interested sense, and her disgust with him based upon his obsessing over her, assaulting her, and now being part zombie—is the central drama behind Max's character, and in that his blood supplies the vaccine, it is a central element in the (partial) victory that Zoe and

Baca are finally able to enjoy. In a twisted way, Max's claims about himself and Zoe being "connected" and that she needs him, play out to be true once the outbreak ensues and he becomes infected. It is his obsessive loyal "connection" to her that brings him to follow her and not kill her, and it is his blood that Zoe needs in order to protect what is left of humanity from the virus. Even when Zoe kills Max, this perverse connection is reinforced by blending in an element of self-contradictory metonymy to Zoe's aggressive refutation of Max and her introduction to her impending destruction of him. After he says his refrain again to her "You are mine," she responds "No, you're mine mother-fucker!" and beheads him with her machete. In refuting him, she perversely legitimates his claim about their connection.

Humanity's pseudo-salvation is due to the perverse connectedness of Max and Zoe, and yet this happens without Zoe expressing any moral attitude toward him other than instrumentality. To an extent this is necessary—if she were to indicate some form of caring about him, for example, it would bring a more objectionable (probably too objectionable, even for a gore-filled horror film) theme to the movie: Zoe caring about her stalker/abuser. Despite this fact, their relationship is also responsible for Zoe's opportunity to devise a vaccine. In this way, Zoe's whole person in relationship to Max inherits the "risk society" ambivalence about science. Her relationship with Max is how the outpost is threatened, and how a vaccine is devised. Max is the subject of much of her work, and in this sense, Max embodies the volatility of science. Zoe, the scientist, has a strange, dangerous, perverse connection with her work that has the power to protect, but also the power to destroy the community.

In several interviews, Johnathon Schaech mentioned the moral transformation of Max upon his turning into a half-zombie as a key feature of his character. Of course, these scenes, where we see Max reckon with his past actions upon his pseudo-death, never made it to filming—which Schaech mentions in one of the interviews (Haley and Schaech 2018). His description of Max is of a character with moral complexity, and he is particularly interested in the moral dimensions of the film and of horror. Schaech describes the moral dimensions to Max's character as dealing primarily with individual—rather than group or institutional—dilemmas.

> I looked it at as when he was human, he was a true monster in how he treated Zoe. When he got bit and transitioned, he faced his own death and all the bad things he'd done in his past. He was making amends with himself for his sins. He met her again and she had to interface with him as the Zombie. During this process, he became like an I Am Legend alpha [...] When a man has to face death, he sees life in a whole new light. He didn't get to get rid of everything—he's half alive and half dead. He tries to say, "I'm sorry," to Zoe, it comes out as "ROAR." It's a big metaphor, and it was easier to play it that way. His physicality, and his dealing with death influences his morality and seeing what he did was wrong.
>
> (Kramer 2018)

Zoe's true romantic interest, Baca, is caught in a tug of loyalties between Zoe and Baca's brother Miguel, the latter of whom tries to sway Baca to his side by claiming that Zoe does have a romantic attachment to Max, and that this betrayal is the real reason she is advocating for him to be kept alive. Miguel complains of Baca's subversion of his command, which was simultaneously a violation of their family bond:

MIGUEL: I'm a commanding officer whose own fucking brother went behind his back and put this whole place in danger! [...] I'm your brother Baca. Your own flesh and blood. Believe me when I tell you she's fooling you. Don't you see what she's doing? Why do you think she keeps this thing alive? [...] That rotter has her name engraved on his arm. Wake up, Baca!

In the next scene, Zoe is standing in front of a mirror cleaning blood off her neck. Baca comes in to talk to Zoe. He tries to comfort and also tells her he needs to hear her say the vaccine will work. Their interaction is a debate, the focus shifting through different personal loyalties. Baca acknowledges Zoe's closeness to Elise (who Miguel recently shot and killed after Elise had been bitten), but then also emphasizes his own difficult place in the responsibility for their deaths: "I ordered them out there for you. For your vaccine. And they died." His words seem to imply—though do not directly state—that his own decisions were based on trust in Zoe. He then questions her on the possible romantic connection between her and zombie Max, a concern of his that had just been sparked by Miguel's questioning of whether Zoe was keeping Max alive (alive as a zombie anyway) for personal reasons. Zoe now tells Baca about their history: "He was a fucking psycho who tried to rape me." She insists she needs Baca to trust her: "Right now I just need you to trust me and believe in me Baca. And if you can't, I'll go it alone." She requests his *loyal* belief.

   Later on, Baca and Miguel have a standoff, and engage in a brief moral deliberation over loyalties in a time of desperation. "Miguel!" says Baca, "Open that fucking door! Lilly and Zoe are still outside!" Miguel replies "I don't give a fuck! The Rotters got in because of that bitch Zoe. That door stays closed." Miguel's reasoning for leaving them outside is not clearly stated, other than his condemnation of Zoe. It is possible that he truly believes he is acting in the best interests of the community, protecting them, but he doesn't actually say this. It's clear, however, that he doesn't care about protecting Zoe and Lilly, which is a mark of his villain-hood. We can only presume that his action is more about self-interest, power, and vindictiveness than about protecting the other people in the outpost.

   As far as what is directly stated, the moral question is one of conflicting loyalties—not between groups, but between close personal connections. Miguel further has the implicit argument that what he says goes because he has rightful command. "Stand down, Baca," he says, pointing his gun at him. This time, Baca uses the family loyalty argument: "You're gonna shoot your own brother now?" Miguel and Baca are (conveniently) spared from having to play out the scenario however, because Miguel is just then tackled and killed by zombies. Soon after, Zoe and Lilly find Baca sitting defeated on the floor, Miguel having been torn apart, Baca himself having been bitten. Baca is holding a gun to his head. Zoe talks him down by emphasizing their connection: "I can stop the virus. Believe me. I can stop the virus. You just have to trust me. I love you Baca." Once again it is trust that is advocated. Baca has to *trust* Zoe in order to be saved (saved from becoming one of the zombies).

The humans win enough, but the virus is not defeated. Zoe develops a vaccine, not a cure. In the final scene, humans are happily living together within a guarded, quarantined area. The outpost, ultimately a military base, is basically secure because of military protection, and the people inside are protected against the illness due to a vaccine. Everyone acts happy in the final scene, but underneath we know there is not a thorough victory, as the world at large is still presumably overrun by zombies. Science and the military are both moderately helpful and explicitly improve the quality of life for those in the outpost, although the larger problem remains as the continuing context that contains the outpost.

Combined summary

In 1985, a variety of angles are held from different characters, and there is even somewhat rich moral debate between Sarah, Logan, Rhodes, and Ted concerning the relations between the humans and the zombies, and between the military and the scientists. Notably lacking in many situations is caring. Sarah—a medical scientist—is the only character who directly voices caring or places any explicit value on caring and bridging. She is our protagonist, positioned against the villain Captain Rhodes, who generally embodies authority, loyalty, and division between groups. Liberal political discourse— emphasizing freedom, human rights, and so on—plays a very minor role, in the form of a couple of ineffective comments from Ted. In the end, the winning moral style is John's simple self-interest and detachment. In some instances, he is maybe caring, maybe loyal, or maybe fair. But resignation, apathy, and self-interest are the dominant virtues of John, and by extension of the story. Identification—whether bridging or divisive—is unimportant, as survival is the key issue and group cohesion may be fleeting.

In 2008, the protagonist Sarah is now in the military, while the closest person to a moral villain is now Logan, who is still a medical scientist working for the military, embodying a flagrant combination of betrayal and self-interest. Rhodes is a minor character, still upholding authority. Political liberty is alluded to early on, via individual characters protesting the military quarantine as oppressive. Ultimately, their protests end up unimportant in what happens (the zombie outbreak) and for human welfare (the zombie issue is much more pressing). Sarah's character is caught in conflicting loyalties between private and public responsibilities (caring for her family vis-à-vis fulfilling her duties as a corporal), and displays ambivalence concerning her identification with or against the infected, particularly surrounding Bud. Her ambivalence concerning Bud is returned by his ambivalence concerning the humans vis-à-vis the zombies, and the mixed outcome of his actions for the welfare of the protagonist group: He gives away their hideout, but later saves Sarah's life, which in turn allows her the time to incinerate all of the zombies in the bunker so that she, Nina, and Trevor can escape. While John's detached style crowned 1985, Sarah's and zombie Bud's ambivalence crown 2008.

In 2018, Zoe (Sarah) is our protagonist both narratively and morally. This time, in her actions with other people she is motivated by care and loyalty, and she—as do all the humans—implicitly accepts the division between human and zombie. This time, Max (Bub/Bud) has a peculiar status. He is not just a zombie, he is a half-zombie, and so carries the eventual vaccine in his blood. Zoe's choice not to kill him (until she figures out the vaccine) does not actually have anything to do with identifying with his human side, or bridging with his zombie side. And perhaps by virtue of his human side being that of an obsessed stalker and abuser, no moral questions are raised regarding the killing of him at the end of the film. In a sense he is outside of the moral discourse. This amorality of his being is coupled with his employing her with the instrumentality of satisfying his obsessive tendencies, his perversely accurate delusion about being "connected," and so on, which has its counterpart in her PTSD flashbacks that prevent her from intimacy with Baca, and the need and opportunity she alone has of *utilizing* his exceptional blood to vaccinate the rest of the uninfected (in the bunker, and perhaps elsewhere). It is a relation that mimics something of the shape of intense loyalty—and in so doing attests to its immense importance—while actually remaining amoral, and oriented to instrumentality. Much of the rest of the drama of the film is very loyalty-centric, and nowhere is there a discussion about the moral status of the infected and their treatment.

The great complexity in the 1985 rendition makes most generalizations about trends over time unreasonable. Yet there are a few which still stand up. First, loyalty becomes increasingly central. In 1985 it is mostly associated with the villain, Rhodes. In 2008 it becomes a point of ambivalence for the protagonist, Sarah. And in 2018, there is no ambivalence; loyalty is simply an overriding motivation for protagonist Zoe. Second, bridging identification withers away. In 1985, Sarah openly supported bridging between the military and the scientists, and Logan practised an intense bridging with the zombie Bub. In 2008, Sarah and zombie Bud are both ambivalent regarding bridging, and that ambivalence plays a key role in the story. The dynamic between scientists and the military is no longer an articulated contest of one group vis-à-vis another, and hence there is no discussion about bridging or division between them. In 2018, the ambivalence is gone. Zoe and all the rest of the humans tacitly accept that zombies are different and deserve no moral consideration. There are no group rivalries among the humans—only personal ones.

The trajectory for the military across *Day of the Dead* renditions is an increase in overall helpfulness, although it is not a simple or linear change. It appears that 2008 was a peak in the overall significance of the military, for good and for ill. Science is also complex, and a bit erratic overall. Science reaches a peak of sorts in 2008 as well, in that it is portrayed as very blameworthy for the origin of the disease. Then in 2018, science per se becomes moderately helpful since Zoe successfully develops a vaccine, yet the person of the scientist risks the destruction of her community and in her pursuit of knowledge she maintains a perverse relationship to her very dangerous work, and is responsible for many human deaths. If there is an overall story here that encompasses both science and military, it might be that in 1985, neither science nor military appear all that effective in any direction, in 2008 both become more active and their overall presence more volatile; and then in 2018 they calm down some again from their 2008 drama. But in 2018, medical science, by way of the person of the medical scientist, inherits the heated ambivalence of risk society. The military leaves the position of debate and contestation that it occupied in 1985 to become unproblematized in 2018, simply moderately helpful, even despite the abrasive personality of Miguel.

Notes

1 Ebert fails to explain what the "real drama" actually is. Presumably, it has something to do with the zombie apocalypse.
2 Logically then, she intervened to stop *John*, who she believes *would* have actually initiated a gunfight in order to protect her.
3 Salazar's bullying and taunting of Bud contains a dialectical element. The permission he gives to himself to act in this way towards Bud occurs when Bud turns, hence when (and because) Bud assumes full *zombie* status. Yet the punchlines of the taunts all revolve around Bud's still-human traits.
4 Having already discussed the context of *I Am Legend* (2007) in an earlier chapter, I refrain here from restating the historical material that I already covered earlier (disease, military, etc.).
5 In fact, the success of the military was originally tempered, but the film company wanted a more optimistic ending. Sands explains: "New Image wanted to have more of a everything's okay moment, with the viral thing, right? The older version was like it's spreading to Boulder, and then we look and see that Nina has a bite mark on her arm."
6 One part of the film takes places in Zoe's old medical facility, post-apocalypse, and here, we get our moment of remnants-of-the-past. Other than the zombies that roam the place, the facility has been abandoned.
7 The psychologizing of Miguel appears in the film too, in a scene where Baca and Zoe are talking about their pasts, and Baca mentions that even as a child, Miguel always wanted to be in control.

References

Bell, A. L., Adams, M., & Griffin, P. (2007). History of Racism and Immigration Time Line: Key Events in the Struggle for Racial Equality in the United States. In *Teaching for Diversity and Social Justice*. New York: Routledge.

Commentary Provided by Jeffrey Reddick, Steve Miner and Cast Members. (2008). *Day of the Dead* [DVD]. Firstlook Studios.

Day of the Dead: Bloodline – Reviving Horror. (2018). *Day of the Dead: Bloodline* [DVD]. Lionsgate.

Ebert, R. (1985). Day of the Dead Movie Review and Film Summary. Retrieved from *RogerEbert.com*: https://www.rogerebert.com/reviews/day-of-the-dead-1985.

Geduld, H. M. (1985). Day of the Dead. *Humanist* 45, 41–42.

Haley, N., & Schaech, J. (2018). Johnathon Schaech of Day of the Dead: Bloodline [Radio Program]. *The Neil Haley Show*. Retrieved from: https://www.blogtalkradio.com/theneilhaleyshow/2018/01/05/johnathon-schaech-of-day-of-the-dead-bloodline

Hall, S. (1980). Popular Democratic vs. Authoritarian Populism: Two Ways of Taking Democracy Seriously. In A. Hunt (ed.), *Marxism and Democracy*. London, NJ: Humanities Press, 157–185.

Hall, S., Critcher, C., Jefferson, T., Clarke, J., & Roberts, B. (2013). *Policing the Crisis: Mugging, the State and Law and Order* (2nd ed.). London: Red Globe Press.

Hawkins, A. (2018). Interview: Johnathon Schaech for 'Day of the Dead: Bloodline'. Retrieved from *Trouble City*: https://trouble.city/articles/2018/1/5/interview-johnathon-schaech-for-day-of-the-dead-bloodline.

Karr, L., & Nicotero, G. (2014). *The Making of George A. Romero's Day of the Dead*. Plexus.

Kramer, G. M. (2018). Re-Animating Day of the Dead: An Interview with Johnathon Schaech. Retrieved from *Filmint*: http://filmint.nu/?p=23250.

Martin, R. H. (1985). An Interview with the Villain. *Fangoria*. Retrieved from: https://www.oocities.org/zodiaczombie/joe2.html

Maslin, J. (1985, July 3). Film: Day of the Dead. *New York Times*.

Putnam, R. D. (2001). *Bowling Alone: The Collapse and Revival of American Community*. New York: Simon and Schuster.

Russell, J. (2014). *Book of the Dead: The Complete History of Zombie Cinema*. New York: Titan.

Schweitzer, D. (2018). *Going Viral: Zombies, Viruses, and the End of the World*. New Brunswick, NJ: Rutgers University Press.

Sontag, S. (1989). *Illness as Metaphor and AIDS and Its Metaphors*. New York: Picador.

Susser, M., & Susser, E. (1996). Choosing a Future for Epidemiology: II. From Black Box to Chinese Boxes and Eco-Epidemiology. *American Journal of Public Health*, 86, 674–677. doi:10.1093/acprof:oso/9780195300666.003.0025.

Tallerico, B. (2018). Day of the Dead: Bloodline Movie Review. Retrieved from *Roger-Ebert.com*: https://www.rogerebert.com/reviews/day-of-the-dead-bloodline-2018.

The Many Days of DAY OF THE DEAD. (2003). *Day of the Dead, Disc 2: Bonus Materials* [DVD]. Anchor Bay Entertainment.

U.S. Department of Health and Human Services. (2019). *A Timeline of HIV and AIDS*. Retrieved from HIV.gov.

Woodger, E., & Burg, D. F. (2006). *The 1980s*. New York: Facts on File.

Conclusion

In the preceding two chapters, within the sample of "Diseased Others" science fiction, themes of tribal morality and confidence in medical science and the military have followed a discernible trajectory, altogether displaying a heightening of some elements of authoritarian populism. This trajectory is one of narrowing moral scope toward loyalty to one's own in opposition to outside groups and embracing military violence as a positive solution to threats to the "normal" population. In general, medical science was also increasingly positioned as dangerous and blameworthy (even if also capable of positive intervention). And this trajectory thus displays a heightening of what I call three "elements of authoritarian populism": tribalism, distrust of rational elites and their institutions, and willingness for violent coercion. This is all consistent with the histories sketched out over Part I of this book.

The notion that American culture is becoming less moral is nothing new. Most of the time, the concern over the decline of "morality" is made by social conservatives over such issues as the loosening of sexual taboos, the decline of the family, the decline of social etiquette, and the general lack of respect for authority. But the path of moral atrophy within the films discussed in this book is different than this. Social progressives today do not typically refer to a "moral" decline, although they do talk about a recent surge of problematic attitudes—racism, sexism, homophobia, and so on. Progressives are less likely to assert that the status of "morality" is at issue, but the framing is clearly normative: These social inequalities are worthy of condemnation, and should be overturned. Of note for the progressive side, the "surge" of intolerance does not mean that there has been a decline from a prior, more tolerant era. The "return to the past" is often voiced by conservatives, while progressives look toward the creation of a different future. The question for the Left of how forms of intolerance have changed since the 1950s is a complex one, too complex to discuss sufficiently here. What we can say is that at a minimum, in America there is a national consensus that the country is suffering from *some* sort of normative deficiency.

A number of social theorists have discussed the moral decline associated with modernity. In difference ways, all of the three major "classical" sociological theorists—Marx, Weber, and Durkheim—dealt at length with these issues. Marx saw the ascendance of capitalism coming to dominate culture and society, which means that the rules of the market would outstrip the norms of tradition, and human relationships would often be experienced as adjuncts to—if not in service to—the economy. Weber saw in the modern project a "disenchantment of the world," a process of "rationalization" where all throughout society reasoning based on normative values would transition to calculating and amoral reasoning. Durkheim saw the threat of "anomie" (normlessness) erupting in modern societies which have undergone rapid change.

More recently Zygmunt Bauman refers to the contemporary general moral disengagement as "adiaphorization," brought on by bureaucracy and consumerism. He defines adiaphorization as "placing, intentionally or by default, certain acts and/or omitted acts regarding certain categories of humans *outside* the moral-immoral axis—that is, outside the 'universe of moral obligations' and outside the realm of phenomena subject to moral evaluation; stratagems to declare such acts or inaction, explicitly or implicitly, 'morally neutral' and prevent the choices between them from being subject to ethical judgment" (Bauman and Donskis 2013, 39–40). Bauman also speaks of moral "deskilling" and attributes an "ethical tranquilization" (Bauman 2006b, 89) to ubiquitous transience and precariousness in contemporary society, or "liquid modernity" (Bauman 2000, 2006a, 2006b).

This same precarious, transient, "liquid" quality of modern life can feed fantasies about returning to a more secure past. Whether and for whom that past was more secure is a good question, but it is also not necessarily the point. Our relationship to the past is through memories and stories, and so imagination and projection always have the ability to run rampant. The romantic vision of a more solid past can fuel conservative desires to return to that lost "golden age." Bauman (2017) refers to these regressive fantasies as longings for "retrotopia," and he considers this sort of envisioning to be an endemic feature of America today. We rarely look forward in our visions of the perfect world. These days we are more likely to look back. These retrotopic impulses are common aspects of far-Right populist movements. Mussolini invoked the Roman Empire, Hitler invoked Valhalla. Today, Trump promises to "Make America Great Again" and Bolsonaro promises to "Make Brazil Great Again."

The liquid quality of modern life is also due to rapid technological change and globalization, as well as the erosion of all forms of rootedness, including the rootedness of the individual within a cohesive community. Erich Fromm (1941/1994) saw this sort of change as endemic to capitalist development and said that it fed feelings of alienation and anxiety that people turn to authoritarian movements to escape. Fromm came up with this idea in the middle decades of the twentieth century, before the neoliberal era began in the 1980s. Yet neoliberalism continues this trend, morally isolating the individual even more. On a cultural level, neoliberalism consistently celebrates the isolated individual, implying a meritocratic world where success and failure are all due to people's relative abilities and efforts. Bauman (2016) also notes that the cultural dominance of neoliberalism has eroded the classical liberal value foundation of American democracy. He notes that a major thread in Enlightenment thinking was to work to safeguard society against tyrannical rule. The separation of powers and the checks and balances of liberal democracy were developed with this purpose in full view. Donald Trump's disregarding of congressional procedure and affinity for instituting executive orders stands directly contrary to this goal. During the French Revolution, the triadic slogan of liberty, equality, fraternity was intended as a system of mutually necessary elements. In particular, liberty requires equality in order to preserve fraternity. Classical liberalism preserved the tripod vision of the French Revolution, but the neoliberal movement eliminated equality as a reigning value. After several decades of neoliberal hegemony, the underemphasis on equality has starved society of fraternity. Neoliberalism leads to barbarism, and barbarism welcomes authoritarianism.

Anthony Giddens comes from a different tradition of social theory, but he diagnoses the same basic problem of moral emaciation. Like Bauman, Giddens (1991a, 1991b) notes that in the contemporary period—what he calls "high modernity" or "late modernity"—people experience less continuity in their lives, and this translates into a state of anxiousness or "ontological insecurity." Along with this, modern life is saturated with calculations about risks vis-à-vis opportunities. We are always trying to "colonize the future," or in other words, to set in place rational plans that will make the future predictable and safe from risk. This preoccupation with risk assessment and avoidance pushes moral reasoning aside. We suffer from an "evaporation of morality" because it runs "counter to the concept of risk and to the mobilizing of dynamics of control. Morality is extrinsic so far as the colonization of the future is concerned" (Giddens, 1991b, 145).

A kind of moral narrowing certainly takes place in the *I Am Legend* and *Day of the Dead* film series, as well as in some of the film series discussed in earlier chapters, such as *Planet of the Apes* and *X-Men*. Ideas in the Frankfurt School and "risk society" traditions may shed some light on this. Yet the trend over time in the stories discussed here is not only towards a kind of impoverishment, an "evaporation" or "adiaphorization," to use the terms of Giddens and Bauman. It is a deep impoverishment, but a thread of moral discourse persists. The value of *loyalty* is maintained. Today it is very often the moral centre of popular science fiction. When loyalty is not centrally pronounced, it is certainly less complex. It was an emphasized site of ambivalence in *I Am Legend* (1954) and *The Last Man on Earth* (1964). There was some detectable ambivalence about loyalty in *The Omega Man* (1971), *Day of the Dead* (1985) and *Day of the Dead* (2008). In the most recent renditions of both films, ambivalence is slim to non-existent. By contrast, loyalty becomes a central theme in Robert's motivation in *I Am Legend* (2007), and is the only substantial *moral* basis for any action or disagreement in *Day of the Dead* (2016). It is not only that morality shrinks and narrows. The morality there is left centres on loyalty to the in-group—to family or those otherwise closest. Contrary to the reification thesis and its derivatives in the Frankfurt School, scientific reason does not rule the day. And contrary to Giddens and Beck, risk avoidance does not drown out other moral considerations. *Loyalty does.*

To be clear, loyalty is not an "authoritarian" or "barbaric" moral orientation. Jonathan Haidt claims there are several "moral foundations" that are grounded in deep emotional sensibilities, which different people orient around to different degrees. Out of five identified domains of morality—care/harm, fairness/cheating, loyalty/betrayal, authority/subversion, sanctity/degradation[1]—Haidt and Graham (2007) discovered liberals tend to emphasize two (harm/care and fairness/reciprocity) while conservatives emphasize the full five. Thus, their Moral Foundations Theory (Graham et al. 2013) suggests that how a person is oriented regarding these various domains is a good predictor of that person's political leanings. The implication here that ostensibly rational positions on political issues are in fact *driven* by deep emotional moral "intuitions," which align according to discernible categories or foundations (Haidt 2001; Haidt and Joseph 2004; Haidt 2012), could be criticized on a number of grounds. For instance, it seems to suggest that conservatives are morally advanced in comparison with liberals, and it implies that rational political discussion is all rationalization, just an extension of more primordial experiences which admit of no rational arbitration. It also implies a causal directionality that runs from moral intuition to political position, which ignores the dialectical relation between emotion and reason.

Regardless, the fact that studies show correlations between political and moral persuasions is hard to ignore (Graham, Haidt, and Nosek 2009). Even without the psychological theory, the categorization scheme can be used as a descriptive rubric, and their notion that morality and politics are connected is relevant for analyzing how historical shifts in moral orientations may correspond to shifts in political orientations. In these terms, what does a liquidation of moral foundations other than loyalty/betrayal amount to politically? What sort of a political orientation would a narrow, loyalty-based moral consciousness correspond with? *Without fairness, loyalty is a tribal orientation. And tribalism is a central element of authoritarian populism.*

Alongside loyalty, the other very common value orientation is in the heated ambivalence toward science, and here too "risk society" is an illuminating theoretical framework. In popular science fiction films, ambivalence toward science is often expressed in plotlines that present a repetitive, even cyclical problem of scientific hubris messing everything up, and then science needing to be called in to save the day, which in turn causes more problems, and so on. This was central to the *Back to the Future* films, and often surrounds the figure of Tony Stark (Iron Man) in recent Marvel films, most notably *Avengers: Age of Ultron* (2015). The volatility of science seems to increase over time across *I Am Legend* and *Day of the Dead* renditions.

Recent studies of survey results support the notion that public confidence in medicine and other social institutions such as education, government, and so on, have been in decline. Confidence in medicine has declined between 1976 and 1998 (Pescosolido et al. 2001), while trust in science has declined for political conservatives (Gauchat 2012). Confidence in large institutions in general was shown to decrease rather steadily from 1972 to 2012 (Twenge et al. 2014).

The increasing volatility of science in the sampled film series, when considered with the declining public confidence in medicine and institutions in general, fits with the ideas of Giddens and Beck about the pervasiveness of risk threat and avoidance in society today. Beck says that in risk society, "social, political, economic and individual risks increasingly tend to escape the institutions for monitoring and protection of society" (Beck 1992, 5). Beck explains that in risk society we become increasingly concerned with the dangers unleashed by our growing technological capacities and come to live under the permanent threat of catastrophe. Many measures are instituted in the interests of fending off or mitigating risk, to the extent that the avoidance of risk becomes a general orientation permeating our culture and institutions. Through repeated experience of systemic and professional failures, "lay" people lose confidence in the "experts" who are ostensibly protecting society by managing the risks. Beck was primarily concerned about environmental risks, but his analyses have been extended to other areas, such as health care and human services (Webb 2006; Rosenberg 2007). Risk society is also global, for instance in the sense that the consequences of climate change are global in scope, especially so in a more interconnected, globalized world. Yet this part of his theory is also very consonant with the issue of emerging infectious diseases (EID) and the discourse surrounding them.

> [T]he nature of contemporary food production means that food risks are no longer limited geographically, and [...] the spread of epidemics such as SARS are facilitated by the ease of modern travel [...] [I]n many ways the media coverage of the risk of EID, particularly after AIDS, seems to follow this *Risk Society* model, highlighting wider contemporary public anxieties, in particular anxieties *both* about the apparent inability of technology (and biomedicine) to contain new threats posed by infectious diseases *and* concerns about globalisation aiding their spread.
>
> (Washer 2010, 75)

Giddens specifically points to a newfound ambivalence in science, on the grounds that we know it can do as much harm as good, and often the harm comes as unforeseen consequences of some sort of intervention that was intended to be helpful. The trajectory of medical science as being portrayed as increasingly powerful and volatile fits very well here. In *The Omega Man*, but especially in *I Am Legend* (2007) and *Day of the Dead* (2008), this is explicitly the case. What is not accounted for by the "risk society" analysis is why the trajectory for the military is so different. Military violence becomes increasingly straightforward as necessary and helpful. Confidence in the military has risen since the 1970s (King and Karabell 2003; Burbach 2017, 2019). In a 2018

NPR/PBS NewsHour/Marist poll, 87 per cent of respondents reported having "a great deal" or "quite a lot" of confidence in the military. This is a far greater amount than for other institutions represented in the poll; "[t]he only institution that Americans have overwhelming faith in is the military" (Montenaro 2018).

One especially glaring element in the recent survey research is a strongly politicized dimension of the changes in confidence. Gauchat (2012) identified a clear partisan trend in the decline of confidence in science: It is located in the conservative political camp. Burbach (2019) likewise found the increases in confidence in the military to be congregated among conservatives. Even beyond the issue of political affiliation, a key difference separates medical science from military violence: One uses knowledge to cure, the other uses aggression to kill. In this light, the loss of confidence in medical science and the growth in confidence in the military might reflect more than just a sense of the salience of the organization and application of techniques from said institutions.

It might also reflect a general decline of faith in reason, knowledge, and the social institutions that embody and promulgate rationality (i.e. science, medicine, education, courts, political bodies, and so on) to help heal society's ills. Alongside a general turning to violence, there is a growing willingness to resort to violence or at least frame it romantically as a tool for security in an uncertain world. This fits both the "liquid modernity" and "risk society" diagnoses. Yet it also points beyond sceptical, anxious, populist, and even egalitarian or democratic dimensions of the loss of confidence in "experts," to the embracing of direct and forceful means toward valued ends, or in other words, to *barbarism*.

While this book focuses primarily on representation, metaphor, morality, and so on, social movements and cultural shifts always have an empirical, "material" dimension. So before concluding, I want to tie all the preceding discussion in with a few theories about demographic change that are also useful for understanding how the United States became so polarized and tribal by the middle of the 2010s. Demographic discussions invariably lead to generalizations about populations based on characteristics like race, gender, class, and sexuality, and for this reason I believe it is important to be cautious and conscientious when discussing demographic trends. Everyone is impacted strongly by their demographic, but everyone is also an individual and much more than the various demographic categories they can be lumped within.

Now that said, the Republican Party tends toward being older white Christian straight men. It is certainly not only older white Christian straight men, nor are by any means all older white Christian straight men Republicans. But the trend is in that direction. It has now been half a century since the 1960s, and during this time the country has become increasingly diverse in terms of race and ethnicity, women have become increasingly empowered, and sexual minorities have gained increased acceptance. Every step of empowerment of women and minorities means a relative loss of power for men and the white majority. The intersection of—at a minimum—religion, culture, race, gender, and sexuality as axes of privilege is a very complex issue, especially when trying to definitively determine influences on not just votes for Trump, but the cultural impetus toward authoritarian populism; for the sake of this analysis I will focus on the issue of racial—i.e. white—privilege. While declines in male privilege, for instance, are certainly very important when considering the right-left polarization in America, I will stick to the racial dimension of white privilege in this analysis, largely for the sake of parsimony, but backed by the conviction that racial privilege is one of the most, if not *the* most, (a) overall prominent axes of tribalism in America, and b) inflamed areas of unrest animating the Alt-Right and Trumpism.

Since the 1970s, a process of "social sorting" has continued whereby people become more and more surrounded by other people who are similar to them in ways such as age, religion, race, and so on (Bishop 2009; Mason 2018). Hence, cross-cutting affiliations are less common, and the clustering is also self-creating, in the sense that people tend to adopt the values of those with whom they associate and whom they perceive as like themselves. In this process then, one would expect different political affiliations to accompany increasingly segregated demographic compositions. And this is in fact what has happened. Thus, for example, older, white, straight Christian men cluster together, have comparably little contact with people different from them, and solidify in-group sentiments with associated Right-wing political beliefs. When people belong to a plurality of cross-cutting affiliations, groups that are demographically different from one another, then it is harder for people to develop strong in-group/out-group hostilities and prejudices. In effect there is political polarization which overlaps with racial and other forms of informal demographic segregation.

The continued immigration of non-white populations over the past several decades has propelled a kind of racial anxiety among the American white population (Major, Blodorn, and Blascovich 2018). In a series of experimental studies, psychologists Craig and Richeson (2014a) found that after white study participants were presented with information about the changing racial demographics in America and the coming "majority-minority" society, they "preferred interactions/settings with their own ethnic group over minority ethnic groups; expressed more negative attitudes toward Latinos, Blacks, and Asian Americans; and expressed more automatic pro-White/anti-minority bias." Craig and Richeson (2014b) also discovered that white Americans expressed more conservative policy positions after being presented with information on the coming of majority-minority society. There is empirical evidence that instead of economic woes, white Trump voters were driven by factors such as racial resentment and fear of whites becoming a minority (Tesler 2016; Mutz 2018). Using data from the GenForward Survey, researchers discovered that "white vulnerability," or "the perception that whites, through no fault of their own, are losing ground to other groups" was a significant predictor of voting for Trump among millennials (Fowler, Medenica, and Cohen 2017).

It is also the case that people belong to fewer groups and institutions than they once did. Specifically, there is less civic engagement, less voluntary association, less enduring family and community ties, less "social capital" (Putnam 2001).[2] In the twenty-first century, this trend has continued for those who are in the lower income brackets of the country (Sander and Putnam 2010). Starting in the 1950s, mass society theorists (Kornhauser 1959/2013) claimed that large, modern, impersonal societies produce alienated individuals who are more amenable to authoritarian social movements (Gusfield 1994).[3] The connection of alienation to authoritarian populism is also theorized in the tradition of critical social theory, for example in Erich Fromm's (1941/1994) *Escape from Freedom*, Stephen Erich Bronner (2014, 2018) and Zygmunt Bauman (2017). The alienated individual often suffers from the feeling of lack of belonging and meaning in life, and may attempt to satisfy the desires for such things by fixating on power, by joining social movements with a strong sense of "we," or—in the case of authoritarian populism—by joining "we" social movements fixated on power. Recent empirical work shows that lack of social integration is indeed positively associated with voting for far-right populist candidates (Gidron and Hall 2017).

When taken all together, the tribal implications of all three of the demographic trends (declining white majority, social sorting, and declining social capital) are black and white (no pun intended). Communities are more demographically homogeneous, people are more isolated and less connected to civic life, and many white people are afraid of belonging to a racial minority. In *I Am Legend* and *Day of the Dead*, the shift over time toward loyalty and away from other moral considerations fits strikingly with these demographic changes and their likely relation to far-Right tribal mentalities. With less civic participation morality has less of a deliberative flavour, and with less social connection beyond the home, those connections within the home become that much more important to protect. With "social sorting," people who have different opinions, lifestyles, or ethnicities seem farther away, less relevant, and so easier to frame in a simplistic, Othered light. And the decreasing majority of whites in the population is fuelling a growing uneasiness about displacement among many white people. Altogether, it is easy to see how these wider social trends might feed into a moral impoverishment and a protect-your-own tribal mentality among white conservatives.

Yet it would be reductive to assume that white conservatives are the only demographic impacted by all of this. Other than the white fear of displacement, the other two trends—social sorting and declining social capital—are not so demographically specific. It is well worth considering that the sudden surge of authoritarian populism in the United States in the form of Trumpism and the alt-Right may be part of a wider cultural phenomenon, one in which many more people participate than just those who espouse white nationalist beliefs. This goes beyond the observation that more white people harbour racist sentiments than admit to them publicly (or even privately).

I would like to suggest that white nationalist authoritarian populism is actually a trend (albeit a rather powerful one at present) in a wider cultural condition that might be framed as a prominent *form* rather than as specific contents: tribal inwardness, intolerance of difference and disagreement, lack of moral recognition for Others, impatience with democracy, and eagerness to entertain violence as a method of social control—if not in practice, then at least in fantasy. Othering, as a whole, might have something of a national style at any given point in history, which mediates and is mediated by the various particular forms of Othering operant (present prejudices, or just tendencies still circulating in cultural memory)—the particulars are separate but they are also related and shape one another. Hate directed towards Asian Americans during the COVID-19 pandemic might carry some of the discourses of the War on Terror, such as fear of bioterrorism and patriotic vitriol about defending the country from brown-skinned persons.

In various works by the Frankfurt School,[4] a crucial distinction is drawn between ideas consciously espoused and authoritarian (sado-masochistic) character types that may be unconscious to a greater or lesser extent. What is crucial about this observation is that the authoritarian character type does not necessarily espouse authoritarian politics—although naturally many do. This theoretical split between the ostensible beliefs and the underlying character harbours the implication that authoritarianism, as a set of character traits, can proliferate much more widely in a culture than a more limited explicit embrace of authoritarian ideologies might suggest. In the work of Fromm and Adorno and others, this is a foreboding explanatory principle. In critical times, authoritarian characters may be susceptible to switching over to the embrace of authoritarian politics.

For those wishing to quell the far-right tide, the question why authoritarian populist movements have sprung up so fervently in Europe and the Americas in recent years is of critical importance. The present project does not address this question directly. To extract from a small sample of film discourse to make global conclusions about wide social trends is of course far-fetched. The relevance of this project is in pointing toward social trends that may be more deeply rooted throughout American culture than most Americans have been aware of over the past several decades; and even now, surely the suggestion that latent "authoritarian" proclivities might be prevalent unawares for many people who consciously reject authoritarianism or white supremacy is not the most common assessment. I say "authoritarian" proclivities not even in the sense of discernibly "racist" orientations, although that could be—and often is—part of it; rather I mean something a proverbial step back from that, something a little less concrete: the *form of Othering*, [5] as well as the loss of faith in *rational* institutions and the increasing faith in military *violence* as a way to cure our ills.

The interpretation I give of the themes uncovered, and the discussion I provide in terms of trends in American culture over the time period surveyed by the films, remains speculative, but I hope informative. My approach to the interpretation of films is broadly psychoanalytic, somewhat akin to an orche-strated dream experience which can be understood as operating according to condensation and displacement; metaphor and metonymy; dream contents on the surface but cathected according to underlying meanings. "Even unin-tentionally, movies can redirect attention to subjects the national psyche would repress" (Haas et al. 2015, 15). But who is the subject having the dream? Certainly, individual viewers have particular intrapsychic dream experiences, but as mass-cultural artifact, the film-as-dream should be understood as a cumulative, socio-cultural event, a sociological dream with flexible imagery that translates into multiple individual forms.

Notes

1 A sixth foundation—liberty/oppression—was later added (Iyer et al. 2012).
2 American individualism may exist in something of a feedback loop with this demo-graphic trend, so that the ideology of individualism supports lifestyles which support social alienation, and feelings of alienation are better tolerated when overlaid with an ideology of individualism.
3 More recently, postmodern theorist Michael Maffesoli (1996) has argued that instead of widespread atomization and conformity, society has turned to a kind of "neo-tri-balism." It has blossomed into a variety of subcultures which provide belonging and community yet retain fluidity unlike traditional society or modern "mass" culture. For Maffesoli, the tribal turn is positive.
4 See Adorno et al. (1950), Fromm (1984, 1941/1994), and Institut für Sozialforschung (1936).
5 For instance, if the trajectory of moral atrophy in us-them relations applies to atti-tudes of whites toward racial minorities, might it also extend to the relation of straight attitudes toward sexual minorities? These sorts of questions are worth exploring further. This connection is not purely hypothetical either. Beyond the self-evidence of there being greater overt heteronormative *and* white supremacist beliefs among the Right vis-à-vis the Left, research has shown positive correlations between various forms of intolerance (Aosved and Long 2006; Aosved, Long, and Voller 2009), as well as positive correlations in undergraduates of prior childhood bullying behaviour with a variety of intolerant attitudes in the present (Goodboy, Martin, and Rittenour 2016).

References

Adorno, T. W., Frenkel-Brunswik, E., Levinson, D. J., & Stanford, N. R. (1950). *The Authoritarian Personality*. New York: Harper.

Aosved, A. C., & Long, P. J. (2006). Co-occurrence of Rape Myth Acceptance, Sexism, Racism, Homophobia, Ageism, Classism, and Religious Intolerance. *Sex Roles*, 55, 481–492.

Aosved, A. C., Long, P. J., & Voller, E. K. (2009). Measuring Sexism, Racism, Sexual Prejudice, Ageism, Classism, and Religious Intolerance: The Intolerant Schema Measure. *Journal of Applied Social Psychology*, 39, 2321–2354. doi:10.1111/j.1559-1816.2009.00528.x.

Bauman, Z. (2000). *Liquid Modernity*. Hoboken, NJ: John Wiley & Sons.

Bauman, Z. (2006a). *Liquid Times: Living in an Age of Uncertainty*. Hoboken, NJ: John Wiley & Sons.

Bauman, Z. (2006b). *Liquid Fear*. Hoboken, NJ: John Wiley and Sons.

Bauman, Z. (2016, November 16). How Neoliberalism Prepared the Way for Donald Trump. Retrieved from *Social Europe*: https://www.socialeurope.eu/how-neoliberalism-prepared-the-way-for-donald-trump.

Bauman, Z. (2017). *Retrotopia*. Cambridge, MA: Polity.

Bauman, Z., & Donskis, L. (2013). *Moral Blindness: The Loss of Sensitivity in Liquid Modernity*. Hoboken, NJ: John Wiley & Sons.

Beck, U. (1992). *Risk Society: Towards a New Modernity*. New Delhi: SAGE.

Bishop, B. (2009). *The Big Sort: Why the Clustering of Like-Minded America is Tearing Us Apart*. Boston, MA: Houghton Mifflin Harcourt.

Bronner, S. E. (2014). *The Bigot: Why Prejudice Persists*. New Haven, CT: Yale University Press.

Bronner, S. E. (2018). From Modernity to Bigotry. In J. Morelock (ed.), *Critical Theory and Authoritarian Populism*. London: University of Westminster Press, 85–105. doi:10.16997/book30.f.

Burbach, D. T. (2017). Gaining Trust While Losing Wars: Confidence in the US Military after Iraq and Afghanistan. *Orbis*, 61(2), 154–171. doi:10.1016/j.orbis.2017.02.001.

Burbach, D. T. (2019). Partisan Dimensions of Confidence in the US Military, 1973–2016. *Armed Forces and Society*, 45(2), 211–233. doi:10.1177/0095327x17747205.

Craig, M. A., & Richeson, J. A. (2014a). More Diverse yet Less Tolerant? How the Increasingly Diverse Racial Landscape Affects White Americans' Racial Attitudes. *Personality and Social Psychology Bulletin*, 40(6), 750–761. doi:10.1177/0146167214524993.

Craig, M. A., & Richeson, J. A. (2014b). On the Precipice of a 'Majority-Minority' America: Perceived Status Threat from the Racial Demographic Shift Affects White Americans' Political Ideology. *Psychological Science*, 25(6), 1189–1197.

Fowler, M., Medenica, V. E., & Cohen, C. J. (2017, December 15). Why 41 Percent of White Millennials Voted for Trump. *The Washington Post*. Retrieved from: https://www.washingtonpost.com/news/monkey-cage/wp/2017/12/15/racial-resentment-is-why-41-percent-of-white-millennials-voted-for-trump-in-2016/.

Fromm, E. (1941/1994). *Escape from Freedom*. London: Macmillan.

Fromm, E. (1984). *The Working Class in Weimar Germany: A Psychological and Sociological Study*. Cambridge, MA: Harvard University Press.

Gauchat, G. (2012). Politicization of Science in the Public Sphere: A Study of Public Trust in the United States, 1974 to 2010. *American Sociological Review*, 77(2), 167–187. doi:10.1177/0003122412438225.

Giddens, A. (1991a). *Modernity and Self-Identity*. Stanford, CA: Stanford University Press.

Giddens, A. (1991b). *The Consequences of Modernity*. New York: John Wiley & Sons.

Gidron, N., & Hall, P. A. (2017). *Populism as a Problem of Social Integration*. Annual Meeting of the American Political Science Association, San Francisco, September. Vol. 1.

Goodboy, A. K., Martin, M. M., & Rittenour, C. E. (2016). Bullying as an Expression of Intolerant Schemas. *Journal of Child & Adolescent Trauma*, 9(4), 277–282. doi:10.1007/s40653-016-0089-9.

Graham, J., Haidt, J., Koleva, S., Motyl, M., Iyer, R., Wojcik, S. P., & Ditto, P. H. (2013). Moral Foundations Theory: The Pragmatic Validity of Moral Pluralism. In P. Devine & A. Plant (eds.), *Advances in Experimental Social Psychology*, vol. 47. Cambridge, MA: Academic Press, 55–130.

Graham, J., Haidt, J., & Nosek, B. A. (2009). Liberals and Conservatives Rely on Different Sets of Moral Foundations. *Journal of Personality and Social Psychology*, 96(5), 1029. doi:10.1037/a0015141.

Gusfield, J. R. (1994). The Reflexivity of Social Movements: Collective Behavior and Mass Society Theory Revisited. In E. Larana, H. Johnston, & J. R. Gusfield (eds.), *New Social Movements: From Ideology to Identity*, Philadelphia, PA: Temple University Press, 58–78.

Haas, E., Christensen, T., & Haas, P. J. (2015). *Projecting Politics: Political Messages in American Films*. New York: Routledge.

Haidt, J. (2001). The Emotional Dog and Its Rational Tail: A Social intuitionist Approach to Moral Judgment. *Psychological Review*, 108(4), 814. doi:10.1017/cbo9780511814273.055.

Haidt, J. (2012). *The Righteous Mind: Why Good People Are Divided by Politics and Religion*. New York: Vintage.

Haidt, J., & Graham, J. (2007). When Morality Opposes Justice: Conservatives Have Moral Intuitions That Liberals May Not Recognize. *Social Justice Research*, 20(1), 98–116. doi:10.1007/s11211-007-0034-z.

Haidt, J., & Joseph, C. (2004). Intuitive Ethics: How Innately Prepared Intuitions Generate Culturally Variable Virtues. *Daedalus*, 133(4), 55–66. doi:10.1162/0011526042365555.

Institut für Sozialforschung. (1936). *Studien über Autorität und Familie*. New York: IfS.

Iyer, R., Koleva, S., Graham, J., Ditto, P., & Haidt, J. (2012). Understanding Libertarian Morality: The Psychological Dispositions of Self-Identified Libertarians. *PloS ONE*, 7(8), e42366. doi:10.1371/journal.pone.0042366.

King, D. C., & Karabell, Z. (2003). *The Generation of Trust: Public Confidence in the US Military since Vietnam*. Washington, D.C.: American Enterprise Institute.

Kornhauser, W. (1959/2013). *The Politics of Mass Society*. London: Routledge.

Maffesoli, M. (1996). *The Time of the Tribes: The Decline of Individualism in Mass Society*. Thousand Oaks, CA: Sage.

Major, B., Blodorn, A., & Blascovich, G. M. (2018). The Threat of Increasing Diversity: Why Many White Americans Support Trump in the 2016 Presidential Election. *Group Processes & Intergroup Relations*, 21(6), 931–940. doi:10.1177/1368430216677304.

Mason, L. (2018). *Uncivil Agreement: How Politics Became Our Identity*. Chicago, IL: University of Chicago Press.

Montenaro, D. (2018). Here's Just How Little Confidence Americans Have in Political Institutions. *National Public Radio, Inc*. Retrieved from: https://www.npr.org/2018/01/17/578422668/heres-just-how-little-confidence-americans-have-in-political-institutions.

Mutz, Diana C. (2018). Status Threat, Not Economic Hardship, Explains the 2016 Presidential Vote. *Proceedings of the National Academy of Sciences*, 119(19), E4330–E4339. doi:10.1073/pnas.1718155115.

Pescosolido, B. A., Tuch, S. A., & Martin, J. K. (2001). The Profession of Medicine and the Public: Examining Americans' Changing Confidence in Physician Authority from the Beginning of the 'Health Care Crisis' to the Era of Health Care Reform. *Journal of Health and Social Behavior*, 42, 1–16. doi:10.2307/3090224.

Putnam, R. D. (2001). *Bowling Alone: The Collapse and Revival of American Community*. New York: Simon and Schuster.

Rosenberg, C. E. (2007). *Our Present Complaint: American Medicine, Then and Now*. Baltimore, MD: Johns Hopkins University Press.

Sander, T. H., & Putnam, R. D. (2010). Democracy's Post and Future: Still Bowling Alone? – The Post-9/11 Split. *Journal of Democracy*, 21(1), 9–16.

Tesler, M. (2016, August 22). Economic Anxiety Isn't Driving Racial Resentment. Racial Resentment is Driving Economic Anxiety. Retrieved from *The Washington Post*: https://www.washingtonpost.com/news/monkey-cage/wp/2016/08/22/economic-anxiety-isnt-driving-racial-resentment-racial-resentment-is-driving-economic-anxiety/.

Twenge, J. M., Campbell, K. W., & Carter, N. T. (2014). Declines in Trust in Others and Confidence in Institutions among American Adults and Late Adolescents, 1972–2012. *Psychological Science*, 25(10), 1914–1923. doi:10.1177/0956797614545133.

Washer, P. (2010). *Emerging Infectious Diseases and Society*. New York: Palgrave Macmillan.

Webb, S. A. (2006). *Social Work in a Risk Society: Social and Political Perspectives*. New York: Palgrave Macmillan.

Index

For Product Safety Concerns and Information please contact our EU
representative GPSR@taylorandfrancis.com
Taylor & Francis Verlag GmbH, Kaufingerstraße 24, 80331 München, Germany